OVEREAGER

EXTRA CREDIT
BOOK 1

GRAE BRYAN

Content warnings: age gap; imbalanced power dynamic (student x professor); cheating (past, off-page, not between MCs)

1
_____

Eli

Eli wasn't generally the type to say things like "Jesus take the wheel," but if he didn't get off the road soon, that could very well change.

"If I perish on this journey, you have to take care of World's Deadliest Assassin for me."

"Tell me the truth, Eli," his sister said calmly, not at all taking Eli's imminent demise seriously. "Are you driving faster than five miles per hour right now?"

"I don't know what that has to do with anything," Eli snapped. "Humans aren't meant to drive with snow on the ground. They simply aren't. It's unnatural."

If anything, five miles per hour seemed *too* fast. Maybe Eli should get out and just ... push the car? Except his loafers didn't have great traction—they were meant for loafing, not heavy labor. It was right there in the name.

It wasn't like he'd been completely stupid. He'd checked the weather back at home, had known it had snowed in Sedona the night before. He'd just expected the roads to be plowed already. Which they had been, until he'd gotten to the turnoff for the dirt road his cabin was on. And now here he was, fighting for his life, his sister the most unsympathetic witness he could ask for.

He'd like to blame it on her being an alpha, but really, it was just her baseline personality.

Following the GPS's instructions, he turned—so very carefully —onto the last stretch of road, a slope with three tiny-home cabins along it. His rental was the last one, a.k.a. the highest up the road.

"If my car starts sliding backward, I'm jumping ship. Who needs a vacation?"

"You do, you absolute loon," his sister told him, sounding suspiciously like she had a mouthful of food. "Even better if you were, I don't know, getting dicked down by some hunky alpha while you were at it."

Eli wrinkled his nose, glaring at his phone in its little car holder. "Gross. We're related. Don't say stuff like that."

"Don't let yourself get into this state, and I wouldn't *have* to say stuff like that."

Eli wasn't in any sort of *state*, thanks ever so. He was ... possibly a tad overworked, sure. And *maybe* slightly stressed from his divorce getting finalized. And potentially just a little bit murderous at the thought of Richard off in the Bahamas with some omega half his age.

Not that Eli *knew* his ex-husband was in the Bahamas with some omega half his age. It just seemed the type of thing for him to do. He was all about clichés apparently.

Like having an affair with his omega secretary.

Eli finally parked his car in the little drive, letting out a sigh of relief. If the snow didn't melt by the time he was meant to leave, he was just going to have to stay forever. Squatters' rights and all. He'd make his classes asynchronous and teach them online.

Maybe the novelty of it would even draw more students in. Professor Miller in his tiny cabin.

"I'm here," he said with a relieved sigh. "Hanging up."

His sister crunched something chip-like loudly. "I feel used."

"As you should. Buh-bye now."

Eli hung up, aware Faith wouldn't actually hold a grudge. She was more worried about him than anything else. Which was silly. He was fine.

So he was thirty-four and already divorced? What of it? He was also thirty-four and already set to get tenure by the end of the year. As an omega, at that. So take that, societal expectations.

He stepped out of his car carefully, mindful of the snow on the ground. He grabbed his suitcase from the trunk and climbed the stairs up to the cabin's deck, stopping there to scope out the main attraction of the whole place, at least for him: the hot tub. It was set on the far side of the deck, with a gorgeous view of the mountains.

It also had a less-than-gorgeous view of the deck below it, including the other cabin's hot tub, which Eli didn't love. There wasn't a lot of space between the cabins, and what if there was some super PDA-y couple staying there? He'd have to watch them grope each other and feel even more horribly single than he did already. The light was on inside, so *someone* was staying there.

Eli would just have to wait and see. In the meantime, he turned the hot tub on, letting it heat while he got settled.

He lugged his suitcase to the front and entered the code for the door lock, shivering from head to toe.

His trembling didn't let up once he was inside either. It was *cold* in the cabin. Eli's eyes locked immediately onto the small heater unit, and he turned it on, setting it to seventy-five. Maybe that was high, but that was what they got for not having the place heated when he arrived.

Eli *hated* the cold. And yet for some reason he'd thought it would be picturesque to visit Sedona over winter break, instead of staying in perfectly temperate Phoenix. And he'd been right—the lingering snow on the red rocks of the mountains was completely gorgeous. That didn't mean he had to like the bone-deep chill that came with it.

Once he had the heat running, he took a look around. The cabin was faux rustic, a new build meant to look quaint. The front door opened into a small area with a little table for meals and a cozy armchair tucked against the window by the front door. Beyond that was a small kitchen with a bathroom off of it. And overhead was the ladder leading up to the sleeping loft.

Overall, it was super cute and would be cozy as hell once it warmed up.

Maybe Eli would come here for his next heat.

Then again, maybe not. When he climbed the ladder to peek into the loft, the bed was big enough, but the ceilings were low, probably too low for an alpha to sit up straight. Some omegas liked cramped spaces like that during their heat, but Eli could see it getting a little claustrophobic.

But then *again*, if it was just Eli, what did it matter? It wasn't like there was going to be some hunky alpha contorting himself into a pretzel to "dick Eli down" as his sister had so horribly put it.

Eli's cheeks warmed. Damn Faith for putting dirty thoughts into his head. She was a menace.

He climbed back down the ladder, taking out the mini bottle of champagne he'd brought and placing it in the mini fridge. Because this was *not* a trip for moping, no matter what his brain thought. Eli was still a relatively young, newly single omega in the prime of his life. His career was on track, and his tenure proposal should be going through by the end of the year.

What else did he really need?

It was approaching sunset by the time the jacuzzi was hot enough to be tempting. Luckily the cabin had also warmed up to the point that Eli could strip down to his swim trunks without shivering.

Swim trunks that had been purchased by Richard and were way too short for decency.

But it wasn't like anyone else was around to see.

Eli popped his champagne and poured a glass into one of the plastic cups provided. No glass in the hot tub—it was in the rules listed on the website.

He resisted stopping in the bathroom to peek at his reflection on the way out. He already knew what he was going to see, and it wasn't anything showstopping. Maybe he should do some sort of midlife-crisis makeover to mark the occasion. He could bleach his brown hair blond or switch out his contacts for those fancy ones that made a person's eyes look like a cat's.

Or maybe he'd just drink his sad champagne in the hot tub and go straight to bed.

Eli went out to the deck, wincing at the knifelike feel of snow on his bare feet, wishing he'd brought shower sandals with him. He laid his towel out on a relatively snow-free part of the small patio table, set his cup of champagne on the side of the hot tub, and climbed in, groaning as his skin prickled with the welcome heat.

He'd only been in there a minute when a voice called out from below. "Hey! Nice night, huh?"

Eli scooted to the edge of the hot tub and peered out over the deck.

There was someone in the jacuzzi below him, on the deck of the other occupied cabin. Someone with a head of loose blond curls and a silver chain around his neck, one tanned arm slung back around the edge of the hot tub, a beer in hand. He looked so friendly—and so young—that Eli couldn't even be annoyed at his silence being interrupted.

"Hello!" he called back. "It *is* a nice night!"

The guy raised his beer in salute. "You just get in?"

"A few hours ago."

"Cool. I've been here a night already. Heading out tomorrow."

Eli nodded, not sure what else to say. Small talk with strangers wasn't exactly his forte lately.

"You want some company?" At Eli's clear surprise, the guy gave a sheepish grin. "A buddy was supposed to come with me, but he had to bail. I guess I'm not good at flying solo. Feel free to say no though." He smiled wide, as if to convey his sincerity.

Eli could tell, somehow, that he *was* free to say no. Even from another building, this guy exuded a certain warmth and carefree vibe, like someone's friendly neighborhood surfer, if that was a thing. He didn't seem the type to hold a grudge.

Maybe Eli still would have said no anyway. But that smile got him. Because the guy was good-looking enough from the get-go— even at a distance—but with that smile? It was outrageous. He had a wide, generous mouth, and his grin transformed his whole face into some sort of ray of literal sunshine.

Eli was just shallow enough to be swayed by it.

Plus, how often did he have a chance to share a hot tub with a hot ... beta? Alpha? Eli wasn't sure, but most likely the guy wasn't an omega. He looked ... tall. Broad.

It didn't really matter either way. Eli wasn't going to *do* anything. But a friendly chat with a cute neighbor wouldn't be the worst thing in the world, right?

Richard wouldn't hesitate, he reminded himself. *He'd probably already have the condoms out.*

"Sure," he said magnanimously, taking a big gulp of champagne. "Come on up."

"Awesome!"

The guy climbed out of his tub, and Eli's eyes widened. Had he made the right call? The guy was ... big. Much bigger than Eli had thought—he must have been slouching down in the water. But standing tall, he was built like a professional swimmer, with wide shoulders and a trim waist.

And his shorts were almost as small as Eli's.

Covered by the water, he'd seemed kind of harmlessly cute—besides the devastating smile—but it was quickly becoming clear he was on a whole different level of hot.

Eli was going to make a fool of himself.

But his new friend was already tugging on a pair of snow boots over his wet feet and walking up the hill in no more than his shoes and those teeny swim trunks.

Too late to back out now.

Eli took a few quick gulps of champagne while he waited to hear the footsteps coming up the deck. He wished he'd brought the bottle with him. He wasn't sure why he was like this—totally fine in a lecture hall in front of hundreds of students, but nervous as hell in more intimate social situations.

Richard had never been able to understand it—why someone so confident in his work needed to be "coddled" (as he so delicately put it) at a dinner party. It was a funny thing for him to be annoyed by, because a stereotypically submissive omega was exactly what he'd wanted in the end.

Hypocrite, Eli thought, but there was no bitterness in it. Not anymore.

And it didn't matter either way because in the next moment, there was Eli's new neighbor approaching—grinning broadly in greeting—and Eli had to fight not to swallow his tongue.

Like, damn. This was the kind of guy Eli had never spent much time with, not even when he was younger.

Or maybe *especially* not then, when he'd been bookish and shy and completely lacking any sort of confidence.

"Hey," his neighbor said, all wet and bare-chested, while Eli did his best not to stare at his nipples. "I'm Noah."

"Hi." Eli gave a stupid little wave, his eyes firmly locked somewhere around the guy's forehead. It seemed like a safe spot. "Eli."

"Thanks for the invite, man." Noah didn't seem to suffer from any of Eli's shyness. He toed out of his boots and climbed in, his half-empty beer in hand. A *glass* bottle too. A certified rule breaker, this guy was. He sighed loudly, spreading his arms out to the sides, tanned chest on full display. "Fuck, that feels good."

No drooling, Eli reminded himself. *Close your damned mouth.*

He took a sip of his champagne, if only to have something to do. He was 90 percent sure this guy was an alpha—with that build, how could he be anything else?—but the chlorine from the hot tub was making it hard to pick out his scent.

Which was good, really. It meant Noah wouldn't necessarily clock Eli as an omega right away either. He could think Eli was a petite beta. Maybe. Possibly.

It wasn't like Eli was ashamed of being an omega, but the lack of clarity gave a certain freedom to the situation. It didn't have to be ... charged, Eli being alone in a hot tub with a potential alpha.

They were just two friendly neighbors on vacation.

He realized Noah was watching him, and coughed on his champagne bubbles.

Noah grinned. He had dimples on both sides, which seemed frankly like too much. Save some charm for the rest of humanity, right?

"So what brings you to Sedona?"

"A little solo vacation," Eli told him, aiming for light and airy but probably falling about a mile short. "And, um, a celebration." He shrugged a shoulder. "Career's going well."

"Right on." Noah grinned at him again. "Good for you, man."

Eli relaxed a little. This was easy enough. Noah was super friendly. He cleared his throat. "What—what about you?"

"Just a little refresh before my spring semester. Business classes are kicking my ass."

Eli relaxed a little more. If Noah was going for his MBA, he was a grad student. Not quite as young as Eli had thought, then. The beer was legal, at least, even if it was in a glass bottle. "And you were supposed to have a buddy with you?" Eli asked, trying to get into the neighborly spirit. "Or—a girlfriend? Boyfriend?"

He flushed, hoping Noah would think it was the heat from the tub. Why was he prying? And so fucking obviously?

But Noah laughed easily. "Just a buddy. Bummer he couldn't make it. But it's nice to make new friends, huh?" He lifted his beer in a little cheers.

Eli met him halfway with his plastic cup, unable to help his own grin. God, how long had it been since he'd made a new friend? He was on good terms with the other professors, sure, but it had been a while since he'd spent time with anyone outside of work or his sister.

They talked for a long time, the sun setting around them. Eli learned Noah was from Southern California originally, although he was studying in Phoenix. (The same city where Eli taught, actually. But Eli's school didn't have an MBA program, so he didn't bring it up.)

Noah was from a big family, with lots of siblings, and maybe his seemingly innate confidence had something to do with that. He asked Eli fun, easy questions. What he'd done or not done around Sedona (nothing besides fear for his life in his car). How he dealt with the Arizona heat summer after summer (air-conditioning and his own pool). Whether superhero movies were classic or overrated (both, depending on the movie).

When it was dark, the light from the hot tub the only thing illuminating their faces, Noah met Eli's eyes, smiling warmly. "So you're celebrating, huh?"

"Yeah. The career stuff and also—" Eli cleared his throat "— my, um, divorce was just finalized, after a whole drawn-out thing."

"Oh." Noah blinked. He had surprisingly thick, sooty lashes, considering his fair hair. "Damn."

"Yeah." Eli frowned down at his empty cup. "Thirty-four and already divorced. Kind of—kind of a bummer, huh?" he asked, echoing Noah's earlier phrasing.

"I'm sorry," Noah told him, sounding sincere. "But hey, you're way ahead of me." He scooted closer, his voice turning low and conspiratorial. "Wanna hear something that'll make you feel better?"

"Hit me," Eli told him, matching Noah's low tone.

Noah made a show of looking around from side to side, as if someone might have been listening in, before leaning in close. "I've never been with anyone at all," he admitted. "I'm still a virgin."

Eli couldn't help it—he choked on his own spit. "*You*?" he finally asked, once he'd gotten a hold of himself.

"Yeah." Noah grinned at him, showcasing those dimples again, apparently not at all offended by Eli's surprise.

"You're lying."

Noah gasped in mock outrage. "Why on earth would you accuse me—your new, dear friend—of lying?"

"Just ..." Eli waved a hand, trying to encompass all that ... *appeal* with only a gesture. "I mean, look at you."

Noah's grin dropped, and he cocked his head, moving effortlessly into seriousness. "But it's about more than just looks, right? It's about ... compatibility. I've got a very sensitive nose." He tapped the bridge of it in demonstration. "Maybe I just haven't found someone whose scent I like."

Eli shifted in place, trying to figure out what to say. It was a little taboo, to talk about pheromones with a near stranger. Or maybe that was just his age talking. Maybe the younger generation talked about pheromones with each other casually, and he was just being some sort of fuddy-duddy.

Noah was still much closer than he'd been at the start of the night, and Eli suddenly had to fight the urge to try to catch his scent. It would have been useless anyway, unless Noah was pumping his pheromones out willy-nilly.

"*You* smell good though," Noah said quietly.

Eli's mouth dropped open. "You can tell? Even with the chlorine?"

"Yeah, I can tell." Noah's gaze had turned oddly intense at some point in their conversation, a new measure of heat in it as he asked, "You're an omega, right?"

2

Noah

Noah kept eye contact with his new omega friend—because Eli *was* an omega, Noah was sure of it—knowing he was toeing the line a little, calling it out so blatantly.

Was it the best idea to ask the secondary gender of a man he'd just met? Probably not. Maybe if they'd met at a frat party, it would have been cool, but it wasn't exactly how polite adults behaved.

But it was true—Eli smelled good. Like, really good. If he was on birth control, it definitely wasn't the kind that blocked pheromones. (And no, Noah wasn't going to ask Eli what kind of birth control he was on. He wasn't a *complete* idiot). Eli's scent wafted through the chlorine fumes every now and then, a clean, citrusy perfume with only a hint of an omega's usual sweetness.

Noah would probably have guessed Eli was an omega anyway, even without the scent. He had the classic look: all fine-boned, with features that tended toward the delicate. Warm honey-brown eyes, a snub nose, and a slightly pointed chin, with no facial hair that Noah could see. His top lip was slightly fuller than his bottom lip, and something about that was driving Noah a little crazy.

He was cute. Really cute. Not just his looks, although Noah appreciated the way Eli's chestnut locks were taking on a slight wave from the steam of the hot tub, and that same heat was putting a pretty pink flush on his cheeks.

Or maybe the blush was a reaction to Noah.

Fuck, that would be nice, if Eli was feeling it the way Noah was.

But Eli's cuteness was also just … him. He'd been so adorable telling the story of his drive up here, exaggerating the way he'd feared for his life because of a little dusting of snow, or telling Noah about his beloved cat, who he'd named World's Deadliest Assassin.

And now Noah was realizing how long the silence had been going on. It was his turn to flush. "Sorry," he said with a sheepish grin. "You don't have to answer that."

"No." Eli cleared his throat. "It's fine. I'm an omega, yes. And you …" The pink in his cheeks deepened in color. "You're an alpha?"

"Yeah." Noah grinned for real now, loving the way Eli's gaze dipped down to his mouth when he smiled. He knew his smile was one of his best assets, and he wasn't afraid to flaunt it when needed. "I'm an alpha. How could you tell?"

Noah was almost positive Eli couldn't smell his scent through the chlorine. Most people weren't as sensitive as Noah was, and he was keeping a tight rein on his pheromones. Otherwise, he'd have been broadcasting "HORNY" all over the deck.

"Your, um … body? I mean—Jesus—" Eli gave an awkward laugh, clearly flustered. "I mean … Shoulders?" He did a weird gesture, as if encompassing the width of Noah's shoulders. "No, um ... build!" he cried out, like he'd just remembered. "That's the word. Your build." He tried to take a gulp of his champagne, even though his cup was empty, his face red as a tomato now.

God, he was cute as hell. He'd said he was thirty-four, but he barely looked it. Maybe he was hiding some grays in that dark hair, but Noah couldn't make any out.

Would he let Noah close enough to look?

He'd seen the way Eli had eyed him as he stepped into the tub, so it wasn't like the omega was completely immune to him. Fingers fucking crossed.

"You like my shoulders?" Noah asked with a teasing lilt.

He was a virgin, but that didn't mean he wasn't a flirt. He'd just never had enough genuine interest to seal the deal with anyone. There was always something off about any interested partners ... something that inner, instinctual part of him didn't take to. His inner alpha, if he wanted to get all macho and claim it.

Eli narrowed his eyes at him, managing to look stern despite his ridiculous blush. "I'm just saying you've got the classic alpha's build, okay?"

"Sorry." Noah raised his hands in surrender. "I'm teasing. You're cute when you blush, is all."

"Don't even," Eli said with a laugh. "I hate how red my face gets." He gave Noah an appraising glance. "For an alleged virgin, you're kind of shameless, did you know that?"

"Is that your type?" Noah asked, not afraid to press his advantage. "Shameless?"

Eli stared at him for a moment, then laughed again, as if Noah were joking. "Oh, the confidence of youth."

"I'm not that young."

"Young enough."

It was Noah's turn to narrow his eyes as he sipped at the last of his beer. He was twenty-one. He could drink. He could vote. He could even register a mating bite.

Eli didn't have one, Noah had already noted. His slender little neck was unblemished. Whoever had married him hadn't taken that step.

Dumb bastard.

And that dumb bastard's loss was Noah's gain. Because Noah may have been picky, but he wasn't afraid to go after what he wanted when he found it.

Eli was cute, and fun to talk to, and he smelled fucking amazing, even mixed up with the harsh scent of chlorine. He was apparently rocking it in his career and was bold enough to let a strange alpha into his hot tub.

Basically, he was a total fucking catch.

Noah had never considered his virginity something precious, but even if he had, this felt *right*. There was nothing about Eli that Noah's instincts didn't like.

His instincts liked Eli a whole lot, actually.

Noah's parents had rented the cabin for a getaway, and then something had come up at his mom's work, and they'd been unable to go. They'd offered it to Noah, and he'd jumped at the chance to escape the family home for the last bit of winter break. He loved his siblings, sure, but he'd gotten used to a certain amount of privacy at school. When his buddy Spencer had bailed, Noah had almost backed out too.

He was so fucking glad he hadn't. There was something surreal about this moment. He was away from his family, his school, his friends. It was just him and this very cute omega, who Noah was quickly realizing he wanted to get to know much, much better.

He was honestly finding it hard to resist scenting Eli right there in the hot tub. Which would have been about ten steps beyond toeing the line, seeing as how he didn't have Eli's permission.

Oblivious to Noah's struggle to control himself, Eli leaned into him. "Another truth for a truth?" At Noah's nod, he smiled shyly. "I'm not used to being flirted with like this."

Noah's stomach dropped. Oh fuck. Was he being one of those horribly pushy alpha creeps, unable to take no for an answer?

"Is it okay?" he asked. "I can tone it down. Hell, I can stop completely," he offered, starting to move away. "Leave you alone to celebrate."

"No," Eli said quickly, grabbing onto Noah's arm. "Stay." He gave Noah another shy smile. "It's kind of nice."

"Yeah?" Noah let the relief flood through him, relaxing his muscles and setting one arm on the back of the hot tub so he was facing Eli more fully. "Then can I ask you something completely inappropriate?"

Eli grinned at him, mischief in his brown eyes. "Why the hell not?"

"You ever taken someone's virginity?" Noah asked, before he could think better of it.

Fortune favored the bold, right?

Eli nibbled on his bottom lip for a moment before answering. "No. I've only been with my ex, and he wasn't a virgin."

"Mm. I bet you'd be a good teacher though."

Noah had expected another shocked blush but not the totally endearing giggle Eli let out.

He cocked his head, unable to help his grin. "What's so funny?"

"Oh, just ..." Eli giggled again. "I *am* a teacher."

Fuck. Of course he was. He was probably patient and kind with his students, just the way he'd been patient and kind when Noah had come to crash his solo celebration.

"I can see that." Noah pressed a finger lightly between Eli's brows. "Just toss a pair of glasses on you. Maybe a tweed suit."

Eli gave him a mock offended look, but he didn't move back

from Noah's touch. "I wear contacts, thank you very much. And no tweed suits. I don't teach at a British boarding school in the fifties."

"I'll just keep that to my fantasies, then." Noah dropped his hand but scooted closer, until their legs were brushing under the water.

Eli bit at his lower lip again, but still, he didn't move away. He cast a sidelong glance at Noah. "You shouldn't be looking for a teacher at all. You should lose it to someone your own age."

"Oh yeah?" Noah pressed his calf more firmly against Eli's. "Why's that?"

"I don't know." Eli shrugged, his leg sliding against Noah's. "Just ... first times should be fun and silly, I think."

"Not romantic? Candlelight and whispered 'I love yous'?"

Eli shook his head. "Mine was kind of like that, and look how it turned out. I think I could have used more silliness. More fun."

"You don't think you and I could have fun?" Noah asked, surprised at the huskiness in his own voice.

This honestly hadn't been Noah's intention coming over. He'd just seen a cute neighbor and wanted to be friendly. But sitting here, with Eli's scent drifting through the steam, it was like a buzzing under Noah's skin. He couldn't let it go. He wanted more than friendly.

He wanted Eli in his bed.

Eli's eyes were heavy-lidded now, golden and dreamy-looking. "I think it'd be ... intense," he told Noah.

"Yeah?"

"Yeah."

"Hey, Eli?" Noah asked, setting his now empty beer on the edge of the hot tub and sliding his arm behind Eli's upper back.

"Yes?"

"I think you should invite me inside."

"We haven't even kissed," Eli told him, even as he let Noah

pluck his empty cup from his hands. "Maybe we're not compatible."

They were compatible. They were compatible as fuck. Noah knew it as sure as anything.

But if Eli wanted a kiss to seal the deal?

Noah may have been a virgin, but he wasn't completely inexperienced. He could handle an audition like that no problem. He grasped Eli's chin, moving in slowly, giving the omega a chance to back away.

But it was Eli who surged up and closed the distance.

Noah grinned against Eli's mouth, then slipped in his tongue, deepening the kiss immediately. He wasn't going to allow some chaste press of lips, not when a night with Eli was at stake.

Eli tasted like champagne, fizzy and sweet. A hungry noise escaped Noah's throat, and he moved his hand down, cupping the back of Eli's neck, his thumb brushing a mere centimeter away from Eli's scent gland. Where a mating mark would lie.

Eli made a little mewling noise that went straight to Noah's dick, his scent blooming into something deeper. He tossed a leg over Noah, clambering halfway into his lap as Noah sucked on his tongue.

Fuck. This was it. This was perfect. Noah grabbed Eli's hip, ready to grind up against him. He was already hardening, the combination of Eli's taste and scent and innate eagerness setting his body on fire.

A hand settled on Noah's chest, pushing him back gently.

Noah broke the kiss with a reluctant groan. Eli was panting, those golden-brown eyes wide, like he was surprised at himself. "So you've kissed before, I take it?"

Noah grinned at him. "Hey, Eli," he said again.

"Yes?"

"Invite me in."

———

ELI'S CABIN was pretty much an exact replica of Noah's, other than small differences in decoration. It was too small to pretend they were just there to extend the conversation, if either of them had been inclined to.

Eli was shivering, even with the heat turned up and a towel wrapped around him. Noah removed his own towel, placing it over Eli's shoulders and rubbing briskly to help him dry off and warm up.

Eli gave Noah another shy, grateful smile, peering up at him sweetly, and for the first time that night, nerves crept in to mess with Noah's head.

Noah really liked Eli already, and he had no idea what he was doing. What if he fucked it up? What if he couldn't make Eli feel good?

He needed to ground himself, and there was only one way he wanted to do it.

"Hey." He tugged his towel off Eli carefully, now that the omega was fully dried. "Can I scent mark you?"

Eli waited a beat before answering—Noah held his breath, afraid to make the slightest movement—and then he tilted his neck. "Of course."

Fuck yeah. Noah stepped in close, lowering his head to the crook of Eli's neck. He rubbed his forehead and cheeks against Eli's soft skin, loosening his hold on his pheromones.

Eli let out a gasp, swaying into him. "*Oh.*"

Noah lifted his head with immense effort. "Okay?" Maybe he'd come on too strong. He was turned on, and way too eager, and it was highly possible he'd just blasted Eli with an overwhelming wave of his scent.

But Eli was already nodding. "Yeah. It's okay. You just—" He inhaled deeply, his eyes going a little hazy. He rubbed his forehead against Noah's bare shoulder, scent marking him lightly in return. "You smell really good."

"Yeah?" Noah grinned at him, suddenly feeling about ten feet tall. "I'm glad. Because you smell fucking delicious."

He really, really did, especially without the chlorine getting in the way. There was a kind of tart freshness to Eli's scent that made Noah want to drink him the fuck up. A delicious little frozen margarita, the kind with more citrus than sweetness.

Noah went back to scent marking Eli's neck, possibly going a little overboard with it. But some of Noah's nerves were already settling, now that Eli smelled like him.

Now that they smelled like each other.

He hummed against Eli's skin one last time before lifting his head. "Gonna ask me up to your loft?"

"Yeah, I—" Eli paused, consternation taking over his features.

Noah stiffened. "What's wrong?"

"I didn't—I don't have any condoms." Eli bit at his lower lip, his brows furrowed. "Do you?"

"No, I didn't—didn't think. *Fuck.*" Noah could feel panic tightening his chest at the thought of this moment getting taken away from him. "But I—I mean, I've never been with anyone. And you —you're—?"

"I got tested when Richard and I separated. I haven't been with anyone since."

Noah let out a breath. "And you're on birth control?"

"Yes."

"Okay." Noah laughed with relief. "I still want to, if you do."

He yelped as Eli smacked him on the arm with surprising strength. "Hey! What was that for?"

Eli wagged a finger in his face. "You can't just take some random omega's word for it that they're on birth control. That's just asking to knock someone up."

It was a good fucking point. Noah wasn't looking to be a daddy anytime soon. He wasn't looking to be a daddy, period.

But he still wasn't letting this chance get taken away.

"Okay." He nodded agreeably, brushing his fingers down Eli's side, already missing the comforting calm he'd gotten from scent marking him. "I won't."

"Okay." Eli let out a slightly hysterical laugh. "Oh god. I'm such a horrible hypocrite. Come on."

He climbed up the ladder, and Noah tried not to drool at the pert bottom flashing in his face. It was a tough battle—Eli's swim trunks were tiny, and plastered to his skin from soaking in the tub.

Noah followed him up, remaining bent down once he was in the loft, mindful of the low ceiling. Eli lay back on the mattress, leaning on his elbows, beckoning with a tilt of his head. "Come here, Noah."

Noah crawled until he was crouched over him, barely daring to breathe. He was hard in his trunks, had been since they'd entered the cabin.

Eli looked him over, his gaze pausing at Noah's throat, where his pulse was no doubt obviously thundering. "You're nervous?" he asked.

Noah was, his previous ease after scent marking Eli having left him at some point on the climb up. He could try to lie, to fake confidence, but his scent was probably giving him away. "A little," he admitted.

Eli's eyes crinkled at the corners with his smile. They were kind eyes, the type that made someone feel at ease with just a look. "We can stop at any time."

Noah nodded. "I know."

"You want to kiss me again?"

Noah didn't need a second invitation. He leaned down and captured Eli's mouth, groaning as Eli's tongue met his, letting his pelvis drop into the cradle of Eli's hips. Now he did grind down, grateful to feel Eli's hardness against his.

Eli moaned his approval, his knees coming up against Noah's sides, his hands delving into Noah's curls.

Noah smiled into the kiss. This he could do. This felt natural as hell. He could have been in his bedroom back home, sneaking Eli in for a clandestine dry hump during his school break.

He made to grind again and froze, cock twitching, as he caught wind of a delicious scent. Even more delicious than Eli's usual pheromones. Richer and deeper and ...

Noah broke the kiss, rising onto his arms. "Holy shit. Is that your slick?"

Eli flushed his deepest red yet. "Oh my god." He covered his face with his hands. "You can't just say that."

Noah cocked his head. "Why not? We're about to have sex. Slick is part of it." He inhaled deeply, letting out a groan. "Oh *fuck*, that smells good."

Eli parted his fingers, peering at Noah through the gaps. "Yeah?"

"Fuck, yeah." The scent was thick and sweet but somehow not cloying. It was just ... enticing. Intoxicating, really. Noah's cock, already aching from grinding against Eli, strained against his shorts.

He let out a harsh breath.

Eli lowered his hands. "What's wrong?"

"I'm just realizing how badly I'm about to embarrass myself."

Eli's eyes dropped to Noah's bulge, and he licked his lips in a seemingly unconscious gesture. "There's nothing embarrassing about being turned on," he told him. "Just, um, you know not to knot someone without permission right?"

Noah gave him a look. "Dude. You gonna tell me not to bite you too?"

Just because he was an overeager virgin didn't mean he was completely unaware of common decency.

"I'm just saying." Eli ran a soothing hand up Noah's side. "It's your first time, so it might start happening. Just warn me and we'll keep it ... outside."

There was something about the matter-of-fact way Eli said it that made it really hit Noah. Holy shit. This was happening. He was about to lose his virginity to the cutest, nicest, most delicious-smelling omega he'd ever encountered.

Coming to the cabin was definitely the best decision Noah had ever made. He grinned, elation filling his chest. "Okay, Eli."

Eli smiled back at him. "Okay."

Noah brushed his fingers against the hem of Eli's trunks. "Can I take your shorts off?"

"Yeah." Eli kicked a foot up, brushing Noah's in return. "But you too."

Noah tugged off his shorts, freeing his aching cock, and Eli's eyes dropped down immediately, his own hands freezing.

Noah tugged impatiently again at the hem of Eli's trunks, grateful when Eli didn't hesitate to slide them off, although his eyes stayed locked on Noah's dick.

His attention was flattering as hell.

Noah's own attention was firmly on the omega lying beneath him. Eli's cock was pretty—jutting out against the light dusting of dark hair on his groin, slim and proportionate to his size, hard and leaking against his hip.

Eli was pretty, all lean lines and flushed skin. His chest was slim, his nipples a beautiful, dusky pink.

But there was more that Noah wanted to lay eyes on.

"Can I—can I see?" he asked, his voice barely above a whisper.

Eli nodded wordlessly, widening his legs, clearly knowing exactly what Noah meant. Noah gripped Eli's thigh, pressing back gently until he saw it.

Eli's hole.

It was already glistening with slick, the thick fluid beginning to leak out between his cheeks.

Noah swallowed hard, trying to remember how to breathe. "I need you to know this is the hottest thing that's ever happened to me in my entire life."

Eli's scent deepened, another small gush of slick escaping him, and Noah let out a helpless groan, his fingers tightening on Eli's thigh.

Yeah, Noah was definitely going to embarrass himself here.

3

Eli

"I need you to know this is the hottest thing that's ever happened to me in my entire life."

Some strange warmth seared through Eli, and he couldn't help the small gush of slick that came out of him with those words.

The hottest thing that had ever happened to *Noah*? What about Eli? He had an absurdly good-looking and ridiculously charming alpha poised above him, staring at his entrance like it was the key to all things good and holy.

Eli had never been looked at that way before in his life.

There was this hint of awe in Noah's gaze, like he couldn't truly believe he was in bed with Eli. Richard had certainly never looked at Eli like that. By the time they'd slept together for the first time, they'd already been dating for a while, and Eli had been, as some would put it, a sure thing.

It hadn't been terrible—they really had been in love at that point—but it had been so serious, so official, and Eli had been so worried about pleasing his then-boyfriend that he hadn't been able to enjoy things as much as he would have liked. Which in turn had set the tone for their relationship—Richard's pleasure first, Eli's as an afterthought.

Eli couldn't really blame his ex-husband—at least not for that —since he hadn't known how to ask for anything better at the time.

But it didn't feel like Eli had to worry too much about pleasing Noah, not when the alpha was so enthusiastic over every little thing Eli did.

Noah's thumb slid back and forth over the sensitive skin of Eli's inner thigh, bringing him back to the present, and that was enough thinking about past relationships, wasn't it? What was happening right here and now was more than adequate to hold Eli's complete, undivided attention.

He relaxed his leg in Noah's hold, and Noah pressed his thigh even further back. Eli should have been embarrassed—he'd never thought he'd be the type to display himself like this, not with slick already running down his thighs from a little kissing and heavy petting—but Eli was Noah's first, and he wanted Noah to be able to experience it all.

If Noah wanted to look, Eli would let him look.

As if he was reading Eli's mind, Noah's gaze shot to his, and the heat in his eyes was molten. "How do you like to be touched, Eli?"

His voice had taken on a deep, husky note, and his scent—a clean, salty medley that reminded Eli of ocean air—was thick and heady, and Eli could already feel a needy omega whine building at the back of his throat. Jesus. Was Noah really nervous about embarrassing himself? Apparently Eli was the one who should be concerned.

"Um. I don't know," he said stupidly. "It's been a while." At Noah's cocked head, he found himself admitting, "A year. It's been over a year since I've had sex."

"I see." Noah kept his gaze locked on Eli's as his thumb slid higher up Eli's thigh, creeping closer to his entrance, Noah's hard swallow the only sign of his nerves. "So I'll need to stretch you open, right?"

Stretching, yes. Definitely that. Noah's cock was … appropriately sized, for an alpha. Thick as hell and slightly curved upward, veiny and angry red at the tip, with the puckered, loose skin at the base where his knot would inflate. It had been a struggle to look away when he'd first undressed—a struggle for Eli to tear his eyes away from that substantial proof of just how aroused Noah was.

The needy whine escaped Eli's throat after all, and Noah's eyes went dark. His thumb swiped across Eli's entrance, and then he lifted it to his lips, tongue darting out.

Jesus Christ.

Eli held his breath as he watched Noah suck his thumb into his mouth, his eyes closing as he hummed. "Fuck, you taste good," he murmured. "Does slick always taste this good?"

"I don't—I don't know." Eli thought Noah might be looking at him now, but his own gaze was stuck on the sight of Noah's wide mouth savoring the taste of his slick. "Most alphas seem to like it. People say they're hard-wired to … you know."

"I bet not all omegas taste like this though."

Eli gasped as Noah leaned over him, pushing Eli's bent leg to the side to make room for his broad form between Noah's hips.

"Try it." And then he was kissing Eli, sliding their tongues together. There was a new, tangy edge to Noah's taste.

Eli's slick.

Eli moaned, sucking on Noah's tongue, more turned on by that than he should have been. Something about Noah's strange mix of confidence and naivety had Eli's hole clenching around air, suddenly empty and aching.

Noah broke the kiss, grinning at him. "Good, right?"

Eli panted, wide-eyed. "You're so …"

"Shameless?" Noah's grin widened. "So you've said." Just as quickly as it had formed, his grin dropped, his expression turning devastatingly serious. "I want to make you feel good, Eli. Really good."

Eli gestured to the slick running down his thighs. "Believe me, you are."

Noah brushed at Eli's entrance with his thumb again. "I've never fingered anyone before."

"That's okay." Eli's leg was getting sore hanging there, so he wrapped it around Noah's hip. "Just touch me the way you like, and I'll tell you if it doesn't feel right."

"Okay." Noah let out a harsh, determined breath, leaning back again so he was kneeling over Eli, Eli's leg across his thigh now, Noah's thumb circling Eli's entrance. Just that gentle pressure felt unbearably good, pleasure pooling in Eli's belly.

"That's good?" Noah asked, his eyes zeroed in on his task.

"Mm," Eli sighed. "Good."

Noah's smile was small but genuine. He spent a long time like that, ignoring his own hard cock and playing gently with Eli's hole, softening him with light, persistent touches. He seemed fascinated by the whole process, all his concentration focused. With alpha pheromones in the air, thick and heavy with arousal, it didn't take long for Eli's entrance to open, and Noah took immediate advantage, slipping the tip of his thumb inside.

"Fuck," he whispered reverently as more slick dribbled out of Eli at his intrusion. He replaced his thumb with his index finger, sliding it in and gliding it back out slowly. "Fuck, you're soft inside. Like velvet."

"Oh god," Eli moaned, more slick escaping him.

Noah crooked his finger in a way that had electricity shooting down Eli's spine. "You like when I tell you how good you feel?"

"I kind of like everything you do," Eli told him, oddly embarrassed to say it.

"Yeah?" Noah looked genuinely delighted at that, his glee washing away Eli's embarrassment. "I should do another finger, right?" he asked, brows furrowing again in concentration.

That was cute. Why was he so cute? And how could he be so cute and hot at the same time? Honestly, Eli might never recover from this. This night was going to haunt him forever.

"Just one more, and then—then I'll be good."

Eli didn't even know if that was true—Noah was fucking huge —but he was losing patience, his insides almost cramping with need. It was miles away from the intensity of a heat, but it was a similar sort of ache. Like Eli's body knew that Noah belonged inside him, and it wasn't willing to wait anymore.

Noah slipped in another digit easily, sliding and twisting his two fingers inside Eli. His other hand slid off of Eli's thigh, moving toward Eli's cock.

Eli grabbed his wrist. "Don't."

Noah froze, his eyes wide.

Eli flushed—or he felt like he did. He wasn't sure if it was possible to be redder than he already was, considering he was hot and flustered, sort of embarrassed but incredibly turned on at the same time. He bit at his lip. "I'll come if you touch me."

"Oh, fuck me," Noah groaned, like it was the best thing he'd ever heard. "Does that mean—are you ready?"

"I'm ready." Eli had a vague recollection that he was supposed to be the one guiding Noah, but he'd quickly swum out of his depth with how turned on he'd gotten. "Are you—are you ready?"

"Yeah." Noah nodded, letting out a shaky exhale. "Yeah."

He scooted his knees closer, one hand pushing Eli's thigh back again. He swiped his fingers through Eli's slick, coating his cock with it, and Eli had to clench his teeth tightly to keep in his moan.

Noah notched the head of the cock against him, and Eli craned his head down to see. It looked absurdly thick, the size of that fat head almost threatening. But Eli wanted it anyway. Needed it.

"Okay?" Noah asked.

Eli nodded frantically. "Okay."

Noah pushed in, and Eli breathed out, willing his inner muscles to relax. But despite the stretch—and fuck, it *was* a stretch—the intrusion wasn't painful. Eli's body seemed to welcome Noah's cock, especially as the alpha lowered to his elbows, his chest brushing Eli's, his body pumping out more of those delicious pheromones that filled Eli's head with fog.

"Fuck. You feel—Eli, you feel—"

Eli had to work to make his mouth move the way it should, the pressure inside him so good and so overwhelming that he was worried he might spontaneously combust. "Good?"

"So good. So soft and wet and warm." Noah let out a breathless laugh. "Fuck. Is this what I've been missing out on?"

Eli wanted to tell him no, that sex wasn't always like this. But who knew? Maybe for Noah, it would be. Maybe he was charming and amiable enough that all sex would feel like the best sex in the world, even when it was just getting started.

Had Eli said first times were supposed to be fun and silly? They were missing the mark by about a mile, then. He'd been right about the intensity. He needed to remind himself that they'd only met a few hours ago. That he was just a convenient excuse for Noah to rid himself of a virgin status he wasn't too keen to hang on to.

"Can I move?" Noah asked, and Eli realized the alpha was trembling.

Eli brushed his hands along Noah's back, trying to soothe his straining muscles. "Please."

Noah drew back, his gaze focused on the sight of his cock leaving Eli's body. And no wonder. It looked absolutely obscene, girthy and glistening, coated with Eli's slick.

Eli's inner muscles cramped again, locking the head into place, and Noah groaned before pushing back in. "Is this okay?" he whispered as he bottomed out again. "Tell me this is okay."

"It's perfect."

It was. Noah was filling Eli so well that even his tentative thrusts were dragging his cock against Eli's walls in a maddening way. Eli slid one hand down to Noah's muscular ass cheek, helping guide him in a smoother rhythm. "Mm. Like that."

He drew Noah's head down for a kiss, and Noah met him eagerly, his mouth warm and welcoming. The familiar gesture seemed to soothe the alpha, some of the tension leaving his frame as he slid in and out of Eli with more confidence.

"Fuck, this feels good," he groaned when he came up for air. "Too good. Eli—Eli, do you feel good?"

"I feel so good," Eli told him, the words leaving him in a frantic rush.

He'd never thought it could be so hot, having someone check in with him over and over, but something about Noah's enthusiasm—his sincere need to please Eli—had Eli's nerves thrumming, pleasure lighting him up from head to toe.

Noah started thrusting more deeply, their combined sweat easing the glide of his body against Eli's, his eyes boring into Eli's as Eli rocked his hips to meet him.

It wasn't long before he held himself still above Eli, his entire body trembling again. "I'm going to come," he said, sounding completely devastated by the fact. "Way too soon. I'm so sorry."

"Don't be sorry," Eli soothed, wrapping his legs around Noah's hips in encouragement. "I want you to come. It'll feel amazing, you filling me up."

"Yeah?" Noah looked so grateful, and so, so handsome, his blond curls plastered to his tanned face, his jaw clenched with the effort of holding himself back. He started up again in a slightly awkward rhythm, but even then, the drag of his cock lit Eli up from the inside.

Eli was close. Closer than he should have been, considering. He ran his hands up to Noah's shoulders. "I'm going to touch myself, okay?"

"Oh fuck," Noah groaned. "Yes, please. Please do that. I want to see."

He rose onto his hands again, putting enough distance between their bodies that Eli could slip a hand around his own cock, thumbing at the tip.

"You should come first," Noah said eagerly. An alpha growl entered his voice for the first time as he watched Eli touch himself. "Make yourself come, Eli."

"Oh god." Eli angled his hips up even further, crossing his ankles and pulling at Noah with them, speeding him up. Noah read the unspoken message loud and clear, driving into Eli deeply with new fervor.

Eli stroked his cock furiously, swiping his thumb over the head again and again.

"Oh fuck." Noah made a sound somewhere between a laugh and a groan. "I'm coming."

He thrust deep—deeper than he had yet, his cockhead practically spearing Eli's womb—and spilled into Eli, hot and thick and gushing.

Eli arched up with a keening moan, his hand working furiously as his own orgasm swept over him, his toes curling and his insides clenching and spasming, milking Noah, whose eyes were shut tight, his face frozen in a pained mask, a low growl leaving his lips. His scent bloomed, deeper and richer, and Eli panted with an open mouth, trying to drink it in, to bathe his insides in it the way they were bathed in Noah's cum.

Even with the overwhelming wave of pleasure, he was half aware he needed to prepare himself for the possibility of a knot, to be ready to pull away if necessary. But it didn't happen—there was no burgeoning pressure at his entrance, nothing that might lock their bodies together. Eli tried his best not to be disappointed by that, even as his hole continued spasming, like it was searching for that extra width.

It was ridiculous. It wasn't like he *wanted* to be knotted by a relative stranger. There was a reason one-night stands didn't allow themselves to be locked together for an hour ... or hours plural.

That would be ... awkward. Not hot.

Definitely not hot.

Noah opened his eyes, and Eli wondered if it was pervy of him, the way he was beginning to crave that worshipful tinge to Noah's gaze. "Holy fuck."

Eli swiped his clean hand—the one not covered by his own cum—through Noah's damp curls. "You liked it?"

Noah laughed, the sound somehow both deep and bright. "That was the most amazing thing in the history of the universe," he declared. "I need to become a poet so I can write, like, a sonnet about it."

Eli giggled, thoroughly charmed. "No poetry, please. I should have warned you about that too. It's one of the hookup rules."

"I didn't knot you though." Noah grinned at him. "I was a good boy."

"I know."

"I was too nervous, I think."

Some part of Eli relaxed at that. Of course. It wasn't that he wasn't a worthy omega (and what was he even doing, thinking like that outside of a heat?). It was just that they were strangers, and it was Noah's first time. The circumstances weren't exactly conducive to a knot.

"Did I make you feel good?" Noah asked, his gaze searching Eli's face for some sign. "Tell me honestly."

"You made me feel amazing," Eli reassured him. And it was true. What Noah had lacked in skill he'd more than made up for with enthusiasm. And a very specific type of intensity, one that somehow turned Eli on without making him feel self-conscious.

"Good." Noah's head dipped down as he rubbed against the crook of Eli's shoulder, scent marking him again. As if they weren't already drenched in each other's pheromones.

Eli tilted his neck, fully encouraging the unnecessary gesture.

When Eli was thoroughly saturated with his scent, Noah finally pulled out. Eli's chest tightened at the obscene gush of slick —why was it so embarrassing sometimes?—but Noah looked positively mesmerized, frozen in place and staring at Eli's entrance.

Eli cleared his throat. "Now would be the time to politely offer to clean up your partner."

"Of course." But Noah didn't move, giving Eli a sheepish grin. "Unless you'd want to ..."

Eli's gaze dropped down, his eyes widening in disbelief. Noah's cock was standing upright once again, covered in Eli's fluids and dripping onto the mattress. "Oh my god. You're hard again. You—" He giggled, the pressure in his chest loosening, leaving him with a light, airy feeling. "You really are young."

"I am," Noah said with an easier smile, his hand stroking Eli's hip. "But also you're really, really sexy."

Eli wasn't. He never had been. He was too serious. Too awkward. Too determined in his work and not focused enough on being the right kind of omega.

But in this moment, with Noah, Eli could almost believe it.

He let his legs fall open completely, uncharacteristically wanton. "Okay, Noah. We can do it again."

———

ELI WOKE UP STIFF, his body sore in a very specific, well-used way. He grinned into his pillow before inhaling not so subtly. His pillow

—the entire loft, really—reeked of alpha pheromones and sex. Neither were scents he'd experienced much lately, and he had to resist the urge to mouth at the fabric like a horny loon.

There was a note on the covers next to him, written on the cabin's stationary. A phone number. And underneath:

Had to go. Roommate emergency. Please, please, please call me.

P.S. Best night of my life. A+ teacher.

Xxx

Noah

4

___

Noah

Noah was twitchy as hell as he drove up to the off-campus apartment he shared with his two roommates, his jaw tense and his fingers clenched on the steering wheel.

Usually he loved coming home to his roomies—that was the advantage of living with his best bros—but he had *not* been ready to leave Eli's bed that morning. The omega had been so soft and warm, curled into Noah's chest, and he'd smelled so good, that tart and fresh scent overlaid with the musk of sex, and Noah could have easily rolled them both over and—

He coughed, shifting in his seat. Okay, probably time to stop thinking about it before he walked into the apartment with a raging alpha boner. He took a deep breath as he parked in the drive, trying to calm himself back down.

But fuck, if Spencer hadn't texted, *It's a disaster. 911. Come home immediately,* and then ignored all Noah's texts and calls afterward, Noah would have stayed until Eli kicked him out. He was almost positive Eli would have agreed to a round three. Because round two had been ...

Well, round two had been fucking *great*. Noah hadn't been quite so quick to lose it as the first time, and he'd gotten to touch Eli, to learn how to stroke him in time with his thrusts until he'd had the omega coming because of *him*. Because of *his* touch and *his* cock, whimpering sweetly and spurting all over Noah's fist.

Well, damn. So much for no boner.

Noah tucked his erection into his waistband and hopped out of the car, stopping outside the front door to check his phone one more time and make sure he hadn't missed a text in the five seconds since he'd last looked. He tried to rein in his pheromones and think of unsexy things. *Spencer hitting on uninterested omegas at a house party. Chase mixing scrambled eggs and oatmeal together for "optimum nutrition" before a game. The state of their shared bathroom after a weekend of raging.*

There it was. Just in time, too, as the front door sprang open before Noah had even touched it. There was Spencer, shirtless and in joggers, his dark hair damp and hanging in front of his eyes. He was munching on a bag of some of his weird protein chips. "Fucking finally," he said with his mouth full. "Took your time."

He walked back inside without waiting to see if Noah was following, and Noah caught up with him in the kitchen. He nodded to their other roommate, Chase, who was hunched over a bowl of cereal at the table, his baseball cap pulled down low over his eyes.

Noah rounded on Spencer, who was acting way too nonchalant for Noah's current state. "Dude, I had to come from fucking *Sedona*. What's the big emergency? And why the fuck didn't you pick up?"

Spencer shrugged. "Had to shower." He pointed to the fridge, a giant silver behemoth Chase's parents had gotten for them, frowning at it. "The fridge isn't cooling right."

It took a moment for Noah to process that the *fridge* was the emergency. "Are you fucking kidding me?"

"Nope." Spencer popped another chip in his mouth. "The food's starting to get, like, warm."

"You called me back, from Sedona—"

"I told him not to," Chase murmured.

"What's the big deal? You texted me yesterday to say you were bored as hell and—" Spencer stopped talking suddenly, swallowing his mouthful and sniffing at the air. He lowered his bag of protein chips, staring at Noah. "Holy shit, dude. You *reek* of omega."

Noah froze like a deer in headlights. But of course Spencer could smell it—he was an alpha, too, and even though Noah and Eli had cleaned themselves up as best they could, Noah hadn't had a chance to shower before heading back.

"He does?" Chase raised his head and sniffed the air, his green eyes widening under the brim of his cap. "Dude. Even I can smell it."

That was ... something. Chase was a beta. He didn't let off any pheromones of his own, but he could smell others' if they were strong enough. Apparently, Noah's morning-after scent *was* strong enough.

Good thing he hadn't made any stops along the way. He'd have scarred some poor gas station attendant for life.

Spencer's mouth was hanging open like a true dope, his tongue piercing glinting in the kitchen light. "Did you—did you get *laid*, Noah?"

"Um—"

"Shit." Spencer sniffed the air again, making a face. "How didn't I smell it first thing? I should have come with you. That omega I was texting with totally ghosted me. If I'd known there'd be, like, a cabin of hot coeds next door ..."

Because of course that had been the reason Spencer had

bailed on the getaway. He hadn't ever quite mastered the ol' bros before hookups rule. Too addicted to the attention he got from romantic hopefuls. Noah had every right to still be pissed about it, but after Eli ... he supposed he was more grateful than anything.

Except for the whole *calling him back for no fucking reason* part.

"Holy shit," Spencer said again, shaking his head. "You lost your v-card." He raised his hand for a high-five, flipping Noah off when he didn't meet him halfway. "I thought you were too picky to, like, ever get down."

"Don't be a dick," Chase scolded mildly. He caught Noah's eye. "You met someone?"

"Yeah. An older omega," Noah told him, glaring at Spencer when the dick let out a wolf whistle. "He was— He's, um ... Yeah, it was really good."

It was the most inadequate description of events ever, but Noah found himself strangely tongue-tied. He would have told his roommates eventually—he was too smitten already to keep things to himself—but he hadn't expected to have to rehash the experience quite so soon.

He should have known. They were way too in one another's business.

Spencer tossed his bag of protein chips aside, scratching at his chest. "Whoa. He broke your brain." He leered at Noah. "That can happen the first time, you know."

Noah rolled his eyes. "I'm surprised you remember your first time. That was, what, a thousand omegas ago?"

"Whoa, whoa." Spencer held up his hands. "Don't take your morning-after regrets out on me. And I fuck all kinds, thank you very much. Omegas. Betas. Alphas. Don't box me in like that."

Noah barely contained another eye roll, but he wasn't actually looking to get into an argument over Spencer's sexual predilections. Not when there were better things to be pissed about. "I can't believe you called it a fucking emergency that the fridge is a little warm."

Spencer winced, looking properly apologetic for the first time that day. "Sorry, man. I didn't know you'd find some omega babe over there." He rubbed a hand over the back of his neck. "It's just —I've already meal prepped for next week. If it goes bad, that's, like, a week's worth of groceries down the drain."

Some of Noah's annoyance settled. Money was tight for Spencer, and as much as the other alpha pretended to just fall out of bed looking carefree and gorgeous, he put a lot of effort into his appearance, including his prepped high-protein meals. He ate more like an athlete than some actual athletes did, trying to keep in peak shape. From what he'd told Noah, he'd been pretty scrawny as a kid, before he'd presented, and it seemed like he had some baggage from that.

Not that Noah would ever say as much to him.

"It's fine, dude. Let me take a look."

Chase stood from the table, setting his empty bowl in the sink. "I told him we can just call the fridge repair guy."

Spencer scoffed. "Why call someone for something we can just fix ourselves?"

He meant something *Noah* could fix, but the sentiment still stood. Chase was the reason they could afford such a spacious apartment so close to campus, each with their own room. His family was loaded, enough that he'd given up his sports scholarship for lacrosse the year before and his parents hadn't even cared. But Spencer and Noah were a little different. Spencer's mom was more broke than he was, and while Noah's parents did fine, they also had a lot of kids. There wasn't exactly a ton of extra money floating around.

He and Spencer were both scared to push Chase's parents' generosity too far.

Luckily, Noah had a good amount of experience fixing things

around the house. Stuff tended to break when you had a pack of kids running wild, like he and his siblings had. "Lemme look. Did you try adjusting the thermostat?"

Spencer gave him a wounded look. "I'm not a complete idiot."

"Debatable." Noah opened the fridge, spotting the problem immediately. "You've just packed it too tight. Your oat milk is blocking the vent."

"The what now?" Spencer asked, looking over his shoulder.

Noah sighed, digging items out of the top shelf. He spent the next ten minutes rearranging the fridge, and then cleaned off the vent thoroughly, just in case buildup was the real issue. When he was done, he washed his hands, telling his roommates, "We'll recheck in an hour, make sure it's cooling right. If that's not the problem, we might need to call someone after all."

He dug his phone out of his pocket, checking it again, even though he would have heard the telltale ding.

Chase settled against the counter next to him, knocking his shoulder. "Texting your omega?"

"I can't. I don't know his number. I left him mine, but—" Noah shrugged, trying to play off nonchalance and probably falling completely short. Maybe he should have woken Eli up after all, made absolutely sure of the number exchange before leaving.

He'd never even considered that Eli wouldn't take him up on it.

"He'll call." Chase knocked his shoulder again, gentle but reassuring. "You know how many omegas have tried to get your number?"

Noah frowned down at his phone. "Not *that* many."

"More than you think. Spence runs interference on half of them."

Spencer grinned shamelessly. "I'm selfless like that." He clasped his hands in front of his chest, all faux earnestness. "Tell us, Noah. Tell us of the one who finally stole your heart."

"Um ..." Noah wasn't sure what to tell. He could talk about Eli's kind eyes. How warm they were, even with a stranger. Or his scent, the way it had caught Noah's interest immediately, lovely and subtle and perfect. Or the way Eli had held himself so seriously in the beginning but giggled like a kid when a bit of humor caught him off guard.

But he found himself wanting to keep all that close to his chest for now.

"He's a teacher," he said instead.

"Oh yeah?" Chase asked. "What grade?"

"Shit." Noah shook his head. "I'm such a dick. I didn't even ask. Maybe elementary school? Or middle school? I could see him being good with older kids. He's ... patient."

"Okay, tell us the truth." Spencer dropped his clasped hands, settling them on Noah's shoulders. "Did you come in five seconds, or did you make it to ten?"

————

MONDAY MORNING CAME MUCH TOO SOON, and Noah had to fight not to put out grumpy dick vibes as the three of them walked to campus.

Chase and Spencer seemed content enough to start classes back up. It wasn't surprising—they were both decent students, and the three of them had all planned similar schedules for the semester, maximizing hang time outside of school and work. Their first class on Monday was at a reasonable ten a.m., and Noah had made them all eggs after Spencer had nagged at him for long enough.

Plus, it was hard to be miserable when the start of spring semester was always so fucking gorgeous, the Arizona heat lowered to a perfect temperature at the beginning of January, the skies sunny and temperate.

Noah should have been just as stoked as the other two, but he was finding it hard to muster the excitement. Eli hadn't texted Saturday. Or Sunday, for that matter.

Maybe he wouldn't text at all.

"Why the fuck are you so gloomy?" Spencer asked, tugging on Noah's backpack and making it clear Noah had lost the don't-come-off-as-a-grumpy-dick battle. "Regretting your decision to take Omega Studies?"

Noah gave him a shove toward the side of the path. "No."

"Why *are* you taking it, anyway?" Spencer let the momentum of Noah's shove land him at Chase's side, slinging an arm around the beta's shoulders. "Think they messed up your designation?"

Noah wished Spencer was still in shoving distance, but he had to make do with flipping him off. "It fulfills one of my gen ed requirements, genius. Plus, my folks think all alphas should be required to take it. For a bit of empathy." He said the last part pointedly, but if Spencer caught it, he brushed it right off.

"Why are *you* taking it, then?" Spencer gave Chase's shoulders a little shake, directing his question to the beta.

Chase shrugged, walking easily despite Spencer's manhandling. "Because I wanted a class with Noah."

"Ugh. Why are you so cute?" Spencer pinched Chase's cheek, avoiding his half-hearted answering punch easily, then leaned over to swipe a hand down Noah's neck in a casual scent marking before veering off in the direction of his own class. "Your funeral, bros! Let's meet for lunch!"

Noah and Chase both stopped for a moment, staring after his departure. "Is it too late to give him back?" Noah asked.

"Yeah, pretty sure we're stuck with him."

It was nonsense anyway, and they both knew it. Their trio had been in the same freshman orientation group, and they'd all just … clicked. Three years later and they were living together by choice, so apparently there was no unclicking to be had.

The two of them kept on toward class, and Chase caught Noah looking at his phone again. "Still no text?"

Noah glared at his phone. "Maybe—maybe I wasn't any good."

It hadn't felt that way at the time. It had felt fucking amazing, the way Eli's body had taken him in. The little sounds he'd made, and the way his legs had locked behind Noah's hips, pulling him in closer. Noah wanted more of it. He wanted Eli to ride him, to see what it looked like with that small frame grinding down on top of him. He wanted to fucking taste him, to part Eli's cheeks and tongue every bit of slick out of him. He wanted to *knot* him, to stuff him full and keep him close for hours, pushing him into orgasm after orgasm.

"Dude."

Noah came out of his horny fog to find Chase staring at him. "What?"

"Are you—?" Chase wrinkled his nose with a cough. "Your pheromones, man."

"Oh fuck." Noah reined them in again with a bit of effort, wincing. "Sorry."

"No worries." Chase gave another awkward cough. "I can barely smell it," he lied. "Just thought you might not want to rock up to the lecture hall putting out sex signals for all to scent."

Noah shoved his phone back in his pocket, irritated with himself. He wasn't some newly presented alpha, letting his rampant pheromones run wild like that. "What's *wrong* with me?"

"You've got a crush." Chase shrugged, turning the brim of his cap backward. "Happens to the best of us."

"Doesn't happen to you," Noah pointed out.

Chase wasn't a virgin, but Noah had never seen him falling hard for anyone either. The beta was kind of ... reserved. It probably would have been good for him to have a crush, actually. He'd been sort of subdued since leaving the lacrosse team last year.

Chase claimed he didn't regret it, and Noah had a feeling that was at least partially true, but he still seemed off.

"That's cause I'm— *Oof.*"

Noah caught Chase's arm as the beta stumbled, having run straight into a broad chest. The man he'd run into was an alpha for sure. And probably a professor, based on how he was dressed, in a tight button-down and slacks. He had a sheaf of handouts in his hands, half of which had dropped to the ground when Chase had crashed into him.

And Chase was just staring at him, wide-eyed.

Noah stepped forward. "Sorry, man," he said. "I'll grab—" He stopped when the alpha professor sent a piercing look his way, a rush of dark, heavy pheromones freezing Noah in place.

Holy shit. That was some intense stuff, even for another alpha.

It was Chase who unfroze first, kneeling and grabbing the papers, handing them back to the professor. "Here you are, sir."

The alpha took them from him, locking eyes with Chase. "There's a good boy," he murmured, his voice a deep rumble. Or at least, that was what Noah thought he'd said, but that would have been, like, way inappropriate, wouldn't it? The alpha nodded. "Carry on, then."

And after one last, lingering glance at Chase, he swept past them, heading into the math and sciences building.

Noah shivered, tucking his thumbs into the straps of his backpack. "Who the fuck was that?"

"Professor Burke," Chase told him, his eyes still on the retreating alpha. "He teaches statistics. I had him last semester."

"How the fuck did you survive? He's terrifying."

Chase shrugged. His cheeks were red—maybe he was embarrassed he'd crashed into the guy and sent his papers flying. "If you're polite, he's actually pretty chill."

"His pheromones are—" Noah let out a heavy breath. "Just be glad you're a beta."

"Yeah." Chase laughed, tugging Noah forward again. "Sure."

They headed into their building, finding a pair of seats a few rows back. The class was structured so that they had a weekly lecture and then split into discussion groups led by TAs twice a week. It was a large lecture hall, and it still looked like it was going to be mostly full.

Noah was mostly looking forward to the class, despite his general grumpiness. He'd heard good things about Professor Miller—the omega professor had positive reviews on the school forums, and his lectures were supposed to be interesting.

Had Eli ever taken a class like this as an undergrad? Noah grinned for maybe the first time that day, leaning down to dig his laptop out of his backpack. He could totally see it, Eli shaking his finger at any presumptuous alphas in his discussion group. *"Alphas shouldn't knot omegas they've just met!"*

And maybe thinking about Eli had Noah imagining things, because he could swear he smelled that tart, refreshing scent, standing out even amid all the random, innocuous pheromones in the lecture hall.

Meanwhile, the cacophony of murmuring students had hushed, meaning the professor had probably arrived.

Noah sat back up, his laptop in hand, and immediately choked on his own spit.

Because there, at the podium, was Eli. *His* Eli.

"Hello, everyone." Eli was dressed in light-colored slacks and a crewneck sweater. He looked ridiculously cute, small in stature but self-possessed, those warm eyes sweeping over the auditorium. "I'm Professor Miller. I'll be teaching you Omega Studies this semester."

5

Eli

Eli's second night in the cabin was incredibly lackluster compared to the first.

He felt stupid for being so disappointed. It wasn't like he'd expected to spend either of his nights with anyone. If anything, this was just things going back to the original plan.

But still ...

How was it possible for Eli to miss someone he'd just met?

A nice beta woman arrived at what had previously been Noah's cabin in the evening, after the cleaning service had left. She waved at Eli from her hot tub but didn't ask for company or invite herself over.

Of course she didn't, because who really did that? Only ridiculously attractive, painfully young alphas with gorgeous smiles and delicious scents who disappeared like smoke in the morning but still left their number, leaving the ball in *Eli's* court, as if he had any idea what to do with it now that he had it.

He thought of Noah often for the rest of his getaway.

Obviously.

Even when he didn't want to, when he was trying to focus on mundane tasks, like washing his dishes in the sink before his departure, Eli would suddenly remember the feel of Noah's hand on his thigh, or the way Noah's features tightened right before he came, or the sound of Noah's voice breaking while he asked if Eli felt good, felt as good as *Noah* did ...

And then Eli would suddenly be fighting for air, or a trickle of slick would be escaping him, and he'd be both turned on and embarrassed by his lack of control.

He kept the slip of paper with Noah's number on it in his pocket, taking it out to stare it at now and then, rubbing his fingers along the edges. He hadn't programmed the number into his phone just yet. He wasn't sure why.

Or he *was* sure, but he didn't know how to articulate it. Didn't know if he was being smart or if he was being foolish.

So on the morning of Eli's departure, the day before the start of the semester, he did the dumbest thing he could do.

He texted his sister to meet him for brunch.

She immediately said yes, of course, and met him at one of their favorite spots, a diner that could be considered pretentious or homey depending how one looked at it. But they served fried green tomato sandwiches with grilled bread practically soaking in butter, so Eli just looked at it as delicious.

Faith was already there when he arrived, immaculately dressed as always, with her dark hair set in elegant waves, sitting in a booth by the window. Eli took a seat across from her, unable to keep eye contact after their initial greeting.

Not with that look on her face.

"You know," Faith said conversationally. "When I told you to get dicked down by a hunky alpha, I was being facetious." She grinned, apparently uncaring that their server was at the table, filling their waters. "I didn't think you'd actually follow my suggestion."

Eli shared a horrified look with their server, who mumbled something about coming back at a later time for their order. Eli waited for the man to leave before dropping his head into his hands. "This is my nightmare."

Faith only cackled.

Eli peered at her through his fingers. "How could you tell?"

He'd showered and hot-tubbed multiple times since his night with Noah. Even with all the extra scent marking, he highly doubted he still smelled like alpha.

"You have that look," Faith told him, twirling her finger at him. "Like you're—"

"If you say freshly fuc—"

"Like you're *embarrassed*," she said, talking right over him. "And a little self-satisfied. And ... guilty." She cocked her head. "Why are you feeling guilty? If it's about Richard, then fuck that six ways to Sunday."

"No, it's not that." Eli hadn't thought about his ex at all since the other night, his head too full of Noah. He bit at his lip, looking somewhere in the general vicinity of his sister's nose. "He was ... young."

Faith narrowed her eyes. "How young?"

"I don't know ... mid-twenties?"

Faith's concern was instantly replaced by a look of fierce delight, but Eli shook his head. "Don't even say it. That's too young for me." He leaned across the booth, whispering, "I took his virginity, Faith."

Faith's jaw didn't exactly drop, but it seemed to be a close call. Eli might have been proud of himself for actually shocking her for once, but he was too mortified to take any real pleasure in it. She took a delicate sip of water. Smacked her lips. Then gave him a Cheshire grin. "Eli Miller, I did *not* think you had it in you."

"Ugh." Eli hid his face behind his menu, sliding down in the booth. "Don't be proud of me."

"Why not?"

"I don't know. Isn't it maybe not a great thing to do with a one-night stand?"

"Was it consensual?"

"Yes."

"Enthusiastically so?"

Eli's cheeks heated at the memory of just how ... enthusiastic the consent had been. "Yes."

"Then so what?" When Eli didn't have an answer for her, Faith popped open her menu, perusing it like she wasn't going to order the same thing she did every time, just like Eli. "But why one night only? That's not usually your thing."

Eli rolled his eyes. "I've been married for the past decade. There is no 'my thing.'"

"You know what I mean." Faith paused, and her pheromones suddenly surged, sharp and protective. "Was this dumb, young alpha *using* you?"

"No!" Eli insisted, grabbing her wrist for a quick, reassuring scent marking. Her pheromones calmed immediately. "And he wasn't dumb," he chastised. "And he left his number."

"But you didn't like him?"

"No, I liked him a lot."

"Okay ..." Faith set her menu down, fixing him with her stern, older sister look. "Help me out here, Eli. I'm good, but I'm not a mind reader."

"He's *young*," Eli said again, not sure of how else to put it. When Faith's expression didn't change, he tried a different tack. "Think of yourself in your twenties. Think of how ... inexperienced you were. He might think he likes me, but he just hasn't seen enough to know."

It was Faith's turn to roll her eyes. "That sounds like you're talking about yourself. Yourself and Richard. Who, we've already established, can absolutely get fucked, and not in a good way."

Their server, who had been bravely approaching again, did an abrupt turnaround.

Eli was never getting his fried green tomato sandwich at this point.

"I'm just saying people change their minds," he said. "And we barely know each other. I think he was just doing what he thought you're supposed to do. Trying to be ... polite."

"Banging and bailing," Faith deadpanned. "How polite. But if you don't think he's really serious about seeing you, then chuck his number, and you can tuck the whole thing into your pocket as a good, unexpected experience. You rebounded!" she crowed, way too loud for where they were, gesturing the server back over. "Finally!"

They ordered, and Eli decided to leave it at that.

Faith would listen, if he really wanted to talk it out more. She was always there for him when he really needed it. She worked in marketing and could have moved to whatever city she wanted, but she'd followed him to Phoenix when he'd gotten his faculty position here. It had worked out for her—she'd found herself an omega wife she adored, who adored her in turn. But still, she'd made the move for him.

And she'd listened, endlessly patient, to all his issues with Richard over the years. All the disappointments and regrets. Eli just didn't have it in him to bring her more relationship drama to dissect so soon. Didn't have the heart to tell her, "Hey, I know I only just finalized my divorce and I've only known this guy for one night, but I might really like him, and I'm afraid to call and find out I was wrong about it after all?"

Faith was right. Eli should just let the whole thing be what it was—two strangers finding temporary pleasure in each other. Noah would meet so many omegas in the coming years, and now that he'd had some experience, maybe he would loosen his exacting standards, let himself experience a little more.

That was what youth was for. Not shackling himself to the first person he found that he liked the smell of. That was the road that led to divorce in one's thirties.

So Eli would leave it at that. And he wouldn't tell his sister he was still carrying the number in his pocket like a pathetic talisman.

Fine.

Good.

Smart.

————

MONDAY MORNING CAME MUCH TOO QUICKLY.

Normally Eli was excited to start the new semester, but he woke up to a heavy weight on his chest. And he didn't just mean World's Deadliest Assassin, although his cat *was* heavy as hell, folded into a loaf on top of Eli's chest and purring at him menacingly.

"You have a robotic feeder," Eli told her, too sleepy to sound properly stern. "So don't look at me like that."

In the next second, the telltale sound of the feeder going off echoed through the house, and Deadly proved his point by hopping off him and running for her breakfast.

Eli was tempted to hit snooze on his alarm and pretend the day didn't exist for another half hour, but he liked a leisurely morning before work, and sleeping through it didn't hold the same satisfaction. So he rolled out of bed to take his shower, donning his robe afterward and pouring himself a cup of coffee to take into the yard.

He fished some leaves out of the pool, sipping slowly, enjoying the cool of the morning.

Should he sell the house?

It was the thousandth time he'd asked himself that question in the past year. It seemed like he should have been making some sort of bid for a fresh start, but he and Richard had only moved there right before the separation—their version of a Band-Aid baby, though *not* the version Richard had wanted—and it wasn't like Eli was dodging happy marital memories left and right.

Richard had barely been at home in the end, and he definitely hadn't put any of himself into the house. It should have been Eli's first sign that things were really ending—Richard not having a thousand fucking opinions for once.

He looked to see Deadly at the door to the yard, her face pressed against the glass, watching him intently. "I won it fair and square in the settlement," he told her, aware that she could probably only half hear him. And also that she was a cat, not a therapist.

Eli liked the house too. It was a cute single-story, two-bedroom next to campus, the perfect size for him. The property was completely walled off, which made for good privacy, especially with the little pool in the backyard, which was crucial for the summertime.

Maybe Eli would start holding wild pool parties with the other professors. They'd drink martinis and smoke cigarettes, and anyone in a couple would have to agree to swing before they were allowed across the premises.

He grinned at the thought. He'd rather die, honestly, but it was fun to have the option.

Although, another option immediately popped into his treacherous brain.

Noah.

Noah coming over all alone, late at night. Noah sliding into Eli's pool completely nude, his big alpha frame lit only by the pool light. Noah fucking Eli up over the edge of it, his arms strong and sure around him, his breath hot in Eli's ear.

Eli took a huge gulp of coffee, yelping as he burned the roof of his mouth.

Fuck.

Bad thoughts, he chastised. *Bad, bad thoughts. We're leaving the poor guy alone, not inviting him over for late-night booty calls.*

But Eli was keeping the house; that was certain. He'd already known he was keeping it—his brain had just been looking for something to fret over. Which apparently it needed to do to not descend into pervy fantasies about Noah at any given time.

Eli headed back inside and had his breakfast before getting dressed, not allowing himself to acknowledge the piece of paper he slipped into his pants pocket. He grabbed his work bag, kissed Deadly on the head, and drove the short distance over to campus.

He busied himself with work for the next hour before class. There was nothing to grade, not yet, but he had emails from the various committees he was part of that he needed to answer.

The important thing to remember was that he was content. He was *not* lonely. Because it would be pathetic to be lonely after being single for only a year, after a decade in a marriage he'd wanted out of for at least half that.

Be honest, Eli, you were for all intents and purposes single for a lot longer than that.

Eli scowled at his laptop. He was beginning to think the vacation he really needed was from his own brain.

By the time he arrived in the classroom, however, he was feeling mostly normal. One of his TAs had set up the PowerPoint for the lecture, and Eli had been able to show up late—or his version of late, which was exactly on time.

He stood at the podium, waiting for the class to quiet down before he spoke. "Hello, everyone. I'm Professor Miller. I'll be teaching you Omega Studies this semester."

He took a deep breath, ready to dive into the class logistics, only to falter, choking on air.

That scent.

Eli knew that scent. Salty and fresh, like ocean air.

His gaze slid unerringly to the third row, drawn like a magnet to a familiar head of loose blond curls. Noah.

Noah was here.

How did he find me? Eli thought dazedly before realizing by the shocked look on Noah's face—he hadn't come here for Eli. He was here for the lecture.

Noah was a student. An undergraduate student.

Eli's student.

There was a rustling from over in the corner where Eli's TAs sat, and Eli realized he'd stopped talking and was staring into his crowd of students like he had more than one screw loose. He forced a smile on his face. "Sorry about that." He shrugged with a little grimace. "Mondays."

The class was gracious enough to let out a few scattered laughs, and Eli pressed on, letting his gaze fall anywhere but the third row. "I'm so pleased you've all chosen to take this course, whatever your reasons may be. There's a lot to cover, so the lectures will go quickly, but you'll have your discussion sections to really get into the nitty-gritty. My office hours are—"

He got through the lecture somehow.

It helped that the first class covered mostly logistics. And that he'd been teaching this exact course for a few years now. It probably wasn't his most engaging lecture of all time—and undoubtedly he was leaving a bad impression for the rest of the semester—but he supposed that was what he got for *fucking his goddamn student.*

He couldn't think about it. Not in the lecture hall. Every time he did, his skin grew hot and his belly swooped with nerves.

He would have liked to run right out of there afterward, but it wasn't an option. Eli always left time for students to come up to him after a lecture, either to say hello or to ask questions. A few did this time, and he interacted with them in some sort of fugue state.

But eventually, the rest of the lecture hall emptied out, and there was Noah, approaching the podium. Another student stood behind him, a generically handsome kid in a backward baseball cap with a confused look on his face, but he headed out after a glance from Noah.

And then there was just Noah and Eli.

"Professor Miller?" Noah asked softly, like Eli was a horse he was afraid of spooking. "May I have a moment?"

Well, fuck.

6

Noah

The lecture had been ...

Well, honestly, Noah had no idea how the lecture had been. All his concentration had been spent keeping his wayward pheromones in check.

Because there had been Eli—*his* Eli—right in front of him, and Noah had wanted nothing more than to run up to that teaching podium, shove his head in the crook of Eli's neck, and scent mark him like nobody's fucking business.

But that would have been uncool to the millionth degree—for more than one reason—so Noah had been forced to just sit there, watching Eli but not being able to touch or scent or speak to him, and it had made something primal in Noah ... frustrated, to say the least.

Chase had cast him more than a few concerned glances, but Noah had only shaken his head at his friend, forcing a smile to let him know it wasn't anything dire. Noah would definitely have to rely on Chase's notes later because he hadn't exactly been soaking in all the info Eli had given them.

Eli. Professor Miller.

Noah knew Eli had seen him. He'd watched the blatant shock appear on Eli's face, had made brief but electric eye contact with those warm brown eyes before Eli had recovered his composure and started looking everywhere else *but* Noah.

But now the other students were gone—fucking finally—and it was just them. Noah and Eli.

It would have been perfect, if not for the completely panicked look on Eli's face, the one that had appeared the second Noah had asked him for a moment together.

"Noah," Eli squeaked, his voice coming out about an octave higher than usual. He opened and closed his mouth a few times, no more words coming out, and right when Noah was about to speak, he finally whisper-yelled (even though no one else was in there, and the lecture hall door was closed), "You said you were a grad student!"

"Um ..." Noah scratched at his jaw, taken aback. "No, I didn't. I said I was taking business classes. And I am. It's my major. My *undergrad* major."

He gave Eli a reassuring smile, since the omega seemed to be freaking out. Or he thought he did, but Eli's panic didn't seem to be lessening, his tasty omega scent taking on a bitter, distressed note. "And you don't, um, teach middle school, I take it."

"Middle school?" Eli said it like it was the most preposterous thing he'd ever heard. "I would never. They'd eat me alive." He stared at Noah for another long moment, then scrubbed at his face with his hands. "Oh my god, I slept with a fetus."

Noah wrinkled his nose. Gross. And a little offensive. He wasn't a *child*. But Eli was going through it—clearly—so Noah let it slide, pressing on through the awkwardness. "I should have known you were a total brainiac," he said, pride welling up in him at the thought. "You have a PhD, don't you?"

"I—what?" Eli took a moment out of his panic to frown at Noah, as if he was offended by the implication that he might not. "Yes, of course I do."

"Awesome."

Eli seemed to register the no doubt adoring look on Noah's face, and even more of his panic receded, suspicion taking over the shell-shocked cast to his features. "Why aren't you freaking out right now?" he asked warily.

Noah shrugged, unable to contain his grin. "I was starting to think I'd never hear from you. And I had no way to find you. But now you're here."

He was. And he looked so fucking good too. Even all dressed up for lecture, there was still something warm and approachable about Eli. He was probably a fucking fantastic teacher. Look at how well he'd taught the class, even with the shock of Noah's presence. Calm under pressure for sure.

"I'm here as your professor," Eli said slowly, like Noah might not have caught that bit, never mind that he'd already called him "Professor Miller."

But Noah didn't want to get into all that right now. Not when they'd just found each other again. He hiked his backpack up higher on his shoulder. "Why didn't you use my number?" he asked, trying not to let the insecurity of the past few days come through in his voice. "You did get my note, right?"

"I—" Eli gaped at him. "You're my *student*."

"Yeah, but you didn't know that at the time." Noah leaned in, lowering his voice. "I missed you."

Eli flushed at the admission, his eyes dropping to Noah's lips. Finally, maybe they were getting somewhere. Noah stepped a little closer, not afraid to press his advantage. It wasn't nearly as close as he wanted to be, but despite his selective deafness re: their student/teacher status, Noah *was* aware Eli was majorly freaking out. He wasn't going to jump the gun and add to that panic.

And, yeah, maybe Noah should have been freaking out, too, but he was just so fucking happy to see Eli. He'd been dealing with this steady, simmering despair at the thought that he'd let the best thing to happen to him in forever slip away, but now he knew he hadn't.

Eli was right there, and that had to be like ... fucking fate, right?

And now that Eli *was* in front of him, Noah was surer than ever that the connection between them had been real. He hadn't imagined it, hadn't exaggerated it in his head. Sure, Eli might have been stressed as hell at the moment, but he wasn't indifferent to Noah. *That* would have been unbearable—indifference. But a case of nerves?

Noah could deal with that. Easy.

"Can I scent mark you?" he found himself asking.

Jesus. So much for not jumping the gun.

Eli spluttered at him for a minute or so, which was pretty fucking cute, before he gathered his words. "What? No. Jesus. We can't—"

"Just a little," Noah told him. "I'm kind of losing it here."

It was true. He might not have been freaking out about the teacher thing—all new couples had their setbacks, right?—but there was a strange, jittery energy dancing under his skin, and it had been there ever since he'd caught Eli's scent in the classroom. It was like the inner alpha part of him was all over the place. He knew he and Eli weren't bonded or anything, but it still felt like *his* omega was here, smelling nothing like him, and that seemed weirdly unacceptable.

Was this a virgin thing? This ... clinginess?

Eli eyed him skeptically. "Our versions of losing it are very different."

Noah threw his head back and laughed.

Eli's lips twitched, but he still looked skeptical.

"For all anyone knows, we could be casual acquaintances," Noah reasoned. "Scent marking wouldn't be totally out of the realm of appropriate."

It was a stretch, and he knew it, but after another moment of studying him, Eli held out his hand. Noah grabbed Eli's wrist immediately, his thumb sliding along the scent gland there.

He let out a sigh of relief, his tense muscles relaxing.

Eli gave him a small smile. "Better?"

"You have no idea," Noah told him with a smile of his own. He kept rubbing his thumb along that gland, willing to stay there as long as Eli would let him. "Why didn't you call?" he asked again.

Eli shrugged, his gaze dancing away toward the back wall. "I thought—I thought maybe you'd have realized it was a one-time thing."

Noah didn't miss the fact that Eli hadn't said *he* had realized it was a one-time thing. Hope blossomed in his chest, and his pheromones swelled before he could stop them. "You did?"

Eli's gaze returned to his, and Noah's breath caught. He was right; he knew it—there was something there. Something real. Something good.

But Eli pulled his arm back, out of Noah's hold. "And I was right."

He twisted away, bending to stuff his laptop and USB stick into his satchel. "This can't happen, Noah. What we had—it was really, really great. But that was it." He turned back, not quite meeting Noah's eyes. "I—I have to get to a meeting. Are you going to be okay?"

Noah recognized temporary defeat when he saw it. It was probably even reasonable of Eli, as much as Noah might hate it. "Sure," he made himself say agreeably. "I'll be fine."

Eli nodded once and then hurried out of the lecture hall.

Noah watched him go. It was easier to handle than it might have been, now that Eli smelled a little like him again.

And really ... a one-time thing? With the connection they'd had?

Yeah fucking right.

———

WITH THE RUSH of the semester's classes starting and the roommates' tendencies to take all their meals together, it was Wednesday evening before Chase cornered Noah without Spencer around.

Noah should have been expecting it, really. Chase may not have had the lock on pheromones that an alpha or an omega would have, but he was observant as hell.

He found Noah sprawled on his bed, surrounded by textbooks, his laptop, and the notebook where he liked to jot the important things down by hand.

Noah's door was open, but Chase knocked on the doorframe anyway, always polite like that. His ever-present cap was off, and his dirty-blond hair flopped from a perfect center part, like some sort of nineties teen heartthrob. "You doing your reading for Omega Studies?"

"You know it," Noah told him. They had their discussion section tomorrow, and Noah wasn't going to be caught slacking in that class, not even by one of Eli's TAs.

Chase came to sit on the edge of the bed. "You knew our professor."

"Yeah." Noah cleared his throat, his eyes on his laptop. "We've, um, met before."

It was weird keeping secrets. Normally Noah would have told his roommates first thing once he'd found Eli, especially after all that moping he'd been doing about not getting a text. But with how freaked out Eli had been about their … statuses, Noah wasn't going to go blabbing it to everyone. He was young—as Eli loved to point out—but he wasn't stupid.

Unfortunately, neither was Chase.

"You said your older omega was a teacher. The one from Sedona."

"Yeah." Noah nodded. Super casual. Super chill. "Middle school."

"You said you *thought* it was middle school," Chase corrected mildly, fiddling with the spine of one of Noah's textbooks. "You hadn't actually asked him."

"Oh. Um. Right."

"And I've noticed you haven't been checking your phone for texts like a fucking maniac. Not since Monday."

"Yep." Noah kept staring at his laptop. He wasn't reading a word—the screen starting to blur as he lost focus—but who the fuck needed to know that? "I gave up. He's not gonna text."

There was a long silence, then Chase spoke, so softly Noah almost missed it. "I'm not going to tell."

Noah finally took his eyes off his laptop. Chase was looking back at him, calm and not at all expectant. Like Noah could tell him it was none of his business and he wouldn't be offended.

"There's nothing to tell," Noah told him, and when Chase gave him a wounded look at the blatant lie, he added, "Because if there *was* something to tell, it wouldn't be my secret. Or, you know, I wouldn't be the one hurt by it in the end. You get it?"

Chase's expression cleared, and Noah grinned. He wasn't freaked out Chase had figured it out, not exactly. Chase wasn't a blab or anything. Noah just didn't want to say it out loud. Not when Eli was the one whose job could be in jeopardy if word got around.

Still, it was a relief to have a friend who might be in his corner, even if he didn't know any of the details.

Noah's grin turned mischievous as he leaned into Chase's space. "Hey, did you know our university doesn't have an official fraternization policy between students and professors?"

Chase's eyes widened. "What?"

"Like, I'm sure it's still frowned upon majorly, but it's not in writing. Some universities have it in writing."

Noah knew because he'd checked. And double-checked. And triple-checked. He was going to be engaging in a battle for Eli's affection, and the battle was going to be between Noah's charm and Eli's common sense. No way was Noah walking into a thing like that unprepared.

Chase nodded slowly, his lips twitching at the corners. "Interesting, man."

"Yeah." Noah grinned so wide it made his face hurt. "Interesting."

And then he let out a loud "oomph!" as he was hit with a twenty-ton weight. A.k.a. Spencer, who'd dive-bombed on top of him on the bed and was now rubbing his nose into Noah's hair, obnoxiously scenting him as Noah fought for his life. "What's so interesting? And don't say homework. You two are nerdy enough as it is."

It was a ridiculous thing to say, considering Spencer had perfect grades. He was anal as fuck about his academic scholarship, and he didn't take any chances with it.

"We're discussing babes," Noah told him dryly, giving up the fight and letting himself be flattened into the mattress. It was the only way with Spencer. If Noah tried too hard to buck him off, he'd just turn it into some all-out wrestling match.

"No, you're not," Spencer said. "Without me?"

He let out an oomph of his own as Chase decked him with one of Noah's pillows.

Noah prepared himself for that to turn into the exact kind of wrestling match he'd been trying to avoid, but Spencer let the pillow bounce off him, tucking his head into Noah's shoulder instead. "Hey," he said, uncharacteristically subdued.

Shit. Had someone died?

"You know I'm sorry about Sedona, right? I didn't know."

"I know you didn't." Noah reached a hand behind his back to blindly pat somewhere in the direction of Spencer's shoulder. "We're good, man." He wasn't going to hold a grudge over something like that, especially not after he'd found Eli again.

"You're not avoiding me?"

Noah rolled his eyes, even though the gesture was lost on Spencer considering their position. "I made you breakfast just this morning."

"Right, right." Spencer only sounded half convinced, but that was his nature. For all that he could be careless, he also needed a good amount of reassurance from his friends. And sometimes extra reassurance about how much reassurance he needed.

It could be a lot for some people, but Noah didn't mind. Neither did Chase. Everyone had their hang-ups; Spencer's were just a little more out in the open than some. "I'm not avoiding you, Spence. I swear."

He could feel Spencer's grin against his shoulder. "So we're going out Friday, then?"

"Can't. I'm working." Noah had taken on a job as a barback at a spot Spencer had set him up at. It wasn't as close to campus as he would have liked, but he supposed that was one of the perks of having a car. "Why aren't you?" he asked. Spencer usually bartended weekends.

"Deb doesn't give me the good shifts anymore."

"That's because you let her blow you and never called her back outside of work," Chase pointed out wisely.

"Doesn't sound like me." Spencer rolled off Noah and started burrowing under his covers. "So no go for Friday. That's chill. We'll get Ash to be your replacement."

Ash was Noah's next youngest brother, and he was attending the same college as them. Noah liked to tell people Ash had followed him here, but really he'd come to stay glued to his childhood bestie.

"You know that would mean Ryder coming with," Noah warned, flipping onto his back and grabbing his laptop again.

Spencer gave an exaggerated shudder. He'd always been intimidated by Ash's unapproachable shadow. Noah got it, but he couldn't quite relate. The guy was practically family at this point, after so many years of following Ash around, and vice versa.

"All right, never mind. We'll do without the Teller family representation for one night." Spencer wrestled Noah's laptop out of his hands, setting it on top of the covers in front of them. "Movie?"

"Sure. Not like I was doing my homework or anything."

Spencer waved a hand. "Good, good. Chase, you gonna make popcorn?"

Noah considered giving Spencer another decking with a pillow, but really, he was done studying anyway. He wriggled down next to Spencer instead, grinning at their beta roommate. "Yeah, Chase. You gonna make popcorn?"

"I hate you both." But Chase stood anyway, making his way to the kitchen.

Noah laughed, settling in for a night of stupid movies and snacks. Tomorrow he'd start plotting again, trying to figure out how to get Eli alone. Noah had already discounted office hours— he had a feeling campus wasn't the place to thaw Eli's defenses. Noah just had to figure out where to make his move. And he *would* make his move.

He wasn't letting his omega get away again.

7

_____

Eli

"**W**as I too harsh, Deadly?"

Eli punctuated the question with a broad gesture that had his wine sloshing almost out of his glass. That was less due to any wildness on his part and more due to his glass still being completely full—Eli hadn't taken so much as a sip yet.

Mostly because he wasn't really sure he should be drinking at all in his current state of mind, but pouring himself a glass in celebration of the week's end had seemed the thing to do at the time.

It was possible his head wasn't on quite straight these days. Or that his brain had vacated the premises.

He'd gotten through the week though. He'd taught his classes, met with his TAs, and attended all his committee meetings, right on time. He'd been a good, *professional* professor.

Noah hadn't shown up to his office hours even once.

Which was *good*, Eli reminded himself. That was *exactly* how it should be. With a little distance and time, they could forget the night at the cabin had ever happened.

Except Eli couldn't stop thinking about it.

It was so stupid. He'd been *married*, for fuck's sake. If anything should have been taking up space in his head, it was that. Not someone who'd been in his life for a single night and one awkward run-in afterward.

But still.

"Was I? Too harsh? I think I was."

Deadly didn't answer. That was because she was a stone-cold bitch when it came to romantic entanglements. Also, she was a cat, and she couldn't speak.

"I was, wasn't I? I should have—should have talked him through it more."

The way you talked him through putting his dick inside you?

And just like that, Eli was wet. It was ridiculous. All it took was the mere thought of his night with Noah and he was practically dripping. He was so fucking *horny* lately.

It wasn't a problem he was used to having. He liked sex fine, but he didn't go craving it twenty-four seven. But ever since that night ...

And god, when Noah had scent marked him in the classroom. It had been the most innocuous scent marking he could have done, and it had still had Eli walking around fighting a boner all day, battling to keep his stupid pheromones in check. And then when he'd gotten home, he'd jerked off like a sex-addled fiend, and it *still* hadn't been enough.

He should have been strong. Should have showered off Noah's pheromones as soon as he'd gotten home. But he'd slept with them still on him, sniffing at his wrist throughout the night like a fucking lunatic.

It wasn't just that Noah smelled good—but god, did he ever. It was also that his pheromones brought Eli right back to that night.

To drowning in them while Noah covered his body with his, rocking into him and looking at Eli like he'd just unlocked the mysteries of the universe for him.

It was just because you were his first. He'd be like that with anyone.

But then what was Eli's excuse?

It hadn't been his first, or second, or thirtieth time. And yet he was fixated on it like he wasn't a thirty-four-year-old divorcé with a decade of marriage under his belt.

Either way, thinking about it wasn't helping. Eli was leaking slick already, and at this rate, he'd have to change his underwear before the night was through.

He turned shamefully away from Deadly's judgmental stare, setting his full glass of wine down and heading to the bedroom before opening the rarely used lower drawer of his bedside table.

It was a pretty sad collection staring back at him, frankly. A dildo with an inflatable knot he never, ever used outside of heats because it kind of scared him. And a small plug he'd bought after the separation from Richard, when he'd thought he might have some sort of sexual renaissance where he'd start using toys or whatever.

Mostly he just jerked off every now and then. Sometimes he was daring and fingered himself.

But now Eli bit at his lip, studying the plug. It would feel good to be full again, wouldn't it? Maybe he'd stop thinking about Noah so much if he could just have one little orgasm where he was properly filled. Properly *satisfied*.

But that plug isn't going to whisper how good you feel. It won't fill you so full that every little movement brushes your prostate. It won't smell like him or feel like him or moan all deep and sexy like he does.

God fucking damn it.

Eli picked up the dildo and the little remote control for its knot, staring at it. Maybe that would be enough. He'd guzzle his glass of wine, take a bubble bath (did he even *own* bubble bath?), and then fuck himself silly until he stopped thinking about alphas altogether.

He should have let Noah knot him.

Fuck. No. No knotting.

His phone buzzed.

Eli yelped, dropping the dildo onto his bed.

Faith was calling. He could ignore it, but if he didn't pick up, she'd just keep at it. She knew he didn't have anything else to do on a Friday night.

He accepted the call. "Heyyy." Super cool. Super casual.

Did he sound all weird and breathy to her or was that just in his head?

"What're you doing right now?"

"What?" Eli squeaked, covering the dildo with his comforter, as if Faith could see it over the phone. "Me? Nothing?"

"Okayyyy," she drawled skeptically. "Then what are your plans tonight?"

"No plans! Me? What?" Eli probably sounded insane, but she'd caught him by surprise, and he couldn't exactly tell her he'd been planning to fuck himself into brainlessness with his underused sex toys.

"You sound deranged, just so you know," Faith told him mildly. "Anyway, you're coming out with me and Liz."

"I am?" Eli frowned at his phone. "No, I'm not."

"You are. It's the first Friday of the semester, and we are not letting you set a precedent of staying in every weekend, mourning Richard and his limp-dicked fuckery."

"I haven't even thought about Richard," Eli told her truthfully. Although, he didn't add it was because he'd been daydreaming about a different alpha's knot.

There were some things a sister didn't need to know.

"Good, then. But you're taking that not-thinking party to the bar with us."

"Faaaith," Eli whined.

"Eliiii," she taunted, in a frankly offensively poor imitation of his voice. Then she brought out the big guns. "Liz misses you."

Damn. She was pulling the wife card. Why did Liz have to be such a sweetheart? Couldn't Faith have married someone as evil and devious as herself?

"Fine," Eli sighed, giving in to the inevitable. "But I'm not dressing cute. And you're buying."

"As if either of those things were in question. Your style is atrocious."

"I'm flipping you off right now," Eli told her as he rummaged in his dresser drawer for a fresh pair of underwear. "You just can't see it."

"We're picking you up in an hour. Dress however horribly you want, but you better not be in pajamas when we get there."

Eli looked down at his pajama bottoms and threadbare tee. "It's Friday night," he scoffed. "Of course I'm not in pajamas."

He hung up on Faith's wicked cackling.

Sisters were the worst.

———

THE BAR FAITH and Liz brought Eli to was more of a dive than their usual haunts. It was a dimly lit narrow rectangle of a building, a long stretch of bar on one side and small booths lining the other, with a single pool table in the back.

Nonetheless, it was already packed, pheromones mingling in the air like a hundred different clashing perfumes. The patrons were a mix of hip, young professionals who'd clearly been at it since happy hour, bar rats who'd possibly been at it since the early morning, and music scene punks killing time before the night's show two doors down.

Despite the crowd, Faith somehow managed to get them a

table within minutes. Eli wouldn't have been surprised if she'd stabbed someone with one of her stilettos for it, but he was willing to put aside his morals if it meant getting to stay seated for a few hours.

"How did you hear about this place?" he asked, raising his voice to be heard over the din.

"One of my clients said it was a cozy spot." Faith glanced around at the crowd, which was lively without being too rowdy. "I have to agree."

By the end of the first drink—gin and tonics for all of them, since Faith had declared she didn't trust the wine selection at a place like this—Eli had mellowed into something moderately human. The alcohol might have been part of it, but Liz's presence helped too. She was a sweet woman with gentle, soothing omega pheromones, and she had a way of putting people at ease without even trying.

Which meant she couldn't have been more of an opposite to Faith, who specialized in riling people up. Yet somehow, they were matched perfectly. Eli had long given up trying to figure it out, grateful that his sister had found someone who loved her exactly as she was.

When they'd all finished their first drink, Eli rose from the booth, gathering their empties. "I'll get this round."

Faith smirked at him, arching a perfectly manicured brow. "I thought I was getting all your drinks tonight. My penance for daring to force you into having a good time."

"Just hush and accept the gesture."

Liz smiled sweetly up at him, her round cheeks dimpling. "Thanks, Eli."

Eli smiled just as sweetly back at her, stuck his tongue out at Faith, and shouldered through the crowd to a less occupied end of the bar. There was a bartender under the bar, tapping a new keg. His head was hidden, but the backs of his shoulders were visible.

They were good, strong shoulders, and for just a second, Eli thought ...

But that was crazy. His horny yearnings were clearly starting to cloud his mind. He just needed to grab fresh drinks and get back to Faith and Liz and the realm of the sane.

And then the bartender popped up, wiping his arm across his forehead.

Noah.

Noah, looking sinfully good in a tight black tee and worn jeans. He was covered in a faint sheen of sweat, clearly working hard, and his pheromones hit Eli like a ton of forbidden, delicious-smelling bricks.

At the sight of Eli in front of him, Noah's wide mouth turned up into an impossibly broad grin. "Eli."

He looked happy to see him. *Why* did he look happy to see him? Shouldn't he be mad at Eli? Upset and disappointed at the very least, given their last interaction.

But Noah looked like seeing Eli on the other side of the bar was the best thing to happen to him in ages.

"Noah," Eli managed to say somewhat normally. Maybe.

Noah leaned over the bar, his biceps flexing in a very distracting way. "You stalking me, professor?"

"I— Uh— What?"

Noah sniffed, not even attempting subtlety, and a dark look crossed his face, his brow furrowing and his smile faltering. "You smell like an alpha."

"I— Who—" Eli was a professor, for fuck's sake. Why was he suddenly incapable of stringing more than two words together? "Sister!" he squawked, grateful the hum of the bar was loud enough to keep this conversation private. "I'm here with my sister!"

Noah's brow smoothed, and he looked behind Eli, presumably trying to scope out Faith, who Eli prayed to all that was holy was not watching this interaction, or he'd never live it down.

Whatever he found had Noah grinning again, his dimples flashing. "And you just happened to come to my bar? Must be fate."

That was ... that was a good line.

Eli frowned at him. "You're a flirt," he accused.

Noah winked. He *winked*. "Only with you."

That was *also* a good line.

Eli hummed doubtfully before he remembered he didn't have a right to care who Noah did or didn't flirt with. He tried to redirect his righteous indignation. "Are you old enough to be behind that bar?"

Noah didn't exactly roll his eyes, but the urge was clearly there. "I'm twenty-one, Eli," he said, exasperation covering up his flirty tone. "And I'm only a barback, anyway. But I can pass your order on to Jolene over there." He tilted his head toward the closest bartender, a gorgeous beta woman Eli suddenly found himself wanting to growl at. What right did she have to work alongside Noah, looking like that? She should cover up. And hide her face. And also switch careers to modeling and leave innocent collegiate alphas alone to barback in peace.

He turned back to find Noah grinning at him, like he was delighted by something Eli had done. "Hey, Eli," Noah crooned, his pheromones blossoming into something rich and salty.

Eli's heart was suddenly beating faster than it should be. "Yes?"

"I have a break coming up in an hour. Spend it with me?"

"Um. I really shouldn't ..."

"I just want to talk." Noah's lips pursed into something akin to a pout, even as his eyes danced. "I think you owe me that much. A real conversation?"

Eli had the vague sense that he was being played. But nothing Noah was saying was *wrong*, exactly. Eli *did* owe Noah a conversation. He'd been too caught off guard earlier in the week, and he hadn't been as kind as he should have been. He'd taken Noah's virginity, for heaven's sake. He should take responsibility.

"Of course." He nodded, hoping the gesture hid the fact that he was surreptitiously trying to inhale more of Noah's heavenly scent. "A conversation."

The grin Noah gave him was blinding. "Perfect. Now what can we get you, Professor? Whatever it is, it's on the house."

8

Noah

Noah could hardly keep himself from literally skipping out from behind the bar when his break came around.

He'd probably been looking like an idiot, grinning widely at nothing as he changed kegs and washed glasses and chopped limes into garnishes, but how else was he supposed to act?

Eli was *here*.

Out of all the bars in the city he could have gone to, he'd ended up at Noah's. Which was a blessed piece of fucking luck, because Noah had been stuck trying to figure out how to get Eli alone. He'd been ready to give in and go to Eli's office hours next week, to try to coax him into being unprofessional enough to at least give Noah his number.

But now Eli was *here*. In a booth Noah had been spying on for the last hour, in the moments he'd been able to spot it through the crowd.

Noah walked straight to that booth now, finding Eli sitting

with the striking alpha woman who had to be his sister—the owner of the earthy pheromones that had raised Noah's hackles earlier, when he'd thought Eli had shown up here on some kind of date.

There was also a pretty, full-figured omega woman who looked to be with the alpha sister, judging from their linked arms and the way she snuggled into her every time she laughed.

Noah wanted to be at that table. He wanted Eli to be snuggling into *him* like that.

For now, though, he loomed over them, grinning way too broadly. But fuck it, Eli liked his smile. He couldn't keep his eyes off Noah when he was grinning, and Noah wasn't afraid to push the advantage.

"Hey."

"Noah," Eli greeted, the word almost a squeak. His eyes were wide and kind of panicked, like he hadn't expected Noah to come over to the table to fetch him.

But how else was he going to get him? And if Eli had just texted Noah like they'd both wanted, they wouldn't have to have an audience like this, would they? So Noah wasn't going to feel too bad about it, even with the way the alpha sister's eyes were narrowing and darting between them, sharklike and predatory, as if she sensed blood in the water.

"It's my break now," Noah announced, giving Eli an out to leave the table and join him without too much more fuss.

But the sister had other ideas.

"Hello," she all but purred, holding out her hand for a shake. "I'm Faith. And this is Liz." She raised a dark brow as Noah shook her hand firmly. "And you are ...?"

"I'm—"

"I already said his name is Noah," Eli grumbled, glaring daggers at her.

Faith flashed him a sickeningly sweet smile. Noah had enough siblings to recognize she was goading her brother. "And how do we know dear Noah?"

When Eli only kept glaring, Noah cleared his throat. "Eli and I met in Sedona."

He hadn't been sure if their connection in Sedona was something Eli had shared with his sister, but Faith's reaction was fairly telling.

"Oh, did you?" Her smile grew as she drawled, "How fascinating."

"Faith," Eli said, a clear warning in his tone.

Faith held up her hands. "Don't let us stop you from ... reconnecting, Eli." She and Liz made eye contact, an unspoken message passing between them, and something newly devious entered her gaze. "In fact, Liz and I need to be going."

"Faith."

"Sorry," Faith said, not sounding sorry at all. She didn't even meet Eli's eyes, too busy sizing Noah up. "I know we dragged you out. But Noah here can take care of you, can't he?"

Noah decided right then and there he loved Eli's sister beyond measure. He would send her a fucking gift basket, if only he knew her address.

"*Faith*," Eli repeated for the third time, through clenched teeth.

This time Faith did look at him. "*Eli*," she taunted. The siblings had a stare off, and then Faith nudged her head toward Noah. "Noah's waiting."

Noah grinned invitingly. Eli looked to Liz, but the omega only smiled gently at him, not even attempting to come to his rescue. Eli let out a heavy sigh—Noah tried not to be offended by that—and rose from the booth, brushing up against Noah as he did so.

Fuck, he smelled good.

Even with strange pheromones layered over him, he was tart and enticing and perfect.

Noah grabbed Eli's hand, unable to keep his thumb from sliding over his scent gland. He nodded at the two women, not even trying to contain his shit-eating grin. "Nice meeting you both."

And then he dragged Eli away.

Noah led him out back, where there was a small break area hidden from the alley by a half wall. It held a dingy metal table with a half-full ashtray and two matching, uncomfortable metal chairs. It wasn't the most romantic spot Noah could have taken Eli, but at least it was mostly private.

"I'm never going to hear the end of that," Eli muttered once they'd closed the door to the din of the bar.

"End of what?" Noah asked innocently.

"Oh, please." Eli narrowed his eyes at him. "As if you don't know. An absurdly hot alpha whisking me away at the bar? That's older sister catnip."

Noah focused on what was important in that statement. "You think I'm absurdly hot?"

Eli glared. "*Noah.*"

"You like to repeat someone's name when you're irritated, did you know that?"

"We can't—"

Noah pulled out one of the metal chairs, gesturing to it. "Sit."

Despite his protest, Eli took a seat immediately, as if unable to help himself, and Noah sat in the adjacent chair, scooting closer until their arms and legs were touching.

Something tense and irritable in him finally relaxed for the first time that week.

This was better. Much better.

"It's good to see you," Noah said softly, fighting the urge to rub his face in Eli's hair like a maniac. "You look good."

He did. It was Noah's first time seeing Eli in regular clothes, and he looked wonderfully unpretentious in a worn sweatshirt and equally worn jeans, his dark hair messy and falling into his eyes.

Eli looked down at what he was wearing. "I don't though." Before Noah could protest, he cocked his head, taking in Noah's scanter outfit. "Aren't you cold?"

Noah shrugged. "A little." It was deep enough winter that even the Arizona nights were chilly, but he hadn't grabbed his jacket before coming out here. Mostly because his work tee was tight as hell, and he'd seen the way Eli had eyed his shoulders at the bar. He wasn't going to waste an opportunity to remind his omega of their mutual attraction.

He nudged Eli's knee with his own. "You want to warm me up?"

"*Noah.*"

Noah felt like he was in grade school again, trying to tug an omega's pigtails just so they'd look at him. Not that he'd ever done that, but apparently he was making up for lost time. "Can I scent mark you?" he asked eagerly.

"You already did," Eli scolded. Clearly he hadn't missed Noah's little move inside. But he still held out his wrist for another round.

Fuck that though. They weren't at school now, and Noah didn't have to hold back.

He ducked his head and rubbed his face against the crook of Eli's neck, where the skin of his scent gland was bared by his sweatshirt's loose collar.

Eli sucked in a sharp breath. "*Oh.*"

Oh was right. Noah could have crowed when Eli didn't pull away.

"So I've been thinking ...," he began, taking full advantage and running his nose along Eli's shoulder, inhaling deeply as he went.

"You have?" Eli asked, his voice wonderfully breathy.

"Mm-hmm. I've been thinking a lot, actually. About your TAs."

"My—" Eli shook his head, as if to clear some fog. "What?"

"Yep." Noah pulled back with some sort of herculean strength of will. Too much longer drowning in Eli's scent and he was going to embarrass himself by sporting a hard-on for the rest of his shift. "I looked over your syllabus again. You have TAs who do your grading, and lead discussions, and proctor exams. There's no part of my work or grade you'll be directly overseeing."

"I—"

"So there's no conflict of interest." Noah wasn't usually in the habit of talking over omegas he was trying to woo—not that he'd ever tried to woo an omega before—but he wasn't going to let Eli talk himself out of this before Noah had his say.

Eli's brow furrowed as he stared at him. "It's still not allowed."

"It's not a written rule."

"It's common sense!" Eli protested. "And I'm up for tenure this year. If we were found out ..."

A small pang of guilt had Noah almost hesitating, but in the end, it wasn't enough to sway him. He wanted this too fucking badly. "We can be discreet," he argued.

For as long as we need to be was the unspoken end of that. One day Noah wanted to be public. Very public. Eli bitten and claimed as his mate kind of public.

But he could be patient. Probably.

He leaned in close, every word deliberate. "I want you more than I've ever wanted anything in my life, Eli."

Eli shook his head. "You haven't lived very long. You haven't *known* me more than a day."

This again? Noah cocked his head. "Okay, Mr. Thirteen Years My Senior. Can you honestly say you feel any different?"

Eli's answer was a hard swallow.

Yeah, that was what Noah had thought.

"Come sit at my bar," he coaxed, bumping Eli's leg with his again. "Keep me company. I'm off at one thirty."

"One thirty in the *morning*?"

Noah laughed. "Hey, that's early. We're lucky I'm not the closer. Come on." He grabbed Eli's hand, tangling their fingers. "Give me something nice to look at. Protect me from the drunk barflies trying to slip me their numbers."

Eli's scent sharpened, taking on a bitter note, and wasn't that all kinds of interesting? Noah should have played the jealousy card sooner. He would have, if he'd known it would be this effective.

Eli nibbled at his lower lip in thought, and Noah waited it out. Finally, Eli nodded slowly. "I'll stay." He held up a finger. "Only for a little bit."

Fuck. Yes.

———

ELI STAYED for more than just a little bit.

Noah had been able to sweet-talk a regular into moving down the bar so Eli could sit across from where Noah ended up the most during his shift—the glass washing station. It meant they could chat while Noah washed dirty glasses, or when he had a little downtime between the busy rushes.

Which, frankly, wasn't often enough—Noah would have liked to stay glued to Eli's side the whole night, not just catch him in snatches—but it was better than nothing.

Eli started off stiff and reserved, but Noah was able to coax him into talking about his work, and it didn't take long for Eli to get super into it, telling Noah all about his time working on his doctorate, and the research he still hoped to do.

Noah had been right, of course—Eli was smart as hell. And determined. And passionate. He was almost shy about it, modest in a way that had Noah suspecting someone had made him feel guilty about his ambition in the past. It wouldn't have been unheard of. There were still plenty of people in the world—mostly alpha assholes—who thought omegas belonged in the home.

Still, the thought of anyone making Eli feel bad about how fucking awesome he was had Noah wanting to punch something.

His unhelpful violent inclinations aside, Noah ate it all up. He wasn't a scholar himself—he was more practical than academic—but it was cool as hell that Eli was.

What Noah ate up even *more* was the little flash of possessiveness Eli revealed when someone tried to slip Noah their number after all. Eli let out the cutest omega growl Noah had ever heard, death-glaring at the beta woman who'd dared try to pick Noah up.

But Eli's growling cut off abruptly when Noah grinned and told her he'd actually just started seeing someone, his death glare replaced by a sweet, embarrassed flush.

Cute. As. Fuck.

Noah had been worried about his own possessiveness, nervous that he might be fending off interested alphas on Eli's behalf all night. But a sweet omega regular had taken the stool next to Eli, and she and Eli chatted amiably whenever Noah was occupied, sharing cat stories and rolling their eyes in tandem at any alpha who dared approach.

It was all fucking perfect.

Except, of course, the downside of Eli staying the whole shift was that, even with Noah plying him with waters in between drinks, by the end of the night he was tipsy as fuck. More than tipsy. Full-on drunk.

By the time Noah had clocked out and ventured to Eli's side of the bar, Eli was swaying in his seat, his delicious citrus pheromones blossoming in a way that meant he wasn't even trying to keep them under wraps.

Noah put an elbow on the bar, grinning when Eli twisted eagerly to face him. "Hey, there."

Eli blinked at him blearily. Fuck, he really was a lightweight. "You're done already?"

"I am."

"Oh." Eli's lower lip pushed out into a delicious pout. "So we say goodbye now?"

"No." Noah shook his head. Fuck if he was going to let Eli try to get home alone in his inebriated state. "I'm taking you home."

Noah caught Eli's new omega friend glaring at him, and he held up his hands in surrender. "Not for that. I'm just getting him home safely."

Eli's pout intensified. "Why *not* for that?"

Jesus. Did Eli want ... *that*? Noah tried to ignore the unhelpful pang of lust, but he couldn't stop himself from brushing a lock of Eli's hair back from his face. "Because you're sloshed, baby."

"Me?" Eli held a shocked hand up to his chest, like he was offended at the very thought of it.

"Yes, you," Noah told him with a laugh, tugging him gently off the stool and steering him away from the bar. "Come on."

He was able to get Eli into the passenger seat of his car without issue, and he pulled up the GPS on his phone. "What's your address?"

"Noah, you can't *drive*." Eli's voice lowered to a whisper, like there was someone else in the car who could hear. "We've been *drinking*."

Noah bit back another laugh. "*You've* been drinking, Eli. I've been working, remember?"

Eli blinked at him owlishly. "Oh."

It took another few minutes of adorably addled segues before Noah got an address from Eli, but then they were off. It wasn't long before Eli's head started rolling against the seat, his eyes barely staying open. He was going to be out for the count soon. Noah could only hope he could get him inside before they were past the point of no return.

Bonus points if Eli didn't yak in his car.

The house matching Eli's address was a cute single-story number with a walled-off yard. Noah got Eli out of the car with minimal coaxing, and after some finagling, Eli entered the gate code for him, leading Noah past a small inground pool and to a side door, where he fished out his keys, letting them into the house.

It smelled like him, tart and delicious and homey.

Noah was trying to be nosey, but it was tough with all the lights off, and he didn't know where the switches were. And then suddenly he had an armful of Eli, his omega peering up at him through dark lashes. "Are you going to kiss me now, Noah?"

Noah let out a slow breath, reining in his pheromones, which had swelled with Eli's question. "I'd like to," he said, his voice full of regret. "I really, really would. But I'm afraid we need to get you into bed."

"Oh." Eli frowned down at his feet, then his eyes widened. "*Oh.*" He whirled out of Noah's arms, heading off in what was presumably the direction of his bedroom, stripping off his clothes as he went.

Noah was temporarily rooted to the spot, mesmerized as Eli revealed more and more skin, and it took him longer than he would have liked to jump into action, running forward and stopping Eli right before he tugged off his underwear. "Maybe keep these on, babe."

Eli's brow furrowed, his hands on his waistband. "Why?"

"Because you're sloshed, remember?"

"But you're not." Eli's hand shot out, dancing down the front of Noah's jeans, and Noah was only just able to grab his wrist before Eli got to his dick. Eli stared at him beseechingly. "We can still make it work."

So Noah wasn't a rocket scientist or anything, but it was becoming increasingly clear Eli was a horny drunk.

Fuck. *Why* did he have to be a horny drunk? Why couldn't he have been a mean one? Or a sloppy one? Or literally any other kind that didn't involve him trying to seduce Noah when Noah was already hanging on to his morals by a mere frayed fucking thread.

"You're killing me, you know that?" When Noah was sure Eli wasn't going to try to grab his dick again, he placed his hands on either side of Eli's head, meeting his warm brown eyes intently. "Listen. If you still want me in the morning, I will do anything you want me to. Swear to fucking god. Any. Damn. Thing."

Eli swayed in Noah's hold. "Even knot me?"

Noah raised his eyes to the ceiling. *Horny god give me strength.*

He cleared his throat. Cleared it again. Cleared it a third time. "I think we should stop speaking now," he finally said. "You're gonna get me into trouble."

"I'm the one in trouble," Eli mumbled, pouting shamelessly. "I'm the teacher, remember?"

But he turned and walked into his bedroom, flopping face down onto a king-size bed.

God, he had a cute fucking butt.

Noah averted his eyes from it long enough to maneuver Eli under the sheets, covering him with the blanket, and Eli burrowed down immediately, until every inch of him was covered. Could he even breathe? Was he going to suffocate under there?

But a moment later, he popped his head out, blinking at Noah again. "You'll stay?"

"I'll stay," Noah told him, shooting a text to his roommates to let them know he'd be out all night, and immediately silencing his phone before the inevitable flood of questions.

The truth was, Noah wouldn't leave for anything in the world.

He settled next to Eli on top of the covers, still fully clothed. It wouldn't be the most comfortable position to sleep in, but he didn't really trust himself to be pressed up against Eli in his under-wear. Like his body might make a move without his permission.

It wasn't something that had happened to him before, but this was Eli. All bets were off.

"Promise," Eli murmured. His eyelids started drooping, and he opened them with visible effort. "Promise you'll be here in the morning." He frowned, even as he lost the battle and let his eyes fall closed. "Last time you were gone."

"I promise." Noah turned on his side, stroking the hair back from Eli's face. "I'll be right here."

For as long as you'll have me, Eli Miller.

9

Eli

There was a drumming ache behind Eli's eyelids, persistent and terrible.

A headache. Right. Because he was hungover. Because he'd gotten ... Ohhh, he'd gotten very, very drunk, hadn't he? Sitting at the bar and downing gin and tonics while Noah had been working.

And Noah had ... taken him home?

Eli bolted upright in bed, wincing as the sudden movement sent a stabbing pain through his head. The memories came flooding back.

Oh god. He'd been a slutty, handsy drunk, hadn't he? Poor Noah had been forced to tuck him into bed like a wayward child. He'd probably run for the hills, no matter that Eli had made him promise to stay.

Except no, outside of the pounding in Eli's head, there were the telltale sounds of someone in Eli's kitchen. And Eli doubted Faith would have come over to torment him so early in the morning. Or at least, he thought it was early, judging by the soft light hitting his bedroom.

So Noah was still here. In Eli's home. After Eli had not so subtly tried to grab at his dick the night before.

Should Eli pretend to be asleep? Maybe if he kept his eyes closed the entire day, Noah would give up eventually.

Cowardly *and* rude, what a combo.

He grimaced at himself and picked up his phone, a text from Faith staring up at him.

> Faith: I call bullshit on our previous convo.
> That boy is INTO you. Don't fuck it up.

Of course she'd realized immediately that Noah had been the alpha from the cabin. Not that it had been that hard to guess. How many cute alphas did Eli really know, especially after Noah had told her they'd met in Sedona? And then she'd abandoned Eli at the bar, the meddling hussy.

Eli could text her right now, tell her, *He's my STUDENT*, and see if she changed her tune.

But he didn't have the nerve. He didn't want to know what it would feel like when Faith was truly disappointed in him. And she'd have to be, wouldn't she? It was unethical and sleazy and ... bad.

He put his phone down. He wasn't going to send that text. And that more than anything told Eli his next move. The very, very bad decision he was about to make.

He'd probably known last night at the bar, when that beta had tried to give Noah her number. Something deep and primal in Eli had growled out, *No. Mine. My alpha.*

He hadn't said the actual words, thank God. But he was pretty sure Noah had noticed the growl.

It was foolish and old-fashioned to say the very least, to rely on some idea of omega instincts to guide him. But Eli had been running on reason for so long ... what would it be like to trust his gut for once?

He threw the covers back and shuffled to the bathroom before brushing his teeth thoroughly and splashing cold water on his face until he felt semihuman. His dark hair was a mess of cowlicks and tangled waves, but oh well. Noah had put up with him as a drunk mess; surely he'd put up with him as a hungover one.

He downed a few painkillers dry, tugged on a shirt and some sweatpants over his boxer briefs, and headed to the kitchen.

He was distracted on the way by the fact that his house smelled like Noah now. He'd have thought it might feel a bit invasive, to have his house smell like a new alpha after so long of it being just him or Faith.

But it was just ... nice, Noah's fresh, salty scent clearing the fog in Eli's brain.

He found Noah in the kitchen, his broad back turned to Eli, fiddling with Eli's coffee maker. Deadly was on the counter—where she was *not* allowed—blinking slowly at Noah as he worked.

Of course she liked Noah already. He was absurdly likable. Even Faith had been charmed by his boldness the night before.

Eli cleared his throat, and Noah turned with a start. He was still in the clothes from the night before, but he was managing to look unfairly fresh despite that. He probably still smelled amazing, too, the charming bastard.

"Eli! You're up!" He gave Eli a strangely nervous glance, rubbing a hand against the back of his neck. "I, um, made some coffee. I hope that's okay? I thought you might want some when you woke up."

This was what was so endearing about him. That Noah could go from insisting on spending time with Eli, insisting on taking him home, insisting they could have a discreet affair ... to embarrassment that he'd been rummaging in Eli's kitchen without permission.

He was bold but not arrogant. Confident but still eager to please. It was an irresistible combination, and Eli was just … done even trying to resist it.

Eli realized he'd been staring, and his cheeks heated. "Thank you. Caffeine is … very necessary."

Noah let out a relieved sigh, grabbing what happened to be Eli's favorite mug and pouring him a cup. "How do you take it?"

"Creamer, please. Lots of it. It's in the fridge."

Eli should be taking over right about now, not letting Noah serve him up coffee like some long-term boyfriend, but there was something too alluring about Noah preparing him a cup.

How long had it been since someone had made Eli coffee in the morning? Richard never had, not since the early days. He'd preferred to stop and get a latte on the way to work, leaving Eli to make his own.

It had never bothered Eli, but now he accepted the coffee with a grateful smile, pleased when Noah leaned against the counter next to him, quietly watching him drink it.

He'd gotten through half the cup before Noah spoke. "Why is your cat named World's Deadliest Assassin?"

"Um, it's a bit tongue-in-cheek," Eli hedged. "She was a failed barn cat. She wouldn't catch any mice, so they were giving her away." He raised his chin stubbornly. "I'm not making fun of her though. It's more of an … inside joke."

"Between you and your ex?" Noah asked, his scent sharpening despite his even tone.

Eli shook his head. Richard hadn't even wanted a cat to begin with. He'd rather have had a baby. "Between me and Deadly." Eli's ears heated as he admitted to having an inside joke with his own cat. "That's what I call her. World's Deadliest Assassin doesn't exactly roll off the tongue."

"I think it's a great name."

Eli grinned shyly, and Noah's pheromones mellowed again as he continued to watch Eli sip his coffee with intense focus.

Eli cleared his throat. "This is really good. Thank you."

"How are you feeling?"

It was a good question, given Eli's state the night before. He could answer in a number of ways. He could say that his headache had already receded, thanks to Noah's refreshing ocean scent and the coffee he'd made. He could mention that he'd be hungry eventually but wasn't quite ready to risk food. He could admit he was still feeling slightly embarrassed and yet at the same time grateful Noah hadn't left.

Or he could be bold.

And for once, Eli was feeling bold.

He set his mostly empty cup down on the counter and pressed himself into Noah, giving in to the impulse he'd had all morning and rubbing his nose into the alpha's T-shirt. Noah had clearly worn it all night, and it was drenched in his scent.

Eli sighed happily when Noah tentatively wrapped his arms around him. "Thank you for getting me home. Sorry if I ruined your night."

"You didn't," Noah told him, his voice hoarse.

"And sorry if I got ... handsy."

Noah let out a husky chuckle. "Believe me, I didn't mind. I just didn't want to, you know, take advantage."

He hadn't, of course. Eli remembered that he'd been a perfect gentleman. Which was all well and good, but until now, Noah had been making all the moves. Inviting himself into Eli's hot tub, suggesting Eli take his virginity, approaching him in class and asking to talk at the bar.

If Eli really wanted this, it was his turn to show it. It was madness, sure, and it might blow up his life in a horrible, horrible way. He might even regret every minute of it.

But he'd regret it even more if he never tried.

"And did you mean what you said last night?" he asked, his voice muffled by the cloth of Noah's shirt.

"Can you, uh, be more specific?"

"That you want this," Eli clarified. "That you wouldn't mind keeping it hidden."

"Yes." Noah's arms tightened around him. "Yes, I want it."

Eli tilted his head back to peer up at him. "And what about the part about doing whatever I wanted this morning?"

Noah's pheromones swelled richly. "Fuck, yes."

"Hey, Noah?"

"Yes?" Noah was holding himself so incredibly still. Like he didn't dare move, didn't dare break whatever spell had been forming between them.

That was okay. Eli would do it.

He batted his lashes, feeling a little ridiculous but figuring he might as well go all out. "I'm going to take a shower—I'm pretty sure I'm giving off toxic gin fumes at this point. Would you like to join me?"

Eli would have loved to be able to take a photo of Noah's expression at this moment and keep it in his pocket for the rest of forever. The mix of surprise and hope and desire was really something else.

"Fuck, yes, I would."

Eli smiled up at him. "Good."

———

ELI'S BOLDNESS lasted until they were actually *in* the bathroom, and then his nerves decided to make themselves known. A fluttering started in his belly, half anxiety and half arousal.

Noah wasn't helping, uncharacteristically quiet again as he

watched Eli turn the taps in the shower with the same intensity he'd watched him drink the coffee he'd made.

"Well?" Eli whirled to face him, cocking a brow with false bravado.

Noah's wide mouth curled up on one side. "Well, what?"

Eli let out a frustrated breath, then gestured to Noah's clothes. "You're going to shower fully clothed?"

Noah cocked his head, his gaze running over Eli's dressed form. "Are *you*?"

Eli placed his hands on his hips, aware he was probably blushing horribly. "Maybe."

Noah smirked at him, reaching up to toy with the hem of his shirt, revealing a tantalizing strip of bare, tanned skin that Eli did his best not to stare at. "On the count of three?"

It was ridiculous. They'd both seen each other naked already. Noah had been *inside* Eli, for heaven's sake.

But Eli nodded, biting the inside of his cheek to hide his grin.

"One ... two ... three!"

They kept eye contact with each other as best they could while stripping off their clothes, and Eli couldn't help his giggle when Noah tripped while pulling off his jeans and underwear, cursing and catching himself on the bathroom sink.

But the giggle caught in Eli's throat when his gaze landed on Noah's cock, already hard and bobbing in the air.

God, he was big.

Eli was going to have that inside him again, wasn't he?

His hole clenched at the thought, slick escaping him.

Noah inhaled sharply, a low rumble leaving his throat, and suddenly the tension in the air was thick enough to cut with a knife. "You smell so good, Eli."

"I smell like gin."

"Like gin," Noah agreed with a smile. "And like slick."

Well, then.

Eli stepped into the shower, sighing at the warm spray. Heat engulfed his back as Noah followed closely behind. "Let me wash you."

Like Eli was going to argue with that. Apparently it was a morning for pampering, and he'd already decided to let it happen with the coffee. What was one more unbelievably sweet gesture to add to the pile?

He tilted his chin to the bodywash he favored, grimacing when Noah picked up the sparkly purple loofah next to it. "A gift from Faith," he explained at Noah's raised brow.

He turned, presenting his back. If he knew anything about dual showers, Noah was going to half-heartedly scrub at his back and then probably immediately take advantage and toy with his ass.

But Noah turned him gently back around until Eli was facing him, gazing into his eyes as he brushed the loofah over Eli's chest. Eli had noticed before that Noah's eye color was hard to place, a light brown that sometimes seemed green in the right light. His blond curls were plastered to his head by the water, and he still had his silver necklace on.

He was gorgeous.

"How was your week, Eli?" Noah asked politely, as if his extremely large and extremely hard cock wasn't brushing against Eli's stomach at that very moment.

"It was—" Eli coughed as the loofah brushed over his nipple. "Good?"

"Was it?" Noah hummed. "Good. Mine was unbearable. I missed you."

"We haven't spent enough time together for you to miss me."

Jesus. Why did Eli keep doing that? Arguing every time Noah said something sweet?

But Noah only shrugged, running the loofah down Eli's side, his lips twitching as Eli shivered at the delicate touch. "Still."

"Your confidence is alarming."

Noah grinned fully. "I've been told that before." He lifted Eli's arm, running the loofah along it and soaping up his armpit, his tone still conversational. "I kept thinking how it felt to be inside you. How warm and wet you were. You made these breathy little squeaks in the beginning, and then ... Fuck. The sounds you made when you came." He let out a harsh breath, as if remembering. "I want to make you scream like that while I'm fucking you. I want to make you come without touching yourself. I think if we practice enough, I'll get there."

He lowered Eli's arm again, tapping a finger to Eli's chest, and Eli realized he was barely breathing, his throat dry and paralyzed while slick dribbled out of him.

Jesus.

He forced himself to take a breath. "Um ..."

"And of course," Noah continued, as if Eli hadn't spoken, lifting Eli's other arm and giving it the same thorough treatment. "I never tasted you, which is a fucking crime. With how good you smell?" He shook his head, then grasped Eli's chin lightly, his eyes searing into him. "Will you let me, Eli? Let me taste you like I've been dying to?"

"Um ..." Eli tried to remind himself that he had his doctorate and should thus be able to string two words together at a time. Who was the inexperienced virgin between the two of them again?

Noah's grin was knowing. "You can nod if you agree."

Eli nodded dumbly, and Noah turned him toward the wall of the shower, his hands as gentle as ever. "Hands on the wall, baby."

Well, that was ridiculous. Eli was thirteen years older than Noah. And divorced. He couldn't be anyone's baby, could he?

Also, he's your student.

Eli shut that voice down immediately. That voice wasn't allowed in here today. Not when something very, very good was about to happen, thanks to Eli's very, very bad decision-making.

Noah's hands landed on Eli's hips, his breath ghosting over his back as he knelt behind him on the tile.

Eli twisted to look at him. "Your knees."

Noah laughed. "Believe me, my knees will be fine."

He parted Eli's cheeks, staring intently. Oh god. Eli had forgotten the way Noah looked at him during sex. Like he was studying Eli. Like there'd be an exam later and he was making sure he'd pass with flying colors.

Don't think about exams, you idiot.

Noah brushed a finger over Eli's hole. "I can't believe I was inside this tiny space."

Eli made a noise, possibly the same breathless squeak Noah had mentioned before. He couldn't be sure.

"I shouldn't be able to fit," Noah mused. "You're so little, baby." He grinned up at Eli. "But I guess that's what slick is for."

Eli groaned, turning back to the wall and pressing his forehead against the cool tile. He couldn't handle the full force of Noah's smile while he was kneeling at Eli's feet, toying with his hole.

But apparently the smile was the least of Eli's worries, because in the next moment, he felt the wet warmth of Noah's tongue swiping over him.

"Oh. *Oh.*"

Noah let out a deep, rumbling groan. "Holy shit. You taste so good." He licked over Eli's crease again, moaning hungrily. "So fucking good. Oh my god."

And then his thumbs were dipping into Eli's hole, spreading him as wide as he was able, and he placed a sucking kiss over Eli's entrance.

Eli's cock jerked as he howled, precum leaking almost as thick as his slick. Noah grunted, and then his tongue was back, dipping in as far as he could.

His approach was ... ferocious. There was no finesse, no teasing. Just hunger and enthusiasm and a complete lack of shame.

Eli started making noises he couldn't remember ever making before, his knees trembling, barely up to the task of holding him up to be devoured.

At some point he dimly registered the sound of Noah stroking himself. "N-No," he protested.

Noah stopped what he was doing immediately, and Eli peered back at him. There was slick all over Noah's chin, the shower spray barely reaching him to wash it away. "No?" Noah asked, hesitant for the first time. "I'm ... Is it—is it bad?"

"What? No! Jesus. It's um ... very good." As should have been more than evident by the immense amount of slick coating Eli's inner thighs, the steady stream of it too thick for even Noah's greedy gulping to keep up with. "But you can't come yet," he said stupidly. "You're supposed to fuck me."

Maybe he'd forgotten to tell Noah that was the plan?

There had to have been a better way to say it, but Eli's brain was foggy with arousal, his balls tight and his cock painfully hard. How was he supposed to be diplomatic at a time like this?

"Oh." Noah gave him a relieved smile. "I'm gonna fuck you, don't worry." His smile shifted to a look of determination. "And I'm going to last longer than two seconds this time. This is just a warm-up. I can't not come while eating your ass for the first time." He shrugged. "Sorry."

"Oh. Um." Eli turned back around. "Carry—carry on, the— Oh!" The last word was cut off with a moan as Noah speared him with his tongue, growling hungrily like some sort of beast.

Apparently, Eli's fumbling words hadn't ruined the mood as far as Noah was concerned.

Eli was just wondering how to warn Noah he was going to collapse when Noah's hand snaked around, thumbing Eli's cock-head, and that was it. Electricity zipped up Eli's spine, and he began chanting mindlessly, "Oh fuck, oh fuck, oh fuck."

Noah popped off with a growl. "Yes. Fucking *yes*. Come on my tongue, baby."

Eli reached a hand back and shoved Noah back where he needed him. If he was going to come on Noah's tongue, he needed that tongue back inside him.

He wailed as the shattering wave of his orgasm hit him, drowning him in sensation. "Oh my god, oh my god, oh my goddddd."

The roaring in his ears was so loud he barely registered the slick sounds of Noah beating off, or the hot splash of Noah's cum against his leg as his own release splattered against the shower tile.

But he was grateful for Noah's big hands gentling his glide down to the tile as Eli's knees finally gave out.

They sat at the bottom of the shower, both of them panting like they'd just run a marathon (as if Eli would *ever*), and then Noah gave him a glowing grin, his dimples on full display. "So, like, just give me ten minutes." He glanced down at his softening cock and grimaced. "Maybe twenty."

Eli laughed, bright and giddy.

It turned out bad decisions felt really, really good.

10

Noah

Any thoughts Noah had of demonstrating his youthful recovery time had to be stowed away when Eli's stomach rumbled loudly as they dried off from the shower.

Eli flushed immediately, his cheeks a bright pink. "Um ..."

Too fucking cute. Noah had to grin at him. He was very, *very* pleased that Eli seemed so determined for them to fuck, but he could be a gentleman and put aside his horniness to make his new ... boyfriend? ... lover? ... omega professor he was obsessed with ...?

Whatever they were calling it, Noah could make him breakfast before they got down to doing the deed.

Although, he sincerely fucking hoped they'd still be doing the deed.

He needed to stop calling it "doing the deed," didn't he?

"Do you have eggs?" he asked as he wrapped his towel around his waist.

Eli nodded, still blushing as his stomach growled yet again, and then he was handing Noah a soft robe as he tugged on a matching one, both of them pale green and striped.

"Was this your ex's?" Noah asked, fingering the soft fabric. Maybe it was a stupid question to ask, but he couldn't resist. He was curious about the asshole. He couldn't imagine having been married before. Couldn't imagine having that kind of intimacy with someone and then having it taken away.

Couldn't imagine letting Eli slip from his grasp.

But Eli was shaking his head. "No. Richard ..." He shrugged, nibbling at his lower lip. "Well, he didn't leave anything behind. I just liked the robe so much I bought a spare."

Noah slipped it on. It was way too short for him—it wasn't like he and Eli wore the same size clothes—but it was hard to mind when Eli's gaze kept dropping to Noah's bare thighs, his eyes darkening.

Noah groaned, averting his gaze from Eli's lustful one and grabbing his hand. "You're not allowed to look at me like that yet. Not until you've eaten."

He tugged a bashful Eli to the kitchen and set him at one of the counter stools, rummaging in the fridge for eggs and butter. He found a loaf of bread by the toaster and searched the cabinets beneath for a pan. "Scrambled okay?"

"Um, sure." Eli sounded almost hesitant, so Noah turned, only to find the omega looking at him with a kind of fond surprise. "You're very comfortable in the kitchen for a coed."

Noah grinned. "I'm not some sort of culinary genius, just to warn you. But I made stuff for my siblings when my parents had to work late. Or early."

His parents had tried their best to be there for mealtimes, but they'd both worked full-time in demanding jobs, and that had sometimes included overtime. Something they weren't going to refuse with six kids to feed.

"Remind me again how many?"

"Six of us total. There's Carter and me and Ash sort of close together, from our mom's first marriage, and then a twelve-year gap before the twins and then Jess—the baby."

Noah had already told Eli, that night in the hot tub, that he considered his stepdad his father—his birth father had passed early enough that Noah didn't remember him—so Eli didn't question Noah about that. But he did ask, "But Carter's oldest, right? He didn't help your parents out?"

Noah cracked the eggs into a bowl, whisking them with salt and pepper. "He didn't have any interest in helping out. He was a model student, had a ton of extracurriculars. He was pretty much still in grade school when he decided he wanted to be a lawyer. I was just—" Noah shrugged, clearing his throat. "Well, it was easy for me to help out."

There was silence, and Noah glanced over his shoulder to find Eli watching him carefully. "Your parents were lucky to have you."

Noah gave an awkward laugh, turning back to the eggs. Eli was easy to talk to—he had a way of paying close attention without seeming at all judgmental—but it still made Noah uncomfortable, basically admitting he was nothing special. His other siblings had always had so much going on, but Noah ... Well, he'd played soccer up until high school, but he hadn't been amazing at it. It had been easy to put it aside so he could drive Ash to and from piano lessons once he had his license, or be home to pick up the twins and Jess from daycare.

"Tell me about this pool of yours," he said, changing the subject. "How often do you use it?"

He knew he was being obvious, but Eli laughed anyway, letting him off the hook. "Not often enough."

It was easy enough to keep Eli talking about the house after that, and it wasn't long until the eggs were done. Noah buttered toast for them both and plated it up. Then he picked Eli up off the stool and set him on the counter, stepping between his legs before the omega caught up to his own surprise.

Noah grinned at him. "Hello."

Eli's cheeks were a delightful pink. "Hi."

Noah piled a bite of egg on a piece of toast, holding it to Eli's mouth. Eli took a dainty bite, keeping eye contact with Noah as he chewed. Something deep and primal in Noah shifted, pleased at the sight.

"Hand-feeding?" Eli asked quietly after he'd swallowed.

It was Noah's turn to flush. He hadn't really been thinking, other than wanting to feed Eli the food he'd made. But it was mate behavior, what he was doing. Alphas in particular would hand-feed omegas during their heats, when the omegas were too worn out to manage on their own.

Still, he wasn't embarrassed enough to stop. "We're, um ... we *are* dating now, right?"

Maybe that was a stupid fucking question to ask. Eli had been pretty clear earlier, that he was willing to start something. Unless he'd been talking about no-strings sex, but that didn't *seem* like what was happening, not with Noah all cozy in his kitchen, making him breakfast.

Eli didn't tell him off for being presumptuous. Or even tease him for being forward. He just opened his mouth for another bite.

Noah had to hold in a satisfied rumble as he piled another bite of eggs on toast.

When he held the third bite up for Eli, the omega grabbed Noah's wrist in a gentle hold, pushing his own hand toward him and shaking his head. "You too."

So Noah took the bite for himself, holding the next one up for Eli again. They took turns until both plates were done, and Eli let out a satisfied sigh after the very last bite.

Noah wiped a crumb from the corner of Eli's mouth. "Better?"

"Much." Eli cocked his head with a shy smile. Noah wasn't sure how he managed to pull off the sweet and demure vibe after having Noah's tongue in his ass, but somehow he did. "You're spoiling me, you know."

Noah blinked at him in surprise. He hadn't done anything special, had he? Was Eli talking about the coffee? Making him eggs? Wasn't all that just ... normal boyfriend behavior?

Noah suddenly had to ask again, "We *are* dating now, right?"

"Is that what you'd like?"

"I'd like to be your boyfriend," Noah told him immediately, keeping up his steady streak of having absolutely zero chill.

Eli shook his head, but even pressing his lips together firmly, he couldn't quite hide his smile. "Let's start with dating. You might get tired of the secrecy." He grabbed at the tie to Noah's robe, fiddling with it. "It *does* have to be secret," he warned, catching Noah's eye. "I'm getting tenure this year, but it's not final yet. It won't be until the spring. Something big—something like sleeping with a student—could jeopardize it."

Maybe that was meant to scare Noah off, but all Noah could hear was that this whole situation was only a temporary problem. That he just had to be patient.

He could be patient. Especially if he got to have Eli in his arms in the meantime.

He slid his hands up Eli's calves, squeezing his knees lightly. "My lips are sealed."

"I'm being very stupid right now," Eli told him quietly, but his knees fell open wider in invitation.

Noah shook his head slowly, his hands sliding higher until he could brush his thumbs along Eli's hips. "I don't think so. You're very intelligent, Professor Miller."

Eli kicked a heel against Noah's ass in admonishment. "Don't even start with that."

"Okay," Noah said agreeably. He leaned in, pressing a kiss to

Eli's chin. "Eli, then." He pressed another kiss to his cheek. "Or ...
baby."

He caught Eli's lips before Eli could protest the term of endear-
ment, undoing Eli's robe and letting it fall open, leaving the omega
open to his gaze. He took a pause from kissing him to admire the
sight: Eli's pretty cock was already plumping from Noah's teasing
touch, and Noah could smell his arousal, even though the slick
wasn't visible on his thighs yet.

Noah was sure it would be soon. Eli had been dripping with it
in the shower.

Noah still couldn't believe he'd gotten to taste it.

Fuck coffee. Fuck breakfast. Noah had already decided he
could live on Eli's slick alone. He'd never tasted anything that good
before in his life.

He hoped he'd been halfway decent eating him out—the way
Eli had shoved Noah's face against himself as he'd come had been
promising. But Noah had no idea what the fuck he was doing still,
when it came to sex. He'd just have to hope his ... enthusiasm had
been enough.

Eli was still letting Noah touch him, so there was that. Noah
couldn't have been all that terrible.

But fuck it. He could ask, couldn't he?

"Was it okay?" he murmured, breaking another kiss. "What I
did in the shower? Did I do okay?"

Eli let out a slow breath, and the sharp, citrusy scent of his
pheromones deepened. The blood rushed to Noah's cock as he
inhaled deeply, trying to get that scent all the way to his veins. "It
was very okay, Noah."

"Really?" Noah had to kiss Eli's throat to hide his smug grin.
"You'd let me do it again sometime?"

Eli huffed a laugh, his breath stirring Noah's curls. "Oh, I think so."

"What could I do to make it better?" Noah asked, mouthing

some more at the warm skin of Eli's throat. "To make you feel good?"

"You could stick your dick in me afterward."

Noah leaned back, gleefully shocked. "So forward of you," he teased. "I don't remember putting booze in your coffee."

Eli flushed, and Noah watched the pretty color travel down his chest as the omega squirmed on the counter. "I can't stop thinking about that night. Your mouth was—" The scent of slick filled the air as he continued to squirm. "It was really good. But I want to do it again." His hand caught Noah's wrist as his voice lowered. "Need you in me again."

Noah was suddenly caught in a vague feeling of unreality. He'd been wanting Eli, thinking about him, dreaming about him, ever since the cabin. However nonsensical or silly his stubbornness after a single night might have seemed, he'd been prepared to hold out for the long haul.

And here was Eli telling him he wanted Noah to fuck him again.

Now, presumably.

"Well, fuck." Noah tugged Eli's hips forward. His cock was hardening rapidly, his own pheromones surging darkly. "I can accommodate that."

He trailed kisses down Eli's chest, capturing one of his pretty, pink nipples in his mouth, sucking until Eli was grabbing at his hair, tugging him closer with a moan. He undid his own robe without letting up, throwing it somewhere on the counter as he slid his fingers toward Eli's hole, exploring the wetness there.

"You fucked me open with your tongue already," Eli told him, knocking his hand away. "Put your cock in me, Noah."

"Jesus."

Apparently the patient, coaxing Eli from the cabin was on hiatus, and demanding, randy Eli was at the helm. Noah didn't mind one fucking bit. They were on the same page; that was for sure—he wanted back in there too.

He grabbed his aching cock, lining himself up with an annoyingly shaky hand. He watched intently as his cockhead breached Eli's rim, but then his eyes almost crossed at the overwhelming sensation of being sucked inside, and he had to close them.

It wasn't like Noah had *forgotten* what it felt like—how could he have forgotten, when the experience was burned into his brain? —but he'd misremembered the intensity. Eli was so wet and warm and slick around him, even as his inner muscles clenched tightly around Noah's cock. It was … *Fuck*, it was just so good.

But Noah couldn't linger with the sensation, couldn't stand there teasing at the tip. Because Eli's heels were already digging into him, pushing Noah to fill him completely.

Impatient little thing this morning.

Noah tried to catch his breath after bottoming out, his cock encased completely in perfect, tight heat. "Holy fuck. Are you— Is it good?"

He'd done this too much last time, hadn't he? Asked Eli over and over how he was feeling. But Eli hadn't seemed to mind then, and he didn't seem to mind now. He just laughed breathlessly— the action fluttering his muscles around Noah in a way that had him clenching down to resist blowing his load too soon—and pressed his heels in again.

"Move, Alpha."

Oh. Oh fuck. Noah hadn't thought he was the type to get hard from an omega calling him "Alpha." He'd had enough omegas try it flirtatiously at parties, and it had never gotten under his skin.

But now, with Eli's breathy order ringing in his ear, a shiver ran down Noah's spine, heat pooling in his belly like liquid fire, and his pheromones flooded out.

Eli whimpered, and Noah's hips started rocking before he was even aware of it. He braced a hand on the counter for leverage, the other firmly holding on to Eli's waist, and let himself sink into a rhythm. He captured Eli's mouth again, drinking in his little moans.

God, it felt good. So good. *Too* good.

Had Noah really been bragging about how long he was going to last this time? Idiot. His only hope was to make Eli feel as good as possible in the meantime.

He released Eli's mouth after one last hard suck of his bottom lip before kissing down his neck and moving the hand on Eli's waist to his cock, stroking him like he'd seen him stroke himself. "Like this?" he asked.

Eli arched into him. "*Yes.* Yes, like that."

Noah lost himself in it—the hot feel of Eli around him, the warmth of him in his hand. Every now and then Eli would give him a fevered instruction. "Harder, Noah. Faster. No, slower. There. Right *there.*" And sometimes, even better, just moan his name, "Noah. *Noah.*"

When Eli spilled over Noah's fist with a keening cry, Noah felt fucking invincible. *He'd* done that again. Made Eli feel good with his touch, with his cock.

But it was a mistake, watching Eli come. The look of him —the high color on his cheeks, his pretty brown eyes heavy-lidded with want, his cute mouth all slack and open—all that combined with the feel of his muscles spasming around Noah had the pleasure in him unspooling, Noah's cock jerking and his orgasm rushing through him before he was ready.

He was about to pull back and away. Except Eli had said ...

Noah dipped his head onto Eli's shoulder, groaning as his knot began to swell. "I can— Can I? Eli, can I?"

Alphas didn't typically knot with every orgasm—and they needed to be inside an omega or a willing beta for their knot to swell completely—but the memory of Eli asking for it last night was enough to push Noah toward it, the blood rushing to his dick with renewed vigor even as he came inside Eli.

Eli stared at him glassily. He looked almost drugged, either from his orgasm or from the potent mix of pheromones flooding the kitchen. "Yess," he slurred. "Do it, Noah."

Noah pressed forward mindlessly, rocking his hips until his half-formed knot caught on Eli's rim and pushed through, expanding completely once he was sheathed inside, like his body had only been waiting.

The pressure was ... insane. Overwhelming. Noah had never felt anything like it, the way Eli squeezed around his knot.

Eli whined, a distinctly omega sound Noah hadn't heard him make yet. His muscles started spasming around Noah's knot, like he was coming again, only dry this time, his cock still soft and spent. There was the squelching sound of slick trying to escape around Noah's knot.

It was perfect. It was filthy. It was too fucking much.

Noah tried to form words. He needed to make sure, right? "G-Good?" he managed to ask through his tight throat.

"Good," Eli confirmed. He threw his head back with a cry as he spasmed again, and the length of his neck was like sin. Noah could bite. Right there. Just sink his fucking teeth in. He wouldn't, but he could. "Good," Eli repeated. "So good."

They stayed like that for who knew how long, Noah rocking back and forth in tiny, incremental movements, filling Eli up again and again as his knot pulsed.

He'd never knotted anyone before. Obviously, since he'd never fucked anyone before. He'd squeezed his own while jerking off, sure. But this—it was like a continual orgasm, draining his cock almost as surely as it drained his brain cells.

How the fuck did anyone get anything done in this world, if *this* was what knotting someone felt like? How was everyone not just fucking their brains out all the time?

He'd have to ask Eli, when he could form full sentences again.

Eventually things settled, Noah's knot locked in place but no longer pulsing, Eli's channel snug but no longer spasming. The fog in Noah's brain finally cleared a little. They probably had another half hour to go before they could separate—it wouldn't last hours like it would during a rut or a heat, but it definitely wasn't deflating yet.

Eli seemed to be coming to at the same time as Noah. He pressed a hand to his face, his cheeks bright red. "Oh god."

"What's wrong?" Noah asked in alarm, his hands moving frantically but not settling anywhere. "Should I not have—?"

"No," Eli reassured him, peering at him through his fingers. "It's just—" He tilted his chin, encompassing the kitchen, the way he was still sitting on the kitchen counter. "This isn't exactly an ideal location. I know better." He bit at his lower lip, looking sheepish. "I got ... caught up."

Oh. Well, that was hot as fuck—that Noah had made Eli mindless enough to forget where they were. But of course it would be uncomfortable for him, sitting on the hard counter until Noah's knot went down.

Noah reached carefully for his discarded robe and threw it on the tiled floor. "Put your arms around my neck," he instructed.

Eli did, even as he asked, "What are you—?"

He squealed as Noah lifted him, still impaled on his knot.

"Shh, baby," Noah murmured, tucking Eli against him. "I've got you."

He lowered them both carefully—so fucking carefully—to the floor, tilting to his side so they were settled facing each other on top of the robe.

It was still an awkward-as-fuck position—lesson learned there —but Noah managed to slowly lift Eli's leg until it was over his hips, cushioning Eli's head with his arm. He had to make each movement cautiously—every time he moved his knot, it pulled on Eli's rim, and Eli whimpered or moaned in turn.

Eventually they were situated more or less decently. Noah ran a soothing hand along Eli's side. "Better?"

Eli giggled, the sound cutting off into another groan as the laughter jostled Noah's knot inside him. "I can't believe I let you knot me on the kitchen counter. Rookie mistake."

Noah grinned. "Well, I *am* a rookie."

Eli frowned at him indignantly. "*I'm* not."

Noah kissed him. Because he wanted to. Because he could.

"Thank you," he said afterward.

Eli arched his brows. "For leading you astray in the art of alpha-omega sex?"

"For giving me a chance." Noah pressed his forehead to Eli's, putting every ounce of his sincerity into his words. "I'm going to be so good to you, Eli. You won't regret it. I won't let you."

———

EVENTUALLY, Noah's knot deflated, and the two of them showered once again.

(It turned out a lot of fluids were involved in knotting, and while Eli had patiently put up with Noah getting incredibly horny about the ample evidence of their union, he'd also insisted they both clean off afterward.)

Now they were on the couch together, trying to find something decent to watch, neither of them up to much besides vegging out. The knotting had been intense, even with the absurdity of the location, and it seemed like they could both use a little mindless recovery time.

Eli was in soft joggers and a tee, and Noah was in Eli's clean robe (the one not covered in cum and slick) while his clothes went through the wash.

While Eli flicked through the streaming channels, Noah turned his phone on, finally ready for it after a long morning of avoidance. He had … quite a few texts. And some missed calls from Spencer.

Chase would be the safer option.

"I gotta check in," Noah told Eli, who slid his head off Noah's shoulder with a soft but disgruntled grumble, allowing Noah to get up from the couch and head into the yard for some privacy.

Chase picked up on the second ring. "Yo."

Noah could immediately hear Spencer in the background, whining, "Is that him? Why's he calling *you* back?"

"Spencer freaking out?" Noah asked mildly.

Chase chuckled. "To be fair, you've never not come home before."

"I'm fine. Just … met someone."

He could have meant anyone, but Chase obviously wasn't fooled. He was silent for a moment, then asked lightly, "You found your omega?"

Noah debated lying. He really did. But it wasn't like Chase didn't already know at least half of it. "I did," he admitted. "It's, um, going well."

"So we'll be seeing a lot less of you for a while." There was no censure in the statement. And no further questions, for which Noah was incredibly grateful.

Although, Spencer sounded in the background again, unwilling to let anything go. "What does that mean? Why? Why can't he bring the omega over *here*?"

Noah ignored it all, letting Chase know, "I'm at least staying the night again tonight. If he'll let me."

"Cool. I'll manage the head case."

"I'll show you *head case*," Spencer growled, and then there was the distinct sound of tussling.

Noah hung up.

He headed back inside the house, smiling as he reached the couch. Eli looked incredibly soft, his face the picture of drowsy contentment, his pheromones a perfect match. "Everything okay?"

"Yeah." Noah settled next to him, pulling Eli's head back to his shoulder. "I'll have to head back tomorrow. My laptop and everything is at our apartment. I've got homework to keep up with, you know."

"Don't remind me." Eli wrapped an arm around Noah's middle. "But you'll stay tonight?"

Something bubbly and sweet and perfect fizzled in Noah's chest. "Definitely."

"We can get takeout?" Eli asked. "And watch a movie?" He sounded almost uncertain, like Noah was going to disapprove of his plans.

But it all sounded perfect to Noah. "Only if it's a very, very stupid movie."

He was rewarded with a bright grin. "Deal."

11

Eli

Eli walked into his office practically buzzing. He was feeling giddy in that kind of ridiculous way that put a literal bounce in his step.

One that had been there for the past three weeks.

He supposed regular sex and companionship did that to a person. Probably? Maybe? Eli couldn't remember those things ever feeling exactly like this, even when he'd been newly in love in his twenties, but maybe he'd let all the negativity that had happened later color his memories of his early times with Richard.

Or maybe this was just different.

Because it felt so *good* with Noah. Unbelievably good. The past few weeks, getting as much time together as they could—which wasn't nearly enough, given their different schedules and the need for secrecy—had made Eli happy in a way he hadn't felt in a long, long time.

It was just ... easy, in a weird sense. Exciting and nerve-racking in the way all new relationships were, but also ... easy. It shouldn't have been, with their circumstances and the age gap. But Noah made it easy. He was always so happy to see Eli whenever he could, so eager to pull him into his arms and catch up on every moment they'd missed with each other. He'd come over for takeout or clumsy attempts at cooking, and they'd fall into easy domesticity together. Or, on the few nights his roommate wasn't bartending with him, he'd invite Eli out to his work, to sit at the bar and be flirted with shamelessly and glare at any hussies who dared hit on Noah.

(Okay, they weren't hussies. They were just regular, interested patrons. But Eli was allowed to be catty once in a blue moon.)

And the sex. The *sex*.

El had never realized how hot it could be to take so many of someone's firsts. The way Noah acted like every blow job was a gift from heaven above was incredibly gratifying, to say the least. Or the way he explored Eli's body like it was the most beautiful, fascinating thing he'd ever seen. Or touched. Or licked.

Anyway.

Eli shifted in his chair as he took out his laptop. He really needed to learn his lesson about thinking of these types of things at the workplace. He had a class to teach after this—he couldn't go in smelling like shameless arousal. Maybe he needed to get on one of those birth controls that blocked pheromones? But he didn't love the side effects he'd heard about, and Noah *liked* the way Eli smelled. Eli didn't want to take that away from either of them.

He was distracted enough, between thinking about Noah and going over his lecture notes, that he was only half aware of telling whoever was knocking on his office door to come in. It wasn't like he was expecting anyone exciting—Noah was under strict instructions not to come to Eli's office during working hours.

So Eli wasn't at all prepared for the alpha who entered at his welcome, striding in like it was the most natural thing in the world and shutting the door firmly behind him.

All the air left Eli's lungs, but he somehow managed to gasp, somewhere between a greeting and an accusation, "Richard."

The bastard looked good. But then again, he always did. Eli's ex was classically handsome in that Old Hollywood way, with a strong jaw, thick dark hair, and immaculate grooming. But he also had a nice, tanned glow going on today—he'd probably just come back from a weekend in Italy or something.

Objective appeal aside, though, with memories of Noah fresh in Eli's mind, the sight of Richard left him ... cold. Unaffected. Richard had his good looks, yes. He always had. But they were surface deep, and they came tied up with a massive ego. Richard just didn't have the warmth Noah had. The magnetism. The sweetness and care.

Eli had learned that last part the hard way.

Some of Eli's feelings must have been showing on his face, because Richard's greeting sounded almost like a chastisement. "Lijah."

Eli frowned at the old nickname. He'd always preferred Eli to Elijah or Lijah, but Richard had liked to tease him with the alternative. It had seemed charming at first, but now it had the feel of an attempt to take control in any way he could, including twisting Eli's own name.

But Eli didn't have to put up with that anymore, did he?

"Eli, please," he corrected mildly, proud of himself for not sounding nearly as acerbic as he felt. "What are you doing here, Richard?"

He had a weird moment of panic after he asked the question. The papers were finalized, weren't they? There wasn't some terrible surprise waiting in the wings? But no. Eli knew for a fact they were.

Richard smiled easily, like Eli was asking out of curiosity and not because his visit was both unexpected and unwelcome. "Lunch with the dean."

Of course. Business. Never mind that he'd met the dean through Eli and had somehow finagled his way into managing the man's investment portfolio. He'd never thanked Eli for it, never counted it as a mark in his favor when he'd been trying to talk Eli into taking on fewer classes.

Well, whatever. Good for him. Really.

"And you decided to stop by for old time's sake?" Eli asked, arching a skeptical brow.

"I wanted to see how you're doing." Richard tucked his hands into his suit pants pockets, rocking on his feet in a way Eli knew was more practiced than casual. "How you're … holding up."

There it was. The faux concern masking blatant condescension.

Eli straightened his spine and gave him a bright, fake smile. "Really well, actually."

Richard looked him over, most likely searching for the lie. But there was no lie. Eli *was* doing really well. He was sleeping great, eating well, and having perfect, round-the-clock, toe-curling sex.

Eli might not have had an Italy tan, but he was pretty sure he was glowing in his own way.

And apparently he was right, because Richard's lips turned down into a there-and-gone frown. Ooh, he didn't like that, did he? Had he really expected to find Eli lost and miserable and missing him? Bags under his eyes, his pheromones emitting pure, bitter misery?

Probably. Richard was definitely arrogant enough to assume Eli was still falling apart without him.

Richard sniffed the air, not quite subtle about it, not in the way he usually was. "Is that …?"

Eli stiffened. He shouldn't smell like Noah right now. He hadn't spent the night last night, and Eli's clothes were fresh. But the alpha had been over often enough that Eli's belongings could still be carrying his scent lightly enough that Eli hadn't noticed.

Richard's brow furrowed, and he inhaled again. His gaze homed in on Eli sharply. "Are you seeing someone?"

Eli didn't flinch. He made *sure* he didn't flinch. "And how would that be any of your business?"

Richard stepped closer to his desk. "Just because the divorce is finalized doesn't mean I can't concern myself with—"

"That's exactly what it means, actually," Eli told him, maintaining the most even tone in the history of the universe.

"Are we really going to do the whole hostile exes thing?" Richard asked with a sigh, like Eli was being difficult instead of perfectly pleasant.

But Eli was done folding when it came to his ex. If Richard didn't like him acting agreeable, then Eli would pull out the big guns. "You cheated, Richard," he said, although he kept the even tone. "Many times."

"I think we both know it was more complicated than that."

Right. Because somehow it had been Eli's fault, the cheating. Because he'd wanted to work, because he hadn't wanted the baby they'd both agreed early on that they weren't going to have. Because he hadn't fallen on his knees and worshipped at the altar of Richard's perfection.

"I miss you," Richard said, his voice suddenly soft and silky. His pheromones unfurled, slow but steady, revealing their rich, tobacco scent. Eli had once found the dark depths of them comforting. Safe.

Now they were only suffocating.

And he didn't have to put up with them for another second.

He stood from his desk. "I have class."

He started packing his belongings, aware of Richard watching him intently. Eli should have expected this, really. Of course his ex had sussed out somehow that Eli was happy, and he'd come to stick his nose in it. To fuck with it as much as possible, in whatever way he could.

Richard missed him? Richard hadn't missed him when Eli had been *right fucking there*, trying to make things work despite all his better instincts.

He slid past Richard to get to the door, and the alpha should have considered himself lucky that Eli didn't shove him as hard as he might have liked. Lucky Eli was above such things. And also aware that it probably would have just hurt his own shoulder.

Richard's deep voice rang out behind him as Eli stepped into the hallway. "I'll be seeing you, Lijah."

"Not if I see you first," Eli muttered.

And okay, it wasn't his best comeback. But at least he hadn't cried or cowered. Sure, he was sort of running away, but why *should* he stick around to deal with Richard's bullshit?

He was over all of it, had been for years at this point, never mind that the legal side of things had taken time to catch up to his heart.

Eli wasn't the same omega Richard had married, and he never would be again.

———

ELI'S LECTURE WENT WELL.

And, okay, Eli had maybe been a *little* jittery from the unexpected visit, but overall, it was nice to realize a Richard sighting wasn't enough to throw him off his game anymore.

His ex didn't have that power these days.

How fucking liberating.

Eli raced home afterward (or as fast as the speed limits allowed, because he was *not* getting pulled over on date night). Noah was meeting him there, and Eli wanted to get to the house first.

He shucked off his work clothes as soon as he was inside, changing into cozier loungewear, and he was just coming out into the hallway when the side door opened.

Eli had given Noah the gate code a week ago.

Best decision ever.

He was stopped in his tracks for a moment by the sight of him—Noah looked so *good*, his blond surfer curls just on this side of wild, a broad smile already on his lips, so happy just to be entering Eli's home. He was broad-shouldered and strong, definitely alpha in stature, but he had that casual looseness to him that made it so he didn't dominate a space in an oppressive way.

He had presence, but he wasn't overpowering.

And he smelled *delicious.*

Eli wanted him.

Right now.

Here was the alpha with the power to twist Eli into knots, but somehow the awareness didn't feel stifling. Mostly because Noah wouldn't abuse that power over him, even if he was made aware of it. Eli knew that, deep down in his guts.

Which was kind of where he wanted Noah to be right now.

Eli launched himself at Noah, throwing himself into his arms, and Noah dropped his bag on the floor without hesitation, catching Eli under his ass and opening his mouth to Eli's aggressive kisses.

He smelled salty and fresh and perfect. Not suffocating, but ... uplifting. Even as his pheromones deepened and sharpened with want and lust and other delicious undercurrents.

Eli didn't waste any time, darting his hand under the waistband of Noah's joggers, moaning his appreciation at the hot, velvety length of him, already hardening from Eli's attentions.

Eli could get him off just like this, quick and easy with Noah's ... youthful enthusiasm, but Eli already knew what he wanted. He wanted that wide-eyed, desperate appreciation Noah radiated when Eli got his mouth on him.

Eli broke the kiss, dodging Noah's mouth when he tried to start it up again, twisting out of Noah's arms instead and scrambling down his body. Eli tugged Noah's joggers down as soon as he landed on his knees, letting out a harsh breath when Noah's huge, hard cock bounced in front of his face.

Noah let out a breathless laugh. "What—?"

"Wanna suck you," Eli told him, peering up at him from the floor, already fisting the base of Noah's cock. Where his knot might inflate, if Eli blew him just right. "Is that okay?"

"Is that—?" Noah let out a groan, his head banging back against the door, the motion revealing the length of his strong, taut throat.

Eli wanted to bite it.

All in due time.

Meanwhile Noah was agreeing, "Fuck *yes*, that's okay."

Eli let out a happy hum, lapping at the fat, mushroomlike tip of Noah's cock, where precum was already beading. Salty. Musky. Delicious.

Eli mouthed along the length of him, somewhere between hungry and worshipful. After a moment, Noah's hands landed on his head, his fingers running through Eli's strands. He didn't try to lead him to do anything, just kind of grasped and petted, desperate to touch him in any way he could.

Eli liked that. A lot.

He could feel himself getting slick as he sucked Noah's cock into his mouth, working his way as far down as he could, which wasn't even to the edge of where Noah's knot would inflate. He used his hands to make up the difference, squeezing and stroking in the way he'd learned Noah liked.

Noah was *loud* during blow jobs. Lots of "fucks" and "oh gods" and "shit, yeah, that's so fucking goods."

It made Eli wet as hell, and honestly, it was great for the ego.

He got lost in his task, reveling in the heavy weight of Noah's cock on his tongue, but when Noah began pulling at his hair with purpose, Eli peered up to meet his eyes.

And apparently that was all Noah had wanted because he let out a desperate groan, grunting, "God, yes. So pretty. Gonna come, baby. Gonna make me come."

Eli hummed his approval, rubbing at his own hard cock through his sweats, his hole clenching around air. He went as deep as he could, gagging himself, but it was worth it when Noah let out a strangled moan, his salty release flooding Eli's mouth.

Eli swallowed every drop he could, massaging Noah's burgeoning knot with his hands. It wouldn't inflate fully without an omega to take it in, but he knew it was a sensitive area regardless.

Plus, it was fun to squeeze. Like a stress ball.

When Noah was done shuddering, Eli slid his mouth down his length once more, lapping at the side of his half knot. And then he sucked.

Noah yelped, his head slamming against the door. "Oh! Oh *fuck*!"

Eli paused. "Okay?"

The hands in his hair tightened. "Yes. Jesus. Yes. Do it again," Noah begged. "Fucking fuck."

Eli grinned. See? So appreciative.

He sucked around the sides of Noah's half knot, his hand catching at the cum that dribbled out each time he did. It was no wonder it was always such a mess when Noah knotted him, if this wasn't even half of it.

Eventually, Noah either grew too oversensitive or too impatient, and he slid his hands down to Eli's shoulders, pulling him up. He licked into Eli's mouth, sliding his hand inside Eli's underwear at the same time and grasping Eli's hard, leaking cock.

Eli was beyond wet at this point, and Noah took full advantage, stroking him in a smooth, squelching glide.

Eli whined into the kiss, bucking his hips.

"That's it," Noah soothed, his other hand grasping Eli's neck lightly, his thumb brushing tantalizingly against his scent gland. "Come in my hand, baby. Gonna taste you after, suck you off my fingers like you sucked down my cock."

Eli didn't last long after that.

After Noah did exactly as he'd said—sucking Eli's cum off his fingers like it was the finest delicacy—he gave him a deliriously bright grin, his dimples in full force. "So. What did I do to deserve such a warm welcome?"

"I just ..." Eli tried to find the words to express the ferocious need he'd felt, seeing Noah at his door, but all that he could summon was, "I just ... like you."

Noah's eyes softened, his smile growing impossibly wide. "I like you too. So much."

He ducked his head into Eli's throat to scent mark him and then stiffened. "You ... met an alpha today?"

He didn't sound accusing, just ... cautious.

Eli bit back a curse. Fucking Richard and his stupid fucking tobacco pheromones.

He didn't want to tell Noah about Richard's visit, not now. It wasn't like he was hiding anything, but he didn't want to bring that bullshit into this space just yet. Especially after what had just passed between them. This hadn't been about that. It had been about Noah.

So Eli settled for a half-truth. "Some uppity business dude came into my office before my lecture. He works for the dean."

Noah took another sniff, his chest rumbling with a half growl. "Kinda rude with his pheromones," he said, his voice harsher than its usual low drawl.

"Tell me about it," Eli laughed, not sure if he sounded crazed or natural. "It was suffocating."

Noah let out a soft, rumbling noise, and then he scent marked Eli as he'd intended, rubbing his face against Eli's neck until all signs of Richard had been obliterated. "Better?"

Eli let out a relieved sigh, letting his weight fall into Noah. "So much better."

And it was, wasn't it? This thing with Noah. Better in pretty much every way.

If only they didn't have to keep it hidden.

12

Eli

Something was niggling at Eli this morning, even as he lay warm and cozy in his bed with a passed-out Noah drooling on his chest. It wasn't hard to figure out what it was.

Richard's visit.

It wasn't that Eli regretted keeping it to himself last night—not exactly. He was still in no rush to introduce the ugliness that was Richard into his new relationship. It was more about what the visit had brought up for him. The old arguments. The disappointment.

It would be stupid to talk about it so soon, right? Eli and Noah had only just started dating, and while their relationship was easy, it was also ... precarious, if only by the nature of their positions. And Noah was young and inexperienced and just ... didn't need to be thinking about these things.

And yet.

There was potential here, wasn't there? Real potential.

Shouldn't Eli know where they stood before things went any further?

Noah's arm twitched where it was resting across Eli's waist, and his breath shifted out of the deep, steady rhythm of sleep. Eli schooled his expression, relaxing his furrowed brow as he watched Noah wake.

The alpha lifted his head, sleep-bleared eyes landing on Eli's face immediately. He always did this when he woke up—sought Eli out like he couldn't quite believe he was there until he'd laid eyes on him.

Noah wiped his mouth with the back of his hand and gave Eli a soft, sleepy smile. "Hey."

Eli's breath caught at the sight of him, and his answering greeting came out almost shy. "Good morning."

They spent a stupidly long moment giving each other fond, dopey looks, and then Noah's eyes widened, and he was leaping out of the bed with an energy he did *not* usually have first thing in the morning. "Holy shit, the plants!"

He started bounding out of the bedroom, still nude, although he did snag a pair of briefs off the floor as he went.

Eli was left dumbfounded. What the hell had just happened?

He didn't become truly alarmed until he heard the front door close, and then Eli rose quickly, slipping on his robe without bothering to tie it as he hurried down the hall.

By the time he got to the front door, Noah was already back inside, bare-chested in his underwear, carrying a box of ... Well, a box of plants.

Eli was no less confused than before. "What—?"

Noah grinned, still panting from his sprint. "I forgot to bring them in last night. They're herbs."

"Herbs?"

"Yeah." Noah nodded, petting a basil leaf as he somehow managed to peer at Eli from under his lashes while looming a head higher than him. "I keep looking at the ones in your kitchen windowsill. They're definitely past the point of no return. I thought we could try again."

Right. The herbs in Eli's kitchen. They'd been a half-assed approach at a hobby he'd tried in the wake of his separation—one of several failed attempts at opening his life up to new interests when all he'd felt like doing was shutting down. He'd either underwatered them or overwatered them or not said the right magical incantation or whatever, and they'd all died within weeks.

And Noah had noticed. Noticed and bought him new ones. Eli spotted basil and thyme and parsley and what he thought might be chives.

Eli needed to kiss him. Needed to tell him how thoughtful he was. How perfect and sweet he was being when Eli had done nothing to deserve it.

"I don't want children!" he blurted out instead.

Noah stopped petting the basil plant, raising his brows. "Um ... not even plant children?"

"It was— That was a huge reason Richard and I fell apart," Eli told him, tying his robe shut because he could no longer stand being mostly naked for this conversation, the words escaping no matter how hard he tried to keep them back. "We'd agreed, in the beginning. But I guess he thought ... He wanted me to change my mind, but I—I—"

He was having trouble making any sort of sense, and he couldn't stop twisting his hands in the fabric of his robe.

"Whoa, whoa, whoa." Noah set the box down carefully on the floor and gathered Eli in his arms, running his warm hands over Eli's shoulders, blasting calming pheromones while he soothed him with his touch. "Did I—" He gave a strangled half laugh. "Were the herbs that big of a mistake?"

"No." Eli gave in to his instincts and buried his nose in Noah's chest, inhaling breath after breath of his pacifying scent until he could speak again. "They were perfect. It was sweet. *You're* sweet. But most alphas—"

Noah wrapped his arms around Eli's shoulders, pressing him closer. "I don't want kids either."

"You can't just *say* that," Eli groused. "Not if you don't mean it."

And now his eyes were stinging. Oh god, was he crying?

Noah looked down at him in alarm. "Okay. Um. Fuck. How about— Let's get you coffee. You need coffee, don't you? I can't just be springing surprise gifts on you when you're undercaffeinated. That was my bad, for sure."

Eli wiped his eyes and let himself be led into the kitchen and supplied with a perfect cup of coffee. Noah babied him all the while with soft touches and softer pheromones, like it really was Noah's fault and not just Eli having a meltdown for no reason.

He was being way too nice. Eli was definitely going to start crying again if Noah kept being so nice to him.

Once Eli was tucked securely under a blanket on the couch, mug in hand, Noah settled next to him with a water. He slid a bent knee under himself and rested his arm on the back of the couch, placing his head on his fist. "Okay," he said softly. "So. No rugrats."

Right. They were having this conversation. Because Eli had started it out of nowhere, like an idiot.

He took a deep breath. Let it out. Took a sip of coffee. Noah waited him out patiently.

"I've always known," Eli finally said. "I just ... never felt the pull. I like my time to be *mine*, you know?" Noah nodded his understanding, and Eli continued, "And I— My parents were great. Good. Fine. But I don't think they really wanted kids. They just had us because they thought they should? And I know what that feels like. How it pushes you toward any scrap of affection, no matter if the source is ... flawed." He stared down at his mug. "I don't want to be that kind of parent."

"You don't have to justify it, you know," Noah told him, his gaze steady and his tone even. "It's enough that you don't want to."

Eli let out a bitter laugh. "Well, my ex felt otherwise. He started pushing for it, and I just—I *knew* how that would go. It would have been *me* leaving my career behind to care for them, not him. Me giving up everything I'd worked for. But somehow I was still the selfish one for not wanting it."

Noah's tone was slightly less even as he said, "He sounds like a fucking asshole."

Eli shrugged. Faith held the same sentiment when it came to Richard, but it had been hard for Eli to see it. "He changed his mind. He wanted me to do the same. People do change their minds."

As if sensing the pointed nature of that statement, Noah met Eli's gaze square on and told him, "I've known since I was a teenager that I don't want kids." He waited until Eli gave him a stilted nod of acknowledgment before continuing, "I've done it all already. Changed the diapers. Cleaned the spit up. Said no to hangouts and pickup games of soccer because I had to pick my little siblings up from daycare. I want any relationship I have to be something that's just ... mine." He bit at his lower lip, gaze glancing off Eli to land on the wall behind him. "Something intimate and ... quiet, I guess? And I don't care if that's selfish." His hand landed on Eli's knee as he met his eyes again. "I *want* to be selfish, as a couple. To have time for friends and hobbies and travel. I want to be able to decide we're doing takeout all week, or we're going away for a month in the summer, and not worry about anyone else but ourselves."

"Oh," Eli said dumbly.

It was an inadequate response, but he hadn't realized—even with the little hints he'd gotten—how much Noah had taken on for his parents when it came to his siblings, or how much it had affected him.

"Yeah. Oh," Noah told him with a soft smile, some of his intensity lightening. "Besides, I know at least some of my siblings are gonna have kids, and I wanna be a good uncle for them. Take the littles off their hands when they need a break." He grabbed Eli's hand. "I know there will be children in my life, they just don't have to be my own, ya know?"

"Well, when you put it that way, it sounds ..."

"Perfect?" Noah supplied, giving him a cheeky grin.

Eli narrowed his eyes at him. "Suspiciously so." When Noah kept on grinning, Eli let out a sigh. "That's what I always wanted, I think, with—with my ex. To figure out a life we really wanted. To *do* what we really wanted. But even without kids ... his work was like his child, always demanding our presence for one thing or another."

There'd been dinner parties and overnight functions with insufferable snobs. Late nights and weekend after weekend lost to Richard's overtime. And then the working "vacations," the two of them holed up in some rental with a prospective client and their family so Richard could network.

Eli cleared his throat. "And then when I was finally settled in my own career, he changed his mind and said he wanted kids after all. Decided that the two of us weren't enough and were never going to be." Eli's muscles tensed with old, familiar anger. "I think he'd always expected me to change my mind. To give in to my omega instincts or something."

"Is that why he never bit you?" Noah asked, his eyes on Eli's neck.

Right. Eli's lack of a mating bite. His distinctly bare neck. It had been a sore point for so long, and then after the divorce, it had only been a relief—one less way his life had to be torn apart by what had happened between them.

"I think so," Eli said with a shrug. "I was young when we got married, and he'd said things about waiting until we were more ...

established. Making it a sort of vow renewal or some bullshit. But yeah, I think he just wanted to wait until I was willing to be knocked up."

Noah's smile had taken on a brittle edge. "Can I call him an asshole again?"

"No." Eli set his empty cup on the side table, trying to give Noah a stern look and failing. He just looked so sweetly indignant on Eli's behalf. "There's no need."

Noah pushed his lower lip out in a mock pout. "Well, damn. Then will you at least accept my gift?" He gestured back to the box of plants that had been abandoned in Eli's hallway. "I did some internet sleuthing, and I think you must have underwatered. We've got a dry climate here, and people underestimate—"

Eli pressed forward, placing his hands on Noah's wrists, halting the too sweet words about his too sweet gesture. Something else was leaving his mouth without permission, in one hurried rush, "Willyouspendmyheatwithme?"

Eli had a fairly regular cycle, with three heats a year, and he'd managed to sync them up with school holidays. Which meant he had about six weeks still before he needed to bring this up. But he couldn't help it—he wanted Noah there, and he wanted Noah to know it.

Noah blinked at him. Once. Twice. "Yes?"

"It's over spring break," Eli told him. "You might have plans."

Maybe Eli should have felt guilty for even asking him. He could handle it well enough with suppressants and toys, and maybe Noah had visions of jetting off to Florida and getting rowdy on some crowded, drug-filled beach. That was what college kids did these days, right? Or was that just lies reality TV had told him?

"Plans?" Noah turned his wrists quickly, so now it was *his* hands grasping Eli's, keeping him from withdrawing. "No plans. No, sir. All plans canceled." He shook Eli's arms gently, barely containing his grin. "Of fucking course I want to spend your heat with you."

Eli sagged in relief. "Yeah?"

And it was hard to second-guess it, when Noah's pheromones were so warm and pleased, his scent emitting pure satisfaction just at being asked.

"Fuck, yeah." Noah groaned. "Oh my god, it's going to be so hot." His voice dropped into something low and intimate. "You're going to get soaked, baby. I'm going to knot you so many times."

Eli flushed, shifting in his blanket burrito. "Noah ..."

"I've never helped anyone through a heat before. How do you get?" Noah asked him, shameless as always. "Are you needy? Bossy? Feral?"

"Um ... the first one." It was actually kind of embarrassing, how needy Eli got. It was part of the reason he hadn't been brave enough to ask Noah yet. There was a vulnerability to it—to letting someone else see him that way.

"Needy?" In the next second, Noah's brain seemed to catch up with his mouth, and he swallowed hard, his pupils blowing wide. "Fuck ..."

Eli squealed as he was suddenly scooped off the couch, blanket and all.

"All right," Noah said decisively, lifting Eli against his chest. "Back to the bedroom with you. I need to have you immediately. These fucking plants can wait."

Eli giggled all the way back to the bedroom. Any lingering anxiety he'd had left over from Richard's visit was gone, washed away in the gentle stream of Noah's patience and care.

13

Noah

"C'mon, man. You won't tell me anything? Not even his *name*?"

Noah took another sip of his beer, rolling his eyes at Spencer. Maybe that was an asshole move, but he wasn't really in the mood for this interrogation. For one, he was definitely bordering on tipsy. For two, Spencer had been nonstop about it for at least half the night, especially now that Chase had disappeared on them (never mind that he was the one who'd invited them to this party in the first place). And for three, Noah was fighting off a headache. The house party they were at wasn't well ventilated at all, and the heavy mix of pheromones they were swimming in was pushing at his sinuses in a way he always fucking hated.

He wished Eli was with him. Things might be better if Noah could shove his face into the crook of his omega's neck and breathe in his refreshing citrus scent. Or if he could grind with him on the dance floor, teasing Eli with light touches until he was begging Noah to leave, to go somewhere private and get handsy for real.

"Dude."

Noah shook his head, trying to clear the fog of lust and too much beer. "What?"

Spencer narrowed his eyes at him. "I'm talking to you."

"Talk to your date," Noah told him, gesturing to the beta on Spencer's lap, who was looking bored beyond belief while she sipped at her hard lemonade.

The three of them were pressed too close together on a small, overstuffed couch in the living room at the edge of the dance floor. And while the beta Spencer was holding didn't smell like strong pheromones, she *did* reek of pheromone-mimicking perfume. Noah wouldn't mind if she and Spencer went off to a new, private location so he could take a full breath without sneezing.

"She's not my date," Spencer said breezily, reaching around the girl to toss his empty red plastic cup onto a nearby table. "I just met her."

The beta huffed. "Asshole." She rose from his lap and gave him the finger, stalking off.

Just when Noah was starting to like her.

"Nice going." Noah ruffled Spencer's dark hair, frowning when his silken strands fell straight back into their stylish disarray. "Why the fuck does anyone give you the time of day anyway?"

Spencer shrugged. "'Cause I'm pretty. There'll be others." He turned on the couch until he was facing Noah more fully, apparently unconcerned with his prospect for the night disappearing. "Something's up with you. You're never home anymore. You never hang out. And now you're bailing on spring break."

Fuck, not spring break again. Spencer was like a dog with a bone at this point.

"I'm literally here with you right now," Noah pointed out.

"What happened to bros before hookups?"

Noah pointed vaguely in the direction the beta had run off to. "When have you ever followed that mantra?"

Spencer blinked eyes that were bloodshot and hazy from too much booze and weed. "Yeah, but you're like, better than me. 'S different."

Well, that was just sad.

Noah grabbed the back of Spencer's neck, pulling him close until their foreheads touched. Maybe he could get his point though by virtue of osmosis. "Dude. Listen—I really like him. But I'm keeping it private for a minute while we figure some stuff out. You *will* meet him, I promise. Just not yet."

Spencer shook his head back and forth in Noah's hold, not so surreptitiously managing to get his neck passively scent marked by Noah. He was always like that when drunk, trying to get as much touch or scent reassurance as he could get. "Is he married or something?"

Noah barked a surprised laugh. "No. Jesus." He paused, cocking his head. "Well, he is divorced."

"Really?" Spencer asked, perking up immediately. It was annoyingly endearing how quickly he went from pouting to pleased. All it had taken was a tiny crumb of information to placate him. Noah was hit—not for the first time—by a wave of guilt for keeping his bestie at a distance. "Why didn't you say so? The ex giving you trouble?"

"Not exactly."

Although, Noah did have a bad feeling about Richard. It wasn't just that the guy was clearly a dick, from the little Eli had said about him. It was also that Noah still felt like Richard was ... around somehow. That he wasn't done with Eli.

But maybe that was only Noah projecting. *He* wouldn't be able to eject Eli from his life after a decade of having him; he knew that much.

But Noah didn't say any of that to Spencer. He loved the guy, he really did, but Spence would *not* be able to keep his mouth shut about Eli if Noah shared anything else. It just wasn't in his nature to be discreet.

Like that time he'd sprained his groin during a particularly athletic hookup and not only told every single person he saw but pulled his pants halfway down to show them the bruising.

Spencer opened his mouth, clearly about to pester Noah for more details, but he was interrupted by the crowd in front of them parting to reveal the dirty-blond curls of Noah's younger brother Ash, followed by the hulking presence of his ever-present shadow, Ryder.

Oh, fuck yes. Noah grinned like a dope, rising from the couch to envelop his brother in a bear hug, making a bro fist for Ryder behind Ash's back. "Ash! Ryder! What're you two doing here?"

Ash allowed the hug for approximately two seconds before he pushed Noah off, and Noah settled back on the couch. "Spence texted."

Noah glanced at Spencer, who gave him a look of wide-eyed innocence.

Ash snapped in Noah's face to get his attention. "Hey. You. Where the fuck have you been?"

"What do you mean?" Noah asked, frowning at him. It had been a while since he'd been on the bad end of his brother's temper, and he hadn't missed it. Ash was still unpresented—a rarity at nineteen—but Noah wouldn't be surprised if he ended up an alpha. He may have been built like a beta—he was shorter and slimmer than Noah, more wiry than muscled—but he had the alpha aggression down pat. Especially when provoked.

But when the hell had Noah provoked him?

Ash started listing on his fingers. "You don't answer calls. You barely text back. I've stopped by the house three times, and every time, this dickhead"—he gestured to Spencer with his thumb—"is the only one there to tell me you're out. Again."

"Uh ..." Noah tried to think clearly. He knew he'd missed a call or two, but he hadn't thought he'd been *that* absent.

"You doing drugs or something?"

Noah could only laugh. "What the fuck, Ash?"

"I told you, Asher darling," Spencer drawled, kicking a foot out to tap Ash's calf. "He's seeing someone."

Ash flipped Spencer off without looking at him. "No, he isn't. Because Noah would *tell* me if he was seeing someone. Wouldn't you?"

"Uh ..."

Ash's eyes narrowed. "I take that back. Who is it?"

"I told you that too," Spencer said cheerfully, apparently pleased as fucking punch to have an ally in the give-Noah-a-hard-time department. "He's being super cagey."

Noah let out a growl. "Spencer, I swear to god ..." He leaned forward, giving Ash his most plaintive gaze. "Look, it's super new, and I'm keeping it to myself for now. I've just been at his place a lot, I guess. I'm sorry I disappeared. I'll do better."

Ash stared Noah down for a long moment. His eyes were light brown, but they had a ring of black around them, and when he focused all his attention on someone, they were intense as all hell.

"Fine," he said eventually. "But I want to borrow the car soon. We want to head to Flag, see the snow before it melts."

Spencer sat up out of his slouch. "Ooh, snow trip? That sounds—"

"You're not invited," Ryder snapped. He'd stepped out from behind Ash—not that Ash's form was capable of covering much of Ryder's bulk—to glare at Spencer. Noah had known the guy since he'd been a scrawny, malnourished kid, so he wasn't affected by the whole "mean alpha" thing he had going on, but he could see why some might be intimidated. Along with the deep, alpha bark, Ryder had dark hair shorn close to his scalp and an impressive collection of tattoos on his muscled arms. The only person he was ever remotely soft with was Ash.

Plus, his pheromones were something else.

Spencer scowled back at Ryder, but he could only keep it up for a second before he dropped it, his eyes lowering in submission. "Fine. Jeez, wouldn't want to be stuck with you two, anyway."

"Don't be a dick," Ash told Ryder mildly, without an ounce of real censure. His gaze landed on Noah again. "Okay, then?"

Noah shrugged. "Yeah, take the car. Whenever you want."

"Good. I'll text. You'll answer."

And then Ash disappeared back into the crowd, Ryder at his heels.

Spencer laughed, the sound almost manic. "Dude. Ash is such a hard-ass sometimes. How hasn't he presented as an alpha yet?"

"Because his designation is officially 'mouthy little shit,' that's why."

Spencer laughed again, clearly feeling the booze. "I'd let him move in with us just for the entertainment value if Ryder wasn't always with him."

"Ryder's chill unless you're an asshole. You just have a way of pissing him off."

"I piss everybody off."

"At least you're self-aware."

But apparently Spencer was feeling pouty again, because he lurched off the couch with a frown. "I'ma go find Chase," he muttered. "Everybody disappearing all the damn time ..."

He shuffled off into the crowd, and Noah let him go. It was best to let Spencer either drink or fuck his way out of whatever maudlin pit he was falling into. Trying to talk him out of it never seemed to work.

Noah waited where he was for a while, thinking maybe Spencer would find Chase and they'd end up with all three roomies on the couch, but when Spencer didn't come back, he stood and started wandering the house until he found a small laundry room that was unoccupied. The booze and late hour were getting to him, and he was feeling a little dizzy, on the edge of too drunk.

Still, he pulled out his phone, requesting a video call.

Eli picked up on the second ring. "Noah?"

He was lying in bed propped on some pillows, wearing his glasses—he'd probably been reading his book. He looked so cute and cozy that it made Noah's chest ache.

"Hi, baby," Noah said, as soft as he could and still be heard over the music pounding outside the door. "Is it too late to call?" He hadn't checked the time, but he knew it was well after midnight.

Eli shook his head, even though his eyes were heavy-lidded with fatigue. "No, I wasn't sleeping."

"Is that my sweatshirt?"

Eli's cheeks flushed a pretty pink. "Mm-hmm. It smells like you." Fuck that was hot. Eli wearing Noah's clothes when he wasn't around, trying to catch his scent. "How's the party?"

It was Eli who'd encouraged Noah to go when Chase had texted him about some guy he'd been on the lacrosse team with throwing a rager. Noah had been about to bow out, but Eli had told him he couldn't hide away with his older boyfriend all the time, that he needed to keep experiencing the typical college stuff so he didn't regret it later.

The only thing Noah regretted was not being in Eli's bed right now. He'd done plenty of partying his first two years of college, all amped up to finally be away from family obligations, with nothing to be responsible for except his own damn self. He was over it at this point.

"It's fine. Boring. Want you here." Jesus. Apparently Spencer wasn't the only one turning into a pouty drunk.

Eli laughed softly. "I don't think I'd be much fun at a college party."

"We'd make it fun." Noah grinned, waggling his eyebrows. "Find a dark corner and put you on my lap."

Eli cocked his head with a sly smile. "Are you drunk, sweetheart?"

Sweetheart. Noah liked that. He liked that a lot.

"Maybe a little." Probably more than a little, but Noah didn't want Eli to worry. He sighed. "Wanna be touching you."

"Yeah?" Eli shifted, his arm moving something out of sight. "I'd like to be touching you too."

"What's your hand doing over there?" Noah narrowed his eyes, as if that might help him zoom in on the action through the screen.

The pink in Eli's cheeks darkened. "Nothing."

"Show me."

Eli huffed, but he tilted his phone down until his lower half was revealed to Noah. He lifted Noah's sweatshirt, which was at least three sizes too big on him, to reveal his hand shoved inside his briefs.

Noah groaned, leaning against the laundry room door as all the blood rushed south. "Which part of you are you touching, baby? Your hole?"

"Uh-uh." Eli bit at his lower lip. "That's for you."

Fuck. Just hearing that made Noah's dick hard. "You stroking yourself, then?"

Eli shook his head shyly. "Just touching. Like I said, the sweatshirt smells like you."

And being surrounded by Noah's scent was making Eli horny. God.

"Do it," Noah urged. "Stroke yourself. Make yourself come for me. It'll help you sleep."

As if that was the reason for Noah encouraging Eli to jerk himself off over the phone. Altruism.

But apparently Eli didn't need much encouragement, anyway. His wrist began moving as he gave in to Noah's pleas. But the fabric in the way was making it some sort of horrible tease.

"Push your underwear down, baby. Wanna see."

Eli tugged at the waistline of his briefs, pushing until the band was under his balls, revealing his perfect, pretty pink dick to Noah's gaze. He didn't put on a show, didn't act coy or seductive. He just jerked himself urgently, like maybe he missed having Noah in his bed as much as Noah missed being there.

Noah would bet Eli was soaked.

"You're so pretty, Eli."

Eli made some wordless sound of protest, but his motions sped up, his hips lifting into his touch. If Noah was there, he'd push them back down, force Eli to take only what he was given, if only to hear the little whimpers of protest he'd make.

But Noah wasn't there. So instead he crooned, "That's it. So perfect, baby. Take what you need."

Eli did, and it didn't take long for him to come with a muffled groan, one Noah echoed at the gorgeous, filthy sight of Eli's cum coating his fist.

Eli was panting as he tugged his underwear all the way off and used it to wipe his hand, muttering about damp fabric. He looked sleepy and flushed and pleased. "What about you though?"

Noah palmed his hard dick through his jeans. "Don't worry, I'll take care of myself when I get home. Or I could come over?" he asked hopefully.

For a second, it looked like Eli would give in, but then he shook his head regretfully. "You should stay with your roommates tonight. They miss you."

"Yeah." Noah sighed. "You're right. I wish you could meet them," he said, the alcohol making him loose-lipped. "They'd think you're so sweet and pretty. And I think—think you'd like them too. Even Spencer. He's a shit, but he's got a good heart."

"They sound lovely," Eli told him. "Really."

Noah frowned down at the floor. "Want them to know you."

"Eventually. I promise." Eli tugged the covers over himself, his brow furrowing. "It's getting to you, isn't it? The secrecy?"

"A little. Just too drunk, I think. I miss them, but now I miss you too. Want you all in one big room."

Noah needed to stop talking now. He was being unfair, and he knew it. Eli couldn't do anything to change their circumstances, and the more people who knew about them, the riskier it would be for his job.

But Eli didn't call Noah out about it. He only hummed thoughtfully, then said, "You know the only thing I really liked about college parties? The dancing. I think you should find your roommates and dance your heart out, till you're not feeling so down. Drink a bottle or two of water while you're at it, because I think you might need it. And then if you still think the party's boring, drag them home and cuddle in with a movie. You guys can have a big hangover brunch in the morning, soak up all the booze you're gonna be regretting."

It sounded pretty fun when Eli put it that way. Like this was less a stupid party and more a vehicle for Noah to bond with his friends. And Spence would never say no to a movie and a cuddle. Plus, Noah kind of liked the idea of following Eli's secret orders to have a good night.

"And then I can come over?" he asked hopefully. "Tomorrow?"

"Yeah, sweetheart." Eli giggled. "Then you can come over."

Noah grinned dopily. "I like when you call me that."

Eli looked almost embarrassed, tucking his bottom lip between his teeth. "Well, you *are* sweet. And you do have a big heart." He cleared his throat with a frown. "It's been hard on you, keeping the two parts of your life separate. I'm sorry."

"It feels better now." Noah was still a little out of it—dizzy and tired—but he also felt … lighter. Like a bit of weight had been taken off. "Just talking to you feels better."

"I'm so glad, sweetheart. Go have fun, and I'll see you tomorrow."

Noah ended the call, trying not to mourn the loss. He'd have fun with his friends, and then he'd see Eli tomorrow.

It was fine. The secrecy was fine.

14

Eli

"I'm just saying you're acting shady."

Eli pulled the phone away from his cheek so he could make a face at it, never mind that Faith couldn't see him on the other end. "Just because I don't want to introduce you to my brand-new boyfriend means I'm acting shady?"

"Yes, it does," she said, as snippy as she'd been the entire call so far. "Because he's not even brand-new anymore. It's been months. *And* I've already met him. This would be a second meeting. Liz wants to make him dinner," she added, unashamedly pulling out the big guns.

Eli tucked the phone back between his cheek and shoulder so he could keep editing his PowerPoint as he tried to talk Faith down from her meet-Noah-right-this-second crusade. "You're lying. Liz can't cook to save her life."

"Fine. Liz wants to order takeout and put it in fancy serving dishes and pretend she cooked." Eli laughed, but Faith wasn't placated. "Is this just a sex thing, then?"

"No!"

"Are you still worried he's not serious?"

"No ..."

Noah had made it pretty clear he was into Eli in a major way. So clear that even Eli, with all his overthinking, couldn't mistake his alpha's intentions.

But what does a twenty-one-year-old know about intentions?

Jesus. Eli really wished he could turn that stupid, skeptical part of his brain off.

"Eli ...," Faith prodded.

"It's just ... complicated, okay?"

The problem was, Eli still didn't have the guts to tell Faith that Noah was his student. He didn't think he'd be able to handle her disappointment with him. If the person he trusted most in this world thought he was a genuine creep ...

Plus, it seemed hypocritical to stress the importance of secrecy to Noah and then go blabbing to his own sister. But either way, Eli wasn't handling this conversation well. Secrecy just wasn't in his wheelhouse—it was getting to him. It was getting to Noah, too, judging by how mopey he'd gotten last week over the phone when Eli had strong-armed him into going to a party without him.

Well, mopey by Noah standards, which meant he'd still been sweet as pie and absurdly easy to cheer up. But still ...

And it wasn't going to get any easier for them, at least not anytime soon. Eli was getting closer to his heat, and his body was letting him know, mainly by telling him he should be touching and scenting Noah every single second of every single day.

Which meant the lecture he was about to go to was going to be hell. Eli couldn't even wear one of Noah's shirts under his sweater to get him through the thing, for fear of someone catching Noah's scent on him.

"Eli. *Eli.*"

Oops. Apparently Faith had been calling his name. Eli cleared his throat, hopefully projecting full innocence. "Yes?"

"Permission to truth-bomb you?"

Eli saved his PowerPoint edits and closed his laptop, leaning back in his chair with a sigh. "Since when have you ever needed permission?"

"Good point. Here goes." She gave a dramatic pause. "Noah is not you. And you are not Richard."

Eli winced. Ouch. "That's not what I meant by complicated."

"Too baaaad," Faith singsonged. "I'm bringing it up anyway. Because if you're keeping him at arm's length because of the age thing ... Just know you're not exactly unbiased in that department."

"Why are you so adamant about him anyway?" Eli asked. It wasn't like Faith to push him into dating. Into leaving the house more often, yes. Into trying to get a little human touch once in a while, sure. But not into shackling himself to another alpha. "You liked him that much?"

He could almost hear her shrug over the phone. "He had good energy, sure. But also ..." Faith let out a sigh. "I hoped after you and Richard separated that you'd spread your wings a little. Let yourself grow and play and experience new things now that he wasn't there closing you off at every angle. But instead you became ... smaller. It was all work, work, work and nights at home. I want you to open your world up, Eli. You deserve it."

Oh god. The sincerity had arrived, and it was painful. Painful and accurate. "And you think jumping into another relationship is the key?"

"I think the way this Noah kid had you blushing and flustered and off-kilter at the bar was the most out of your comfort zone I've seen you in a long time. And I think some people find it easier to be brave when they have a person in their corner. I think, from the *very little* you've told me about him," she said, in a tone that made it clear how she felt about that, "he seems like the kind of guy who wants to be in your corner."

Eli was ... genuinely speechless.

"Eli?" Faith prompted. "Did you hang up on me?"

"Faith, you can't make me *cry* before my lecture." Eli let out a thick laugh. "Goddamn."

"Ooohh, I hit it out of the park, didn't I?" Faith couldn't have sounded more delighted with herself if she tried.

"Don't be cocky about it. It'll ruin the effect."

"Fine. I'm hanging up while I'm flying high. Your wise, wisdom-y, wizened older sister."

Eli hung up before she could. That was what she got for being smug.

He lingered at his desk, considering her words. He hadn't thought of himself as closed off since the divorce. Just ... focused, maybe. On work. On rebuilding.

Although, what exactly had he built in the year since Richard had officially left? All Eli really had to show for that time were some dead herbs and a lot of lonely nights.

Eli thought of Noah's vision of the kind of couple he wanted to be—quiet and intimate and selfish; wasn't that what he'd said? The kind of couple that lived the life that suited them in the moment. The kind that valued flexibility as well as a firm foundation.

They could really do that, couldn't they? This could be real, what he had with Noah. Really real.

They just had to get through the semester.

And then ...

And then Eli would make it all up to Noah, with everything he had in him.

Eli couldn't exactly go to college parties with him, even when Noah wasn't officially his student any longer, but he'd invite Noah's friends over to the house, let them use the pool and spend time all together. And he'd take Noah to Faith's for dinner and let Faith rib him mercilessly. He'd meet Noah's parents and hope they didn't murder him on sight.

And when Eli's own parents got back from whatever European retirement tour they were currently on, they'd do the perfunctory boyfriend meet, just so Noah knew exactly how much he mattered.

They'd be a real couple. They might even get married someday.

And instead of that thought terrifying Eli like it rightfully should, it made butterflies erupt in his stomach. The good kind, made of spun sugar and fairy dust and whatever other nonsense the good kind of stomach butterflies were made of.

Eli packed his workbags and walked to his lecture in a sort of daze.

As he opened the door to the lecture hall, he sternly reminded his body that they could *not* leap on Noah the moment they saw him. Or leap on him at all, for that matter. There would be no leaping whatsoever. Nor could they steal whatever clothes Noah might be wearing off his body and shove them under their shirt. They had to wait. To be patient.

But it wasn't Noah's salty-fresh pheromones greeting Eli as he entered the hall. Instead it was the heavy, tobacco pheromones of his ex-husband.

All Eli's daydreams popped in an instant.

Fucking Richard was in his classroom.

———

It took everything in Eli to contain his groan.

Stupid, smug Richard, all pressed and polished in his suit, leaning against Eli's podium like he had a right to.

A number of students—and more than one of Eli's TAs—were

making hopeful eyes at the undeniably handsome alpha. Eli wished he could tell them to avert their gazes before an entire decade of their lives was stolen away from them, but he didn't want to sully his reputation as a professor by spouting crazy nonsense at his students.

He'd wait until he had tenure for that.

Noah was nowhere to be seen yet, thank fucking God. But since there were other students in their seats already, Eli couldn't open with the line he wanted to, mainly, "What the *fuck* are you doing here?"

Instead, he had to settle with, "Richard. What brings you to my lecture hall unannounced?"

Mature. Professorial. And totally inadequate to the helpless rage Eli felt. He was too close to his heat for this fuckery. His emotions were heightened, and he wanted *his* alpha, the one who made him feel safe and seen and held. Not this businessman hussy with no concept of the finality of signed divorce papers.

And Eli's pheromones were loose enough in preheat that Richard was able to scent Eli's annoyance, his eyes crinkling in the corners as he gave Eli a condescending smile. "No need to get your hackles up, Lijah. I was simply—"

"In the neighborhood?" Eli finished for him, plopping his bag on the podium with a raised brow. "Having lunch with the dean, perhaps?"

"Why, yes."

"Lotta lunches these days." Eli lowered his voice as he handed his laptop to a TA to get set up. "An illicit affair, maybe?"

Richard only laughed, like Eli was being charming instead of irritable. "We're rearranging his portfolio, is all. You know he's not my type."

"But his secretary, perhaps?"

Richard's mouth pursed into a disappointed moue. "Lijah ..."

Eli was disappointed in himself, actually. Not for the dig about the secretary—that had been perfect—but for playing into this whole thing at all. He needed to get Richard out of here, not vent his anger. "I have a class to teach, Richard."

"I know." Richard flashed white teeth. "I was thinking of observing. I do so miss watching you work."

Of all the bullshit ... Eli contained his huff but only barely. "Funny, because I remember you pressuring me to stop."

"I may have been ... hasty, Lijah." Richard stepped closer, his pheromones pulsing just on the edge of inappropriate. "There was no reason for you to leave your career. Nannies exist for a reason." He placed a hand on Eli's lower back, and Eli was too startled to stop him as he leaned down to say in a low voice, "Like I said, I've missed you."

And of course, just as Richard was pressed into him, whispering in Eli's ear like some sort of welcome guest, Noah walked in.

He didn't notice them at first—too busy chatting with his beta friend, Chase—but he looked over before taking his seat. He *always* looked over before taking his seat, like he couldn't resist laying eyes on Eli as soon as he could.

Eli watched in horror as Noah froze mid-step, the smile dropping from his face as his nostrils flared. No doubt he recognized Richard's pheromones—they were distinct.

Please sit down, Eli begged in his head, brushing Richard's hand off his back. *Please sit down and let me explain later.*

But Noah stood where he was, barely ten feet from the podium, practically vibrating with tension. "Do we have a guest lecturer, professor?" he asked, his voice stilted and unnatural.

Richard raised his head in surprise, noticing Noah for the first time, a genial smile already on his lips. "Just a visitor, son."

Jesus. He couldn't possibly have sounded more dismissive.

"One who is *leaving*," Eli said desperately.

"Lijah ...," Richard chided, although his voice was warm—

putting on a show for their audience, no doubt. "Not even five minutes for your husband?"

Fucking hell.

As Eli rushed to correct, "*Ex*-husband!" as if that was really going to help anything—a surge of dark, bitter pheromones filled the air. Like a beach after a storm, salt and seaweed and decay.

Noah had never smelled like that, not once since Eli had known him. It was heavy and stifling, a clear alpha warning.

Richard wrinkled his nose. "Back in my day, students had a better handle on themselves."

A loud rumble filled the air. Dear god, was Noah *growling*?

Eli had to put a stop to this. He put a placating hand on Richard's arm, trying to distract him from the damning noise. "Richard. Please. I have a class to teach. You have an ... intimidating presence. Some students aren't used to that." He looked over to Noah, pleading with his eyes as he ordered, "Mr. Teller, please take your seat."

He wasn't sure if Noah would have, if not for Chase tugging on his arm, practically dragging him away.

When all this was over, Eli was going to buy that beta flowers.

Richard leaned into Eli again, murmuring, as if it was some kind of joke, "I think someone's got a crush on teacher."

Now that Noah was safely seated and out of Richard's eyeline, Eli took his hand off Richard's arm, hissing, "I need you to *leave*. You're distracting my students."

"I see your preheats are the same as ever. Moody, Lijah?"

Now it was Eli's turn to let out a growl. It was horrible of him. Completely unprofessional. And he could hear students whispering in the background, no doubt eating up all this drama.

But he *hated* being railroaded like this. He had thought signing the divorce papers would put an end to this dynamic. What right did Richard have, to show up and humiliate Eli in front of his class? His omega studies class, no less?

His next words made it out through clenched teeth. "If you don't leave in the next five seconds, I'm calling campus security. This is your final warning."

Richard blinked at him in surprise, and Eli almost laughed. Had Richard really thought that even after a year apart, Eli would have forgotten to grow a backbone? Or was he really going to force Eli to put his money where his mouth was right now and call security on him?

But then Richard was leaving, walking out the door with one last disappointed shake of his head.

Eli cleared his throat, trying to get control over himself and his now completely wayward pheromones. He couldn't look at Noah, even as he faced the rest of the students. He was too afraid of what he'd see.

Too afraid to witness what he might have just ruined.

"All right, class. Apologies for the ... distraction. Let's get started, shall we?"

15

Noah

The day had started out so well too.

Noah had been jazzed—he was going to spend the night at Eli's tonight, and they were going to have a discussion about heat expectations. He knew it was supposed to be, like, a serious, adult conversation, but he couldn't help the fact that it was also going to be so fucking hot.

He hadn't been able to get the dirty thoughts out of his head ever since Eli had said he was going to be ... needy.

Which was kind of ridiculous to obsess over—most omegas were needy during their heats, to some extent, at least.

But this would be Eli. *His* Eli, needing Noah on a basic, primal level, more than he ever had before.

It was heady as fuck. And Noah had known there was no way the discussion was going to end with anything other than them doing filthy, filthy things to each other.

So Noah had walked into class on a happy, horny cloud, chatting easily with Chase, who'd proven how well he could keep a secret by just how *not* weird he was every time they entered the Omega Studies lecture hall.

And then Noah had scented them—those strong, tobacco pheromones that had been lingering on Eli's skin a few weeks ago. The pushy businessman, Eli had told him. Except as soon as Noah had looked over and seen the man—the definition of tall, dark, and handsome—looming over Eli, his hand on Eli's lower back, possessiveness in every inch of his body language, Noah had known.

This was Richard. The ex-husband.

And now Noah was frozen in the middle of the classroom, unable to take another step.

He couldn't make a scene; he knew that. He'd fuck everything up for Eli if he did. But Noah couldn't make himself walk away either. Not while that dickhead was standing over Eli like he had a right to, pushing his pheromones at him like he had any. Fucking. *Right.*

"Do we have a guest lecturer, professor?"

Noah didn't recognize his own voice, the tense, gravelly edge to it. Chase was whispering at him urgently, telling him he needed to go sit down.

And Eli just looked ... Well, he clearly wanted Noah to sit the fuck down too.

And then the ex-husband spoke to Noah, smug and dismissive as all hell. "Just a visitor, son."

Son? *Son?*

Fury raced through Noah's veins, hot and swift, even as Eli insisted Richard was leaving.

Eli, who hadn't told Noah that Richard was back, sniffing around. And Noah couldn't even blame him, at least not if he was thinking clearly. Alphas could be weird. Territorial. He knew he wouldn't have handled the news well—he would have ached to scent Eli every day before school, just in case the asshole appeared again. Which Noah wasn't allowed to do. Because they were a secret.

He should have realized anyway, shouldn't he? Of course Richard was back. Of course he'd walked away only to realize there wasn't anything better than Eli out there for him.

Noah would almost feel sorry for him, if he wasn't currently resisting the urge to rip the guy's throat out with his teeth.

And then Richard called himself Eli's husband—present fucking tense.

Noah lost it.

His pheromones surged, heavy and thick and bitter as hell. He hated this man. He didn't care if it was immature or stupid. He hated him. Hated that he'd gotten a decade of Eli and had been willing to fuck it all up but somehow still couldn't slink all the way off into the horizon like the pest he was. Hated that Eli and Richard looked good together, standing there with their matching dark hair and eyes and their fucking age appropriateness. Hated most of all that even though Richard was the *ex*-husband, *he* was the one allowed to be up there with Eli. Touching him. Scent marking him.

Claiming him.

Richard said something smarmy, and Noah was growling. Here was the scene he wasn't allowed to be making. But even worse, here was Eli placating Richard, a hand on his arm and a plea in his voice. And then Eli was turning to Noah and calling him Mr. Teller, asking him to sit down. To leave Eli there with Richard.

Noah supposed he should be grateful for Chase pulling him to sit down. He wasn't sure what he would have done otherwise. Probably jumped over the podium and thrown Eli over his shoulder, abducting him to somewhere safe and private where Noah could scent mark every inch of his perfect, soft skin, where he could erase Richard from Eli's body and his mind and ...

Well, it didn't matter. Noah wasn't allowed to do any of those things.

He watched like a hawk, vibrating with tension in his seat, as Eli told Richard to leave. Noah's omega was no longer placating the handsome alpha. He was fierce instead, letting out an omega growl that had Noah's chest rumbling with satisfaction.

But that feeling didn't last long, even as that asshole finally left and Eli started his class, composed and professional.

Noah could hear the whispers around him. The "Who was that?" And the "Oh my god, so hot." The "Did you know Professor Miller was married?"

The gossips were loving this. Loving the thought of their pretty omega professor being swept off his feet by the handsome, repentant alpha who'd just walked out the door.

It hurt.

It hurt to sit there, Noah's omega right here and yet worlds away, smelling for all the world like his ex-husband and not Noah. It hurt to pretend to be strangers when Noah needed reassurance the most.

It just ... hurt.

———

NOAH GOT to the house before Eli.

It was unsurprising, considering he'd driven like a bat out of hell, and he'd known Eli would need to at the very least pack up his laptop and dismiss his TAs.

For that matter, Eli technically still had office hours, but Noah had a feeling he'd cancel them.

A feeling that turned out to be justified when Eli burst through the door ten minutes after Noah's arrival, barely dodging Deadly dancing between his feet as he cried out, "I'm so sorry!"

They needed to talk about it. They 100 percent needed to have a serious discussion. But first ...

Noah prowled toward Eli and gathered him in his arms, rubbing his face against Eli's cheeks, his neck, his shoulders, stroking his hands over Eli's back, his arms, his wrists.

Scent marking the motherfucking life out of him.

Eli—wisely—went completely limp in Noah's hold, even letting out a tiny, relieved sigh that did a little something to soothe Noah's raised hackles. It was a reminder that Eli wanted to smell like *him*, not that dick he called an ex-husband. A reminder that he was *Noah's*, not Richard's.

When Eli was as covered with his pheromones as he could possibly be—short of Noah fucking him right there in the front hallway—Noah dropped his head onto Eli's shoulder. "I hate him," he murmured, ragged and worn. "I've never hated anyone before, but I fucking hate him."

Eli stroked Noah's curls with a tentative hand. "I know, sweetheart. I'm sorry."

"You lied," Noah accused, though there was no real heat in it. "Before."

"I did." Eli wrapped his other arm around Noah's waist, holding Noah against him. The angle was awkward with their height difference, but Noah didn't care. "I didn't want him to—to ruin things just by existing, I guess."

Noah huffed a breath against Eli's neck, his hands landing on Eli's hips. "You think I can't handle your history?"

"I think you shouldn't have to, this early on."

That was wrong. Eli was wrong. Older didn't always mean wiser, did it? "Why is he around now?" Noah asked, feeling like he already knew the answer. "He wants you back?"

Eli's fingers never stopped their stroking. "I don't know. I don't know why he would, after everything."

"I do."

Eli let out a short laugh. "You're biased, sweetheart."

Noah groaned, his fingers tightening around Eli's hips. "I hated seeing him up there with you. I hate that he's allowed to touch you in public."

Eli leaned back to look at him, raising his hands to cup Noah's face. "He's not though." His brow furrowed as he stared into Noah's eyes. "He's *not* allowed. I was caught by surprise. It's not going to happen again."

"If he wanted you back, would he have a chance?"

Eli gave him a wounded look. "You have to ask?"

Something eased inside Noah. "No." He shook his head. "I don't."

He had already known, hadn't he? But he couldn't have helped asking either. After what he'd seen and who he'd scented. He circled his thumbs over Eli's waist. "I'm sorry. But trust goes both ways, right? You need to trust me too. As a full partner. You need to —need to tell me things. Yes, you have some baggage. But I'm not a child. I can handle it."

"I know. I—" Eli stopped mid-sentence as Noah's phone rang.

Noah silenced it without looking, and it immediately rang again. And again.

Eli's lips curled into a wry smile. "Maybe you should check who it is?"

Noah sighed, but he took a hand off Eli's waist to look. Ash was calling.

Fuck. Fuck, fuck, fuck.

The car. Noah was supposed to have left it at campus for his brother.

He picked up on the next rang. "Hey. I'm sorry, I—"

Ash cut him off. "Who do you know who lives on Elm?"

Something sank in Noah's gut. Eli's house was on Elm. The house they were at now. "What? Why?"

"We called a car already. We're on our way."

"How the fuck do you know—"

"That stupid friend tracking thing you set up on my phone."

Of course. Noah had insisted on it when Ash had arrived on campus. He'd wanted a way to find him if anything happened to him. It had been silly, overprotective older brother stuff.

But now Ash knew where to find Noah. Here. At Eli's.

Noah released Eli from his grip and dug his keys out of his pocket, turning toward the door. "Listen, I'll come to you."

"Too late," Ash said flatly. "We're here. I see the car. And I'll see you in less than a minute."

It sounded like a threat. Noah supposed it kind of was.

He looked helplessly to Eli, whose brow was furrowed in concern. "My brother's about to be here."

Eli's swallow was audible in the quiet of the house. "Your brother?"

"I promised him the car." Eli's face paled, and Noah rushed to reassure him. "Listen, he's never taken Omega Studies. He shouldn't recognize you."

A firm knock on the front door rang out. With one last look at Eli, frozen there in the hallway, Noah opened it to reveal Ash, looking annoyed as hell, with Ryder behind him. They both carried backpacks filled to the brim.

"Hey," Ash said. He looked immediately past Noah's shoulder to nod at Eli. "You're the boyfriend?"

Eli cleared his throat, his arm raising in a half wave. "Hello."

And then Ryder made a small, surprised noise. "Professor Miller? I had you last semester."

Jesus. Fuck.

Noah and Eli froze at the same time. They couldn't have had a more deer-in-the-headlights reaction if they'd tried.

Why the fuck hadn't they just hidden Eli in his room? Would Ash really have insisted on meeting him? Noah could have just told him his boyfriend was in the shower.

Ash bristled, drawing up to his full height as he looked between them. "What the fuck?" He stepped into the house, zeroed in on Eli. "You're a teacher. Are you *his* teacher?"

"Ash." Noah stepped in front of his brother, blocking Eli from his view. "It's not like that."

"What's it like?" Ash bent sideways to scowl at Eli from around Noah. He pointed a finger. "What the *fuck* do you think you're doing with my—"

It was too much. Richard's presence in the classroom earlier. Ash shouting at Eli now. Eli, who was so fucking close to his heat it was setting Noah's teeth on edge to even have Ryder—an alpha he knew and trusted—around him in such close quarters.

For the second time that day, Noah's pheromones surged. This time they were aimed at his brother. "*Out,*" he growled. "Fucking *now.*"

Ash dropped his hand, his rage melting immediately into hurt. Noah had never yelled at him before, never once used his pheromones against his little brother.

Ryder instantly had an arm over Ash's shoulder, glaring at Noah like he was an asshole as he pulled Ash away, shutting the door behind them.

Noah *was* an asshole.

He looked helplessly at Eli, whose face was distressingly blank. "I'm going to go handle this."

"Of course," Eli said faintly.

"I will be *right* back."

"Uh-huh. Sure."

Noah went out the door, hoping to explain things to Ash in a way that wouldn't mess up Eli's life. Or his own relationship with his brother.

16

Eli

Eli paced his living room, hot and flushed and feeling somehow too big for his own skin.

How had the day gone so awry? First Richard and now this.

He wished he could hold Deathly and soothe himself with her purrs, but she'd hidden away somewhere, no doubt pissed at the intrusion of strangers into her home.

Not exactly a stranger though. Noah's brother. Ash. A boy who'd looked at Eli with such *anger*. Such disdain.

Of course he had—he'd been looking at the seedy professor lusting after his older brother. He'd looked at Eli and seen some lecherous creep taking advantage of a student.

Everything was wrong. The situation was tilting sideways.

His pacing lasted only a minute, and then he couldn't help himself—he scurried to the living room window that looked out onto the street, pulling aside the curtain. There were Noah and

Ash standing at the open passenger door of Noah's car, having a heated discussion, by the look of it. There were raised hands and probably raised voices to match. The Ryder guy was standing close enough to hear them, and he was facing toward Eli's window, but his expression was unreadable.

Eli watched them argue, his heart in his throat, only jumping away from the window when Noah finally turned and strode back toward the house, leaving the other two men to drive off in his car.

When Noah returned through the front door, looking all shades of miserable, Eli was back to his pacing, unable to keep himself from wringing his hands like some sort of caricature of a distressed housewife.

For once, Noah didn't rush to take Eli into his arms. He stayed where he was, standing by the door, his intense gaze focused on Eli.

Eli stopped his pacing, and they faced off. At least, that was what it felt like. The tension between them was strange and heavy, and Eli didn't know exactly what to ask.

Does your brother really hate me? The answer to that was obvious.

Have you forgiven me for Richard? That one was less obvious but also possibly irrelevant, in light of what had just happened.

What came out instead was "I thought your brother was unpresented."

Noah ran a hand through his curls, his brow furrowing into a confused frown. "He is."

"He smells like an alpha."

Ash had been emitting a dark, woodsy scent. Definitely not the neutral notes of an unpresented male.

Noah let out a breath. "Those are Ryder's pheromones. People can be ... weird about the unpresented thing, and he gets protective. It's a besties thing."

Eli wasn't so sure about that. It hadn't smelled like a "besties thing." It had smelled more like a claiming.

But he wasn't going to argue the point. Not now, after what had just happened. He cleared his throat, wishing Noah was closer but too unsure to bridge the distance between them. "How—how did it go?"

Noah gave a bitter laugh, leaning back against the door. "Well, he's not gonna call the cops."

It was obviously a joke—Noah was well above eighteen—but it made Eli's stomach twist anyway. Eli was scum, wasn't he? Or Noah's brother thought he was, at the very least.

Whatever Noah saw on Eli's face had him stepping forward, his hand held out in a placating gesture. "Eli, no. It's okay. He's pissed, but that's just Ash. He'll calm down, and we'll have a real talk."

Eli started twisting his hands again, unwilling to accept the reassurance. "That's two people who know now, Noah. Your brother and his friend. Two *students*. Ones who don't like me very much right now."

Noah ran a hand over his face with a wince. "Is now a good time to tell you Chase knows too?"

"*What*?" Hot, fresh panic ran through Eli's veins. He hadn't been expecting that. Chase was in his *class*, for fuck's sake.

"I didn't tell him, but he ... figured it out."

"And you didn't think to tell *me*?!" Eli didn't exactly screech the words, but it was a close thing. He knew he should take a breath, try to lessen the rising panic, but he was too flustered by what was beginning to feel like hit after hit after hit.

Noah's answer was decidedly calmer, if just as devastating. "Like you didn't think to tell me about Richard?"

It felt like a low blow, even if it was a fair one. "I guess this is the thing with a secret relationship," Eli mused, feeling like his brain was separating from his body. "You get too used to keeping secrets." He let out a bitter laugh, his shoulders sagging. "Jesus, I'm going to get fired."

"Chase won't tell anyone. And I'll convince Ash. We'll get through this, Eli."

"*We* will?" Eli shook his head. "It's *my* job on the line, Noah." He thumped a hand to his chest, old wounds coming too close to the surface, making him feel too raw and too tender. "*My* career."

He'd been so close too. They'd be making the official decision after spring break, but it was basically a formality at this point. Eli had only needed one more week of classes, his heat to get through, and he would have at least had tenure. A leg of sorts to stand on if things went sideways like this.

"It's your career, yes. But I'm your partner." At Eli's silence, Noah narrowed his eyes. "You *do* see me as your partner, right? You see this as long-term? Or is this just some sort of distracting fuck while you wait for your tenure to go through?"

His words fell like a slap across Eli's face, and Eli blanched accordingly. "What did you just ask me?"

Were those Ash's words Noah was giving voice to, or was that something *he'd* been feeling? Had Eli been envisioning a future together while they weren't actually on the same page at all?

"Shit." Noah ran his hand through his hair again, tugging harshly on the strands. "I'm sorry. Fuck. I didn't mean that. I'm all worked up. Richard and then this. And you smell—" His face fell, shoulders dropping as he crossed his arms. "Maybe we need to take some space."

Space was the last thing Eli wanted. It felt like all this might be falling apart, and he wanted Noah closer, not further away. Even with the jumble in his head, the panic and the misery, he wanted Noah to hold him, to tell him things were going to be okay. He wanted to be bathed in some of that eternal optimism Noah usually carried around so effortlessly.

But Noah had never asked Eli for space before—if anything, it had always been the opposite—so if he was saying he needed it now ...

Well, Eli had to grant him that, didn't he?

It was probably for the best, anyway. They had another week until Eli's heat, and that would give Eli time to ... recalibrate. Time to figure out if he was going to be handing in his letter of resignation at the end of the week. Time to figure out what his life was going to look like if the worst happened.

But what *was* the worst that could happen? Losing his job? Or losing Noah?

Eli swallowed through a thick throat. It took concerted effort to rein his pheromones in, to avoid signaling his distress in bold, vivid colors. But he was the older, more experienced partner. It was his responsibility to be calm and reasonable.

He owed Noah that much.

"Okay." He cleared his throat—it wasn't closing up, not really. He knew that, even if it felt like it was. "Yes, of course. It's, um, hard to think right now. Space would be—would be good."

Noah didn't look pleased by Eli's acquiescence. If anything, he looked even more pained. He started nodding absently, his gaze darting everywhere that wasn't Eli. "Okay. Okay, good. I'll get a car."

"I'll drive you," Eli offered quickly. The thought of Noah being driven away by a stranger was for some reason untenable.

But Noah was already shaking his head, still not meeting Eli's eyes. "Not a good idea. Nosy roommates, remember? Chase knowing is one thing. Spencer would be another." He came forward to press a brief kiss to Eli's cheek, and his touch was a consolation, if a small one. "I'll call you soon."

And then he was out the door.

———

"Stop looking at me like that."

Faith's expression didn't change. "I'm not even looking at you. I'm looking at Deadly."

"But your *face*."

"This is what faces do in these situations," Faith told him, and apparently things were serious enough that she didn't even make it sound like a taunt. "It's my thinking face. Just chill out."

Eli threw his hands up as he stood from the couch, unseating poor Deadly off his lap. "*How?*"

He'd realized shortly after Noah had left that, while time apart may have been what Noah needed, time *alone* was only going to be the recipe for Eli to have an anxiety spiral of epic proportions.

And since two of Noah's people knew about them already—no, make that three; Eli couldn't forget about Chase—Eli no longer felt so sneaky calling in the big guns.

He'd told Faith everything.

And now she was here in his living room, lounging in the armchair across from him, and her face was doing a *thing*, and Eli didn't like it.

"You hate me now, don't you?" he asked, covering his own face with his hands. "You think I'm a despicable sleaze?"

Faith muttered something suspicious about preheat hormones before clearing her throat and fixing Eli with a firm look. "I do *not* think you're a despicable sleaze, Eli. What the fuck? I'm just ... surprised."

"That I'd do something so despicable?"

Faith rolled her eyes. They were going to get stuck that way if she kept doing it so dramatically. "Stop it. You told me how all this started. You didn't know. You're not some perv lording the possibility of an A over a vulnerable student. I'm just ... surprised you'd risk your career."

Eli had, hadn't he? He'd risked everything. For a *boy*. He

lowered his hands, searching Faith's face. "You think I've made a huge mistake, don't you?"

"Eli." Faith made his name sound like an admonishment. "Sit. Calm the fuck down. Drink some tea, for Christ's sake."

She'd made him a cup—herbal, since she'd claimed he was too jittery for caffeine ("vibrating like a damned washing machine")—even though the weather was warming up with the appearance of spring and it wasn't tea weather *at all*.

When he didn't sit and drink as commanded, Faith let out a weary sigh. "I didn't say you're making a mistake. It's just ... even with all Richard's bullshit ... your career was the one thing you were firm about. You never wavered. Even *I* thought you might at one point. But you didn't."

"It's different with Noah," Eli said automatically, the statement too true to require any thought at all. He glared at her for some reason, as if daring her to object.

"Okay," Faith soothed, gesturing to the couch he'd abandoned. "So sit. Tell me why."

Eli finally did as she asked, picking at the tassels on the closest pillow, trying to figure out how to put what had been until now an unexamined gut feeling into words. "Well, for one, Richard saw my career as a threat. Some sort of barrier in the way of making me an ideal omega. Noah doesn't see it that way. It's a complication for us, sure, but he *likes* that I'm smart. That I'm driven."

"That's great," Faith said easily. "Score one for Noah. What else?"

"It's just ... a feeling." Eli frowned down at his feet. "I loved Richard in the beginning, but it was ... I don't know, that love lived in my mind, you know? Because he was intelligent and handsome and he did all the right things. Because he seemed to care for me more than anyone else ever had, except for you. But with Noah ... that feeling lives in my body." Eli pressed a hand to his chest, right over his sore, wounded heart. "Like ... a sense of safety. Of warmth. I just feel ... *good* around him. And I know he feels the same way. It's instinctual. It feels solid and real and important, even if logically the situation's a mess." He looked up at Faith. "Is that stupid?"

Faith leaned forward, squeezing Eli's knee in reassurance. "No, it's not. It's really lovely, Eli." She leaned back, brow furrowed thoughtfully. "So are you saying, even if this went south—as far south as it could go—it might be worth it?"

Eli shrugged with a lightness he wasn't sure he really felt. "There are other colleges. Other career paths in academia even, beyond teaching. But there's only one Noah. Maybe ... maybe I wouldn't be giving up my career. Maybe I'd just be redirecting it."

"Yeah, this isn't even that great a school."

"*Hey.*" Eli threw the tasseled pillow at her. "I like it here."

Faith caught the pillow easily before it could hit her in the face. "I'm just saying. If it was, like, your all-time dream university ... But you're right. It's just one school." She crossed her legs, leaning back in her chair. "So what else is holding you back?"

"He's young ..."

Faith waved a hand, like that was inconsequential. "And what exactly about his youth bugs you? You think he'll get itchy feet? Cheat the way Richard did?"

Jesus. They were really getting into it, huh? Eli was going to need to pay her for therapy services at this point. But he didn't have any energy left to be prideful about relying on his sister this way, not after the events of the day. "No, I'm not worried he'll cheat. I'm worried he'll ... change."

That was what had predicated the cheating, wasn't it? Richard changing his mind about what he wanted, about how he wanted Eli to be.

Faith laughed, and he wished he had another pillow to throw at her. "Jesus, Eli. Of course he will. You both will. That's what people do when they grow together." Her laughter dropped off, and the look she gave him was sympathetic. "Not all change is bad. Not all change is the reveal of a secret baby obsession and wandering eyes. I'm not saying your situation is ... ideal. I'm just saying you seem to already know what you want. You're just afraid to give in."

"But I fucked it all up." The panic rose in Eli's throat again. "I drove him away."

Faith cocked her head and, to her credit, didn't roll her eyes again. "One night of space is driving him away?"

"It is if he never comes back," Eli said mulishly.

There was already an ache in Eli's gut, telling him it was wrong to have Noah so far away. Noah should be *here*, holding Eli tight while Eli spilled all his panicked thoughts. Eli should be positively reeking of Noah's alpha pheromones, instead of huffing the lingering traces off his shirt from where Noah had last touched him.

"Take the night, Eli," Faith said with uncharacteristic gentleness. "Sleep off some of this—" She waved a hand to encompass Eli's general craziness. "—and call him tomorrow. His feelings might be hurt right now, but it's nothing you can't talk out."

Right. One night. One night was fine. Eli would be *fine*. He bit at his lip, giving Faith the most pathetic look he could. "Will you stay though?"

Now Faith did roll her eyes. "Of course, you loon. But I get to choose the movie. And at some point, when you're not freaking out, you'll have to answer to keeping this a secret from me."

"You'll pick something with too many explosions," Eli argued, focusing on the important part of that statement.

"That's the price you pay for my sage wisdom, baby," Faith told him, rising from her chair with her phone in hand. "Lemme just call Liz to let her know."

She walked out of the room for privacy, and Eli took out his own phone and sent a message before he could think better of it.

I'm sorry.

He put his phone away immediately, determined to put it out of his mind and give Noah the space he'd asked for.

17

Eli

Eli woke up flushed and aching, his lower belly cramping tightly. He was in his underwear only, having kicked off his pajama pants and the covers at some point in the night, but his skin was still damp and hot to the touch.

He moaned weakly. *Fuck.*

His heat was here. An entire week early.

It was still building to the first real peak, considering Eli was still relatively clearheaded and not writhing for a knot, but based on the feel of things, that would change by the end of the day.

Maybe sooner than that, considering the damn thing had sparked off seven whole days before it was supposed to.

Eli stumbled out of bed, dragging on his discarded pajama bottoms, even though the material itched at his skin. Faith was a disturbingly early riser, and she was already in his kitchen, immaculately dressed with a mug of coffee in hand.

She immediately wrinkled her nose, covering her face with

one hand. "Oh my god." She set her coffee aside with a choked sound. "No wonder you were acting batshit yesterday."

Eli covered his own nose in a mirror of her actions. Normally he found his sister's earthy scent soothing, but right now it was ... wrong.

Wrong alpha, his instincts were telling him.

"It's early," he whined, knowing he sounded like a child but unable to help it. "A week early. I'm screwed. It's midterms this week."

"It'll be fine," Faith told him, her words muffled by the covering of her hand. "Just call in your heat exemption, and they'll get a sub for you. Not everyone's heats cooperate as neat and timely as yours usually do."

Eli's anxiety was unappeased. "Noah's supposed to help me through it."

Eli didn't have his usual dose of suppressants from the doctor, and the thought of using toys after planning to have Noah with him all this time ...

Faith shrugged. "And?"

"He has *class*," Eli practically wailed. "Exams."

"Students get heat and heat-partner exemptions same as professors, Eli," she reminded him, emitting her pheromones in a way that was probably supposed to be comforting but was setting Eli's hair on end instead. "He's an alpha partner of an omega in heat. You two can get a doctor's note afterward, if his professors ask for it. The names will be confidential."

Eli knew all this. He really did. But he couldn't stop the growing sense of panic.

Everything was all wrong. His alpha wasn't here. Eli hadn't even started building a nest. Noah was supposed to bring him clothing over the next week, but they hadn't had a chance, and now his heat was here, and there was no alpha and no nest and—

"It's early!" he yelled again, slamming his open palm on the kitchen counter. "Why is it early?"

He couldn't see Faith smile behind her hand, but he could hear it in her damn voice. "Jesus. I forgot how you get." Before he could fly off the handle, she added, "You've been spending your days with a compatible alpha, and you just had a big emotional upheaval. It makes sense for things to have gone offtrack. You just need to call Noah."

"What if he won't come?"

Just saying it out loud had the panic rising higher in his throat, Eli's stomach cramping harder than it had so far. Noah needed to be here. He was Eli's alpha. Why wouldn't he be here?

It was stupid. Eli had spent heats alone with medications and toys. But he hadn't been expecting to spend *this* one alone.

Why was Noah making him spend his heat alone?

"Eli." Faith's voice broke through the fog of his anxiety. "Call him now. I'm going to get Deadly packed up."

"What?" Faith was taking his cat? "*Why*?! What's wrong with her?"

To Faith's credit, she didn't call Eli out on his losing his mind. "To babysit her," she said evenly. "You're going into heat for days ... maybe longer, with a new alpha in your life."

"He's going to fail all his classes!" Eli cried, forgetting that two seconds ago, he'd been convinced Noah was abandoning him.

"Eli. Call Noah. *Now*." Faith added a hint of alpha command into the last word. Eli didn't technically have to follow it—omega bodies had evolved since the dark ages of real alpha commands— but it did add a little bite that cut through the fog again.

He bolted to his bedroom and grabbed his phone off his bedside table. His room didn't smell like the wrong alpha, but it didn't smell like Noah right now either.

That was bad. And wrong. And ... bad.

Usually Eli had a bigger vocabulary than this.

"Eli?" Noah picked up on the first ring, but he sounded sleepy, like Eli had woken him. In Eli's hypersensitive state, he also thought Noah sounded a little wary.

Oh god. He hated Eli now, didn't he?

"Noah?"

"What's wrong, baby?" At whatever he'd heard in Eli's voice, Noah no longer sounded the slightest bit sleepy. "Are you okay?"

Eli sniffled. Jesus. He was a grown man. He wasn't crying over a heat. "It's here early. My heat."

"Oh. *Oh.* Oh shit."

Eli bit back more tears. Noah was going to say no. Of course he was. He'd said they needed space, and Eli was asking him to be all up in his business for days on end without air. And Noah had midterms. *Midterms.*

"Okay, baby," Noah soothed. "Okay. You stay put. It's going to take me just a little bit to get everything together. But I promise it won't be longer than an hour. Okay? Is that— Can you wait that long?"

Eli held the phone away from his face, staring at it like he could somehow make sense of everything that way. "You're still coming?"

"Of fucking course I'm coming."

"But ... your classes."

"I'll get a heat-partner exemption. I'm literally emailing my professors right now. We'll just get a doctor's note afterward."

It was exactly what Faith had said.

"And you don't ... hate me?" Eli asked, unable to help himself.

"Jesus. No, Eli. I'm sorry." Noah sounded a little breathless, like he was moving around on the other end of the phone. "I was being an asshole, and I needed a breather so I could ... Well, so I could not be an asshole anymore."

"Oh." Eli wiped at his eyes. "You never responded to my text."

"Well, um, for the record ... an 'I'm sorry' text with no context after a fight kind of sounds like you're breaking up with someone."

"Why would an apology be a breakup?" Before Noah could answer, another horrible cramp hit Eli, and he moaned in pain.

"Oh fuck." The panic Eli had been feeling since he'd woken up was reflected in Noah's voice now. "I'm coming, baby. Okay? Hang on. Just getting some stuff together."

"Don't hang up," Eli said hurriedly, afraid to lose the comfort of Noah on the other end of the line.

"No?" Noah asked. Then, "No, of course I won't. I'm gonna tell you everything I'm doing. You just sit tight. Right now I'm putting some of my clothes in a bag. Ones I haven't washed yet ..."

Oh. That was good. Clothes for Eli's nest. Clothes that would smell like Noah.

Eli let out a breath, some of the tension temporarily leaving his body. He sat on the edge of his bed and listened to Noah narrate all his actions. This was all okay. Noah was coming. Eli just had to wait a little longer.

His alpha would be here soon.

———

By the time Noah pulled into the driveway, Eli was sweating.

Faith had left some time ago, reassured by Noah's presence on the other end of the phone that Eli wasn't going to completely fly off the handle. Eli had promptly stripped down and put on his lightest silk robe, usually the one thing he could tolerate as his heat was approaching.

But already it was too much. The stupid thing itched against Eli's oversensitive skin, clinging to the backs of his thighs, where the first trails of slick were accumulating with every fresh cramp.

Eli wanted to be naked. But he needed to wait. He couldn't greet Noah at the door naked. Or even better, at his car.

Could he?

No, no, he had neighbors ...

"Okay, baby," Noah said through the phone. "I'm getting out of the car. I'm going to hang up so I can grab everything in one go. But I'm right here, I promise."

Even though Eli could *see* through the window that it was true —Noah's car was in his drive—he still felt momentarily bereft as the line went dead.

Where was his alpha?

But he barely had time for distress before his door was opening and there was Noah, beautiful and bright, his arms full with a giant duffel and assorted shopping bags and other things Eli didn't care about.

Eli threw himself at him, trusting Noah to drop all that rubbish and catch him. Which Noah did.

Good alpha.

Eli shoved his face into Noah's neck and moaned.

There it was. Perfect and salty and *his*. Eli's tense muscles loosened, some of the cramping in his belly easing already, even as fresh slick dribbled down his thighs.

Noah was saying something, something about "I'm sorry" and "God, you smell fucking amazing," but Eli was distracted by all the annoying fabric in the way of the skin-to-skin contact he was searching for.

He unwrapped his arms and lowered his legs to the floor, needing better leverage. There was too much clothing here. He tugged at Noah's shirt.

"You want this off?" Noah asked, like it wasn't obvious.

Eli only grunted, already working on tugging down Noah's joggers.

"Okay," Noah laughed, pulling off his shirt and letting Eli do his thing. "Um, I brought some fruit and protein bars. Easy stuff for mid-heat. But maybe you should eat something more substantial now while you still can? I read it's important to—"

Eli shook his head with another grunt. No. No food.

Noah lifted his feet one at a time so Eli was able to tug his joggers all the way off, keeping the fabric in his arms afterward. They were soft and smelled strongly of Noah. They would be perfect for the nest.

Eli froze.

His nest. He hadn't made one yet. Why hadn't he made one yet? He'd been ... distracted. Worried. Worried Noah might not come. That he might not be here for Eli's heat.

But why wouldn't Noah be here? Of course he was here. He was good and sweet and smelled like the ocean, and he was going to knot Eli so perfectly as soon as they tumbled into the nest.

The nest that didn't exist.

Eli whined in distress.

"Baby?" Noah's big hand cupped Eli's chin. "Tell me what's wrong. We'll fix it."

"Nest," Eli mumbled, biting worriedly at his lip.

Noah tugged Eli's lip out from between his teeth with his thumb. "You're worried about your nest?"

"I haven't— There isn't—"

"It's not ready yet? That's fine," Noah soothed. He pressed a kiss to Eli's forehead. "That's easy. And my fault, anyway. I should have brought this stuff over sooner."

Clad only in his underwear now, Noah bent low—his movements slow, like he was worried about spooking Eli—and opened the giant duffel bag.

Oh, that smelled *good*. Like delicious, salty Noah.

Eli crouched, inching closer as Noah pulled out a fleece blanket that smelled fucking amazing. "I've been sleeping with this the past few weeks, whenever I've been at my apartment. Haven't washed it."

Eli snatched it, adding it the shirt and joggers he'd already stripped from Noah. "What else?" he asked, trying to peer inside the duffel.

Noah laughed, pulling out more perfect-smelling items. "Some, um ... gym clothes. Unwashed." He raised his brows, looking sheepish. "Too much?"

Eli snatched those too.

"One of the pillows from my bed."

Eli grabbed the pillow and straightened, holding his new treasures to his chest. He headed in the direction of the bedroom, pausing when Noah stopped at Eli's thermostat instead of following him.

"I'm turning up the air," Noah told him. "You're sweating, baby."

Cool air would be good, yes. Good thinking. *Good alpha.*

Eli hurried on to the bedroom. Some omegas had separate rooms for their nests, some used their own beds, but Eli had a particular favorite spot, a large space between his bed and the wall. It was far from the door and the room's lamp, making it feel secluded and cave-like when tended to properly.

He dropped his armful and pulled the comforter off his bed, using it as a base, then got to work. He weaved in the offerings Noah had brought with his own favorite items he dug out from under his bed—soft, worn blankets he saved for heats, a few choice pillows he lined up against any hard barriers.

Noah had arrived at some point, and he stood at a respectable distance, handing Eli things when he asked. *Good alpha.*

When it felt right—when it *smelled* right—Eli perched in the middle. He'd lost his robe at some point, having added it to the nest—and now he knelt naked, cocking his head and peering up at Noah through his lashes coyly.

Noah's smile was the widest Eli had seen it. "All done, baby?" At Eli's small nod, he praised, "It looks perfect. So cozy."

Eli preened. He was out of practice—he barely nested when he used suppressants and toys to get through a heat—but the body remembered. Of course it did.

"Can I—can I come in?" Noah asked, hesitant and almost shy.

Eli nodded again. He was ready to drag his alpha in if necessary, but it was good Noah was coming willingly. Less hassle.

Noah stepped into the nest, and Eli couldn't help it—he leaned forward, wrapping his arms around Noah's legs and drinking in his scent from where it was the strongest—the sizable bulge in Noah's underwear. Eli rubbed his face against the length of it, moaning.

Noah made a choked sound. "Oh fuck."

Eli ignored him, pulling Noah's underwear down, pleased when Noah's thick, hard cock bobbed out, already leaking precum for Eli to taste. That was good. That was perfect. Eli licked at the tip, moaning again, and then he sucked Noah down.

Yes, good and perfect. Noah's cock was fat and heavy on Eli's tongue, and his taste soothed some of the frayed edges in Eli's mind.

Except ...

Eli whined as another cramp hit him, sneaky and awful. It wasn't enough right now, was it? He needed Noah's cock elsewhere. But he didn't want to let it out of his mouth either. Noah tasted so good. Smelled so good. Eli didn't want to lose it.

Noah's strong fingers cupped Eli's jaw once more. "What's wrong, baby?"

Eli whimpered around the cock in his mouth.

"You need more?" Noah stroked his jaw tenderly. "I can give you more."

Eli nodded as best he could while still sucking.

Noah bit back a groan, tapping Eli's cheek. "You gotta—gotta let me go first, baby."

Eli's brow furrowed, sucking even harder. He didn't want to let go.

"Don't worry," Noah soothed, although his voice sounded a little strained. "I'm going to fill you right back up. Take care of that needy hole, okay? I promise."

That sounded ... good. Sounded right. And Noah had been a very good alpha so far—Eli could trust him with this.

After a last, lingering lick, Eli let Noah's cock fall from his mouth.

He moaned at the loss and turned hurriedly onto his knees, placing his chest on the floor and lifting his ass in the air. Presenting for his alpha.

There was another choked sound, and Eli looked back over his shoulder at Noah.

His alpha had a hand around the base of his big cock, gripping hard, like he was fighting not to come too soon. A smug purr escaped Eli at the sight.

Noah groaned again. "You look so fucking—"

Eli's doorbell rang.

"Ignore it," Eli pleaded. He raised his hips invitingly. "Need you, Alpha."

Noah cursed, stepping toward Eli.

But the doorbell rang again. And again.

"What the fuck? Can't they scent the heat pheromones?" Noah grabbed the spare robe from the back of Eli's bedroom door, throwing it on with jagged movements. "I'm so sorry, baby. I'll get rid of them so fast. I'll be right fucking back. Don't—" He waved his hands. "Just stay right like that."

Eli whimpered in protest, but he wasn't so far gone that he didn't know this had to be dealt with; otherwise, it would be a distraction he wouldn't be able to tolerate. Things were supposed to be calm and peaceful and quiet in his nest. He even had a "Do not disturb" sign for these occasions, but he'd forgotten to put it up.

As Noah left the room, Eli rested his head on his forearms with a whimper, his ass in the air and slick coating his thighs, waiting for his alpha to return.

18

Eli

Eli was left waiting longer than he should have been for Noah to come back.

Long enough that Eli's head grew a little fuzzy again, trying to remember why his alpha wasn't there. Why Eli was waiting in his nest alone.

Had he not made the nest inviting enough? Was it not good enough for his alpha?

Eli straightened onto his knees and peered around his nest. It smelled good—smelled *right*—but there could be improvements. He rearranged a few errant items while Noah did whatever he was doing, weaving their scents back together in a way that no alpha should be able to resist.

Eli was vaguely aware of the sound of raised voices, and then Noah yelling fiercely—which made Eli's belly cramp in a not nice way—and then the front door slamming. Maybe Eli should be concerned? But it was hard to grasp onto, the feeling flickering out of his grasp in the next moment. That was all *outside* the nest stuff.

All Eli could focus on was Noah coming back *inside* the nest. Eli needed him here. Right here. Needed Noah inside him.

He pressed a hand to his lower belly, and it twisted painfully, as if in confirmation.

And then Noah did come back into the room, looking flustered and smelling faintly of cigarettes on top of his own distressed pheromones. "I'm sorry. That was—"

Eli whined, wrinkling his nose and holding out a hand to keep Noah from entering the nest. Eli needed him here, definitely, but he needed him smelling ... not like that.

"Right," Noah muttered. "Later. We'll deal with all of it later." He took a few deep breaths, and his scent slowly lost its harsh edge, blooming back into the salty, rich deliciousness Eli was craving. It grew thick enough that it covered the gross tobacco scent as well. No more cigarettes.

Maybe Eli had imagined it all?

Noah's eyes softened as he stared at Eli. "You look so beautiful, baby. Your nest looks amazing."

Words. Too many words. Eli didn't have it in him to perch prettily and look coy anymore. He knelt back on his elbows and spread his legs instead, his urgency growing with every passing second. "I need—"

Noah's throat bobbed as he swallowed hard, his pupils blown wide. He shrugged off the robe he'd thrown on before. "I know. I'm sorry I've made you wait. Do you want to—would you like to present for me again?" He asked the question in a tone that made it sound like it might be what *he* would like, his hands clenching at his sides. His knuckles were bruised. Strange.

But Eli didn't need to be asked twice. He whirled around, chest down, ass up. He heard Noah lower onto his knees in the nest, shuffling in behind him. He whined as Noah's warm hand landed on his hips, stroking the skin there.

"Look at you," Noah whispered, hushed and reverent. There

was the squelching sound of him stroking himself, and Eli bit back another whine at the thought. "So ready for me."

"Yes," Eli moaned, his belly cramping again. "So ready."

Noah's hand trailed down Eli's inner thigh, swirling in the mess of slick coating Eli's skin. "God, I want to eat you out so bad. Lick up all this slick."

Eli growled in protest. *No.* No tongues. No fingers. Only Noah's cock. His knot.

"I know, baby," Noah soothed, spreading Eli's cheek with his thumb, baring Eli's hole to the cool air of the room. "I know. Another time. Let's fill you up, huh? Stop you hurting."

He didn't tease after that, the stroking sounds petering out as he lined up right where Eli wanted him.

Eli keened as the fat, blunt head of Noah's cock finally slipped into his soaking hole. Yes. *Yes.* This was it. He was finally going to get filled the way he was supposed to. The way he needed. He canted his hips higher, pushing back, forcing more of Noah's cock inside. The cramping in his belly eased with each hard-earned inch.

Noah pressed a hand to Eli's lower back, deepening the arch of Eli's presentation as he bottomed out. "So good," he praised, sounding breathless. "So—so perfect. Does that feel good, baby?"

Eli moaned, pushed his hips back harder, urging Noah to move.

Noah obliged, fucking into him as he murmured, "I'm so lucky, baby. So fucking lucky."

Eli was the lucky one. His alpha had a perfect cock. Big and thick and wonderful. And Noah's knot was going to be even better; Eli just knew it. It was going to fill all those sharp, hurting places and soothe Eli perfectly. Fill him up with cum and lock it deep inside.

Noah fucked him with slow, deep thrusts. They were perfect

until they weren't enough, and Eli keened, the sound breaking off into a sobbing moan as Noah sped up the pace.

There. That was it. Good and perfect and—

"More," Eli pleaded, only half aware of what he was saying. "Please."

"More?" Noah asked, the roll of his hips pausing.

Was that a question? Why was Noah asking questions? Eli didn't have any answers. He only had his *own* questions, like why the fuck had Noah stopped?

But then Noah slid an arm under Eli's chest, pulling and rearranging them until Noah was on his knees with Eli's thighs spread over them, still speared on Noah's cock, his back pressed tightly against Noah's chest.

Eli groaned, his head rolling against Noah's shoulder. *Yes. Fuck, yes.* So deep like this.

And then Noah shoved his face against Eli's neck, scent marking him as he pounded up into him, just as fiercely as before.

Yes, this was—this was— *Ungh.* Good. Perfect. Surrounded by Noah. Reeking of him. Filled by him.

Eli opened his mouth to tell Noah how good it was, but what came out was "More."

Noah let out a dark chuckle, his breath cool against Eli's overheated neck. "Yeah, baby?" he panted. "You ready for my knot?"

Yes. *Yes.* That was what Eli wanted. Something was building in him, something wonderful, but he needed ... Yes, he needed *that.* Noah's knot.

Noah kept thrusting into him furiously, the sloppy, wet sound of Eli's slick loud in the otherwise quiet room. "Gonna come, baby," he warned. "Gonna fill you up. Gonna knot you, keep it all inside."

"Yes, yes, yes," Eli chanted mindlessly. He wanted all that. Was ready for it.

Noah's arms tightened around Eli as his hips stilled and he

shuddered, filling Eli up just as he'd promised. Eli squirmed around the sensation, soothed by the cum even as he whined at the lack of movement. It still wasn't ...

But then he could feel Noah growing, feel himself stretching around him. Noah started moving again, gentle rolls of his hips as he lodged his swelling knot deeper inside Eli.

Eli helped him by writhing and wiggling and whining. Or maybe that didn't help. He didn't know. All he knew was that eventually he was perfectly filled, and then all it took was the slightest grind of Noah's hips and Eli was finally coming, his cock leaking cum like a fountain as his belly released the last of its cramping, his inner walls clenching around Noah's knot, milking more of Noah's cum inside him.

It was like a fever breaking, or a fog dispersing. Eli was still a sweaty, shuddering mess, but suddenly he could feel the cool air of the room against his skin, hear the quiet stillness of the nest, scent Noah's deep, primal satisfaction.

He let himself go limp, leaning back into Noah. His alpha.

Noah stroked him, up his sides and down his flanks, like Eli was a racehorse cooling down after the finish line. "Better?" he asked softly.

"Yeah." Eli let out a long, relieved breath, nuzzling his head back into Noah's neck. "Sorry, I got a little fuzzy for a bit there."

"Don't be sorry," Noah scolded, kissing Eli's sweaty cheek. "Hottest experience of my life."

Eli's laugh was half a sigh, as he was too tired suddenly to manage a full chuckle. "You say that about everything we do."

"And it's the truth every time." Noah shifted until he was leaning back against the nest's pillows, his body curled around Eli's, his knot lodged firmly in place. It probably wouldn't go down for another hour at least. "Anything else I should know, while you're lucid?" he asked. "We never got a chance to go over ground rules."

Eli hummed in thought. He was feeling so loose and satisfied that it was hard to focus, but they might not get a better chance than this. "My heats are pretty standard," he told Noah. "I mean, don't go biting me just because I'm so irresistible."

He could feel Noah roll his eyes behind him. "Of course not. I'm not a caveman."

Some people did consider claiming bites a relic of the caveman days. A leftover tradition from when they'd all roamed together in packs. It had once been a sign of a mating bond that couldn't be contested or—some would say—an alpha's ownership over an omega (and vice versa, in Eli's opinion).

But studies showed that a bite melded a couple's pheromones in a very real way, one that made it possible to have a deeper understanding and feeling for each other's moods and health status.

They weren't permanent—they *could* be broken, though it was a sad, painful process—and not everyone went for them these days. As evidenced by Eli not having Richard's bite, even after a decade of marriage (although the prick had always lied about "one day").

Not everyone believed in them as a necessary sign of partnership, but Eli was realizing, now that he was with the right person, that maybe *he* did. He had a feeling Noah did too.

He cleared his throat, banishing the idea from his mind for now. It was a little too dangerous to be thinking about claiming bites when he was hormonal and locked onto Noah's knot. "Anyway, the lucid periods will get shorter. I'll need your knot more and more as we approach the peak. Your body will get the message, so it shouldn't be a problem for you. With how fast it came on, it could burn bright and be over in a few days, but I wouldn't count on it."

Noah was stroking Eli's lower belly now, tracing the outline of the bulge his knot was making. It was distracting, but Eli still was fairly certain he was listening.

"Noah?"

"Yeah, baby?"

Eli needed to say it now. While he was still lucid. "I do see a future with us. I promise."

Noah's hand paused its stroking, and then he was hugging Eli so tightly against him it dislodged the breath from Eli's lungs.

Noah loosened his hold immediately. "Sorry. I just— Yeah, I do too. A really, really good one."

Eli kind of wished they were facing each other now, but that wouldn't be possible for a while yet. He laid his hand over Noah's, relaxing back in his alpha's arms. "Good. I'm glad."

They held each other in silence for a long time, and then Noah pressed a kiss to Eli's head, telling him, "I'm gonna shift us so we're lying down, okay? You should get a little catnap while you can."

Eli nodded his agreement. A catnap sounded good. His eyes were already getting heavy just at the suggestion.

"I should have brought snacks in here." Noah cursed as he shifted them horizontal. "I should be hand-feeding you while we're knotted. And fuck—water. I'll grab it all when we separate." He growled, the sound full of self-recrimination. "I'll do better, Eli. I promise. I'll learn to take such good care of you."

Eli stroked a soothing hand along Noah's arm, the one wrapped like a comforting band around his chest. "Sweetheart," he murmured, his eyes falling closed. "You came when I called. You're here. You don't need to do any better than that."

19

Noah

Noah rocked his hips in a gentle rhythm as he held the strawberry to Eli's mouth. "C'mon baby. One more bite. Do it for me?"

Eli whined in protest, his eyes shut tight as he pressed back into Noah, inner muscles clenching around Noah's cock as he tried desperately to milk Noah's knot for more. He'd get it too. They'd been locked together for over an hour already, but Noah's knot wasn't going to subside anytime soon, not with how things had been going tonight.

They were on the third day of Eli's heat, and as far as Noah could tell, things were reaching their peak. Eli was barely coherent, only speaking to beg for Noah's cock or his knot. He was at the point of needing to be filled pretty much all the time, and the only way Noah could get him to eat or hydrate was to offer things while they were locked together, when Eli was slightly more relaxed and compliant.

Slightly being the key word.

Eli still wasn't taking much at this point—Noah was only able to coax him into some of the sliced fruit he'd prepped and some sips of water—but that was how it went during heat. Omegas inevitably went into a calorie deficit at their peak as their bodies focused on the main drive of heat—mating.

Noah had known all that, but it was still hard not to stress over it in the moment. Eli was so small, and his body was working so hard. Noah was bigger and stronger, and he was barely keeping up, making do by hastily eating protein bars in the brief periods of time when Eli was passed out and Noah's knot was deflated. He'd eat as quickly as possible, then try to catch as much sleep as he could afterward, recharging as best as he was able.

Just do what you can, he reminded himself now, the food he was offering still uneaten. *Go with what feels natural. Eli needs you calm. He needs you present and focused.*

He kept rocking his hips, holding the strawberry to Eli's lips, and sure enough, after another disapproving whine, Eli finally took the strawberry from him, sucking the juices off Noah's fingers afterward. He then tilted his head back for a kiss, and Noah gave it to him, capturing Eli's mouth lazily, his hand cupping around Eli's throat.

They were spooning, Noah wrapped around Eli's back. It was the most comfortable position when they were knotted together, and comfort was key at this point, with Eli needing Noah's knot so often. Eli's cozy nest was absolutely saturated with their scents— their scents and their cum. The last shower Noah had been able to get Eli to take had been early yesterday morning, and that had only happened because Noah had fingered him throughout, then fucked him furiously against the shower wall afterward.

They'd left the shower messier than they'd started.

Now Eli broke the kiss with a little whimper, his head falling down onto Noah's bicep as his eyes shut. He was finally falling asleep again.

Eli hadn't lied about being needy during his heat. From what Noah had learned in sex ed, all omegas craved a knot during one, but for some, that was it. In between knots, they wanted their own space, wanted their alpha to leave them be while they napped in the nest on their own. But Eli needed to be touched at all times, it seemed. Needed Noah wrapped around him whether they were fucking or not. Needed to be kissed and petted to sleep.

He wasn't snappish or demanding about it. He'd whine or keen sometimes when Noah wasn't quick enough, but when Noah gave him what he needed ... then Eli would *melt*. It was gorgeous to see him like that, really. So sweet and trusting and grateful.

The classes and books hadn't lied about the intensity of a heat either. It was the most grueling workout of Noah's life, keeping Eli satisfied these past three days, his body barely fueled by the meager energy bars and spare fruit he was managing to get in.

And yet it was maybe the happiest Noah had ever been. To be needed like this, to *provide* like this ... it was heady, the responsibility and the care it involved.

Noah had been needed before, obviously. As a helper to his parents, as the dependable older brother to all his younger siblings. But not like this. Not by someone who was his and his alone. Noah couldn't even articulate why it was different—it just was. And it lifted something in him.

Home, his heart was telling him. This was home. This person, this nest, this bond.

Eli.

It was a well-known cliché, falling in love with someone during a heat or a rut. But that wasn't what was happening here—Noah had *been* falling in love with Eli, almost from the first moment he'd met him. It was the reason he'd acted like such a dick when Eli had freaked out about Ash. It had been Noah's gut reaction to the bone-deep fear that the person he loved was going to leave him.

He knew it had stressed Eli out to have his heat come early, but Noah was almost grateful. It had given them both a reason to get their heads out of their asses quickly. It had allowed Noah to be here now, with his partner, his boyfriend, his future mate.

The exhaustion may have been out of this world, but so was the satisfaction. They were safe and content in a cocoon that consisted of only them, no outside world or responsibilities involved.

Although, that would come, wouldn't it? And soon.

Noah flexed his hand, the faint burn still running along his knuckles. They had things that needed to be dealt with when Eli was coherent again. That asshole Richard ...

Noah wouldn't think about it now though. If he did, the rage would seep into his pheromones, and then Eli would scent his distress. Noah needed to keep things calm and peaceful now. He needed to protect his mate while he was vulnerable.

When Eli's heat receded and he finally came to fully, then Noah would wash them both, make Eli the biggest meal of his life, and make sure they sat down and talked it all over. They would plan for whatever came next, and they would do it together.

Part of Noah couldn't wait, despite the complications they needed to manage. He was eager to get through this, eager to head toward the future where Eli was allowed to be his. The future where Eli could meet the other people in Noah's life properly—his roommates, Ash, even his parents. The future where Noah could walk through the world with Eli on his arm, proudly displaying this brilliant and kind mate he'd found. His bright and beautiful omega.

Eli shifted against him with a quiet exhale, the soft skin of his ass sliding along Noah's pelvis. Noah had thought he'd already fallen asleep, but then Eli shifted again, the push of his hips clearly purposeful.

"You need more, baby?" Noah asked, keeping his voice soft.

He didn't wait for an answer, just started rocking his hips again, rubbing his knot against Eli's inner walls. Eli moaned, his eyes still shut tight. Noah trailed his hand down Eli's belly to find his omega's cock hard and standing at attention.

"Poor baby," he soothed, rubbing his thumb along the swollen head. "You're aching again, aren't you?"

Eli's reply was another moan, this one slightly plaintive, as if agreeing with Noah's "poor baby" assessment.

Noah hiked up Eli's thigh to get at a better angle, fucking him as best he could. He couldn't thrust with any sort of leverage when they were locked together like this, but he could get a little movement, enough to get Eli where he needed to be. Noah started rutting against him, his hand stroking Eli's cock as lightly as possible, aware that Eli's skin was oversensitive right now.

And then Noah was the one moaning, a husky groan he couldn't contain. The way Eli clenched around his knot ...

Jesus, there was nothing like it in the world.

Eli tossed his head back against Noah's shoulder, his dark hair damp with sweat, his neck arching like the world's sweetest temptation. That rich lime scent filled the air, and Noah's gums itched with the urge to bite down—to claim.

He wouldn't do that though. He would never break this trust between them in such a stupid way. One day they'd *both* agree to a bite—Noah was fucking sure of it—but it wasn't today.

So he kissed Eli's neck instead, laving at the salty skin there with his tongue afterward. "So sweet for me," he crooned. "My beautiful omega. You feel so fucking good."

Eli threw his hand back, his fingers digging into the meat of Noah's ass, and Noah sped up his rocking. "That's it, baby," he urged as Eli panted and gasped. "Let go. Let it all go."

Eli shuddered as he came, a weak spurt of ejaculate coating Noah's fingers. His poor omega was drained and empty at this point. Noah should have been, too—without the heat pheromones saturating the air, he would have been—but as Eli's inner muscles spasmed and clenched around him, Noah emptied another thick burst of cum, fucking it deep inside Eli.

Filling him with pups, if they were back in the old days, before heat-effective birth control.

Oh fuck. Noah groaned at the thought, moving his hand to cup Eli's belly, swollen with Noah's knot and cum. Noah didn't want that in this life, but just for a moment, it was something to imagine, this belly of Eli's swollen with Noah's pups instead. Something about that thought pleased the primal, vicious part of Noah that lit up in delight every time Eli begged for his knot. His inner asshole alpha.

Noah wasn't ruled by those urges—he could separate the reality from the fantasy—but he could admit they were a little bit fascinating, here in the hazy cloud of heat pheromones.

Eli's hand landed over his, gripping Noah's fingers tightly as the rest of his body relaxed fully, limp and sated in Noah's arms. He made a soft sound of contentment, his cheeks and forehead flushed and sweaty. He looked so beautiful like this, his handsome face softening into sleep.

The break wouldn't last long, not at the peak like this. He'd wake again as soon as Noah softened, no doubt needing him again immediately. Earlier in the heat, Noah had been able to soothe him with his fingers and tongue in between bouts of knotting, but that wouldn't work now.

It would be a long and arduous night as Noah's body worked to respond to Eli's demanding needs.

Noah tucked his head into Eli's neck, letting his own eyes fall closed as he breathed in that perfect, citrus scent, rich and thick and sweet with heat. He let out his own sigh of exhausted contentment.

He'd rest now, sleep while he could. Until his omega needed him again.

20

Eli

Eli woke slowly, his skin wonderfully cool for the first time in forever. Cool and ... sticky. Crusty? Not clean; that was for sure. By the feel of it, he was definitely covered in multiple layers of dried sweat and who knew what else.

He opened his eyes—his bedroom was dark and dim, but there was a little daylight coming in from under the door to the hallway. The air was thick with the rich, heady mix of sex, slick, and alpha cum.

Noah's arm was wrapped firmly around him, his broad body spooning Eli's back. They no doubt had been knotted together when they'd fallen asleep, but they were separated now.

Eli was empty for the first time in ages.

He twisted in small, careful movements until he was facing Noah. The alpha was deeply asleep, his wide mouth half-open, his blond hair the wildest nest of curls Eli had ever seen it. He had dark circles under his eyes, and Eli had to resist the urge to trace them with his finger.

Poor Noah. Eli must have really worn him out.

He flushed, biting at his lip. He remembered, of course. His heat hadn't been a total blackout, just … fuzzy around the edges. But Eli remembered begging. Lots of begging. Begging for Noah's touch, his kiss, his knot. Over and over and over again. He also remembered refusing food and water, only barely coaxed by Noah's mouth or fingers or cock into taking care of himself even the slightest.

Well, Eli *had* warned him.

Noah stirred, as if sensing the weight of Eli's searching gaze, his thickly lashed eyes blinking open blearily. He immediately sat up, hovering over Eli. "Baby?" he asked, voice thick with sleep. "What's— You ready for more?"

Eli wanted to tease him—Noah barely looked like he was capable of standing, let alone dicking Eli down one last time—but Noah seemed so sincerely worried that Eli smiled gently instead. "My heat broke," he told him. "It's over."

"Oh." Noah blinked some more, running a hand through his hair, only for it to get stuck halfway. He jerked his fingers out of the tangles with a wince, relaxing slowly back onto the blankets. "Oh, thank God."

Eli's lips twitched. "Was it that bad?"

Noah threw his bicep over his eyes with a tired laugh. "Are you kidding? It was amazing. Transcendent. Fucking *spiritual*. I'm just drained, baby." He lifted his arm to give Eli a sly look. "You took all my cum. Sucked it out of me like an incubus, every last bit. Past, present, and future."

"Your *future* cum, even?" Eli tried to look appropriately alarmed, but it was difficult to manage with the smile that wanted to escape.

Noah nodded somberly. "Mm-hmm. I'll be shooting blanks for the next decade. If I even shoot anything at all."

"Oh my."

Noah uncovered his eyes with a much more robust laugh, the sound trailing off as he looked at Eli with fresh concern, his large hand reaching over to cup Eli's hip tenderly. "How are you feeling? You must be hungry. Thirsty." He sat back up with a groan. "I'll go and—"

"Hey. *Hey*." Eli ran a soothing hand over Noah's arm, grateful when even that gentle touch was enough to stop him from getting out of the nest. Noah was clearly still in caretaker mode, and Eli needed to get him out of that headspace. He met his alpha's eyes with a small smile. "You did such a good job taking care of me, sweetheart."

Noah's gaze softened immediately. "I did? You—you remember?"

"I do." Eli swept his hand up Noah's arm and over his shoulder, finally cupping his cheek. "And you were amazing. But you can relax now."

Noah shook his head. "You're still weak though. And—"

"You're equally worn out," Eli argued. At Noah's stubborn look, he laughed. "Okay, how about this? We'll take care of each other. Regain our strength together."

Noah held out for a long moment, but he finally sighed, leaning his head into Eli's touch. "Okay. Together, then."

Eli glanced around the nest, wrinkling his nose at the mess they'd made of it. And themselves. It was to be expected, of course, but still—the *fluids*. "Shower first, I think. Then we can toss all this in the washer."

He thankfully received no argument from Noah, and they took a luxurious shower together. They kept things chaste, neither of them attempting anything they couldn't finish. They soaped each other up but didn't linger anywhere salacious, taking turns washing each other's hair instead, Noah leaning down awkwardly so Eli could reach. They exchanged tender, exhausted kisses that didn't go any further. Both their bodies needed some recovery time.

Recovery time and a mountain of food.

There was a beautiful intimacy to it all, and Eli hated that there was a teeny, tiny part of himself waiting for the other shoe to drop. It was *this* part of heat that had always been a bit ... fraught in Eli's marriage. Richard had hated the recovery phase, when he'd been too drained to work or socialize, and Eli had always been racked with guilt for having been so needy that he'd put them both there.

Eli knew better at this point than to compare Noah to Richard. But some emotional reactions were ingrained after years of habit. The fear of disappointing and being disappointed in turn. The hesitance after asking for so much.

But Noah seemed happy to be here with Eli, even weak and exhausted like this. A little worried about Eli, maybe—he'd mentioned breakfast five times in the shower already, as if convinced Eli was still going to refuse food—but certainly not resentful, even with the week of exams he'd had to miss.

After they'd each carefully toweled the other off—Noah adorably taking the time to make sure each of Eli's toes was perfectly dry—Eli led them to the kitchen. Noah was clearly going to freak out for real if he didn't get some food in Eli soon.

With the early heat, Eli hadn't had a chance to stock his fridge properly for postheat recovery, but he had eggs and bacon and plenty of coffee. Noah sliced more of the fruit he'd brought, while Eli whisked the eggs, and he even found a loaf of bread in the freezer Eli had forgotten about.

What they lacked in variety of ingredients, they made up for in quantity.

So. Much. Food.

When it was all done, they sat at the kitchen table. Or, more accurately, Noah sat at the kitchen table and then promptly pulled Eli into his lap.

So Noah clearly wasn't sick of touching him, was he? There was no hint of resentment over taking care of him.

Eli finally released the last of his lingering worry in a slow breath. *Time to let go.* There was no other shoe dropping anywhere. This was just the way Noah was. Thoughtful. Caring.

Loving.

Eli relished the delicious relief flooding through him, sinking back against Noah's broad chest.

Noah placed a kiss on the top of his head. "Can I— Will you still let me feed you?" he asked, almost shy.

Eli tilted his head back to gaze at him. "You want to?"

"Yeah." Noah's grin was embarrassed, his cheeks lightly pink. "I think it'll help me feel better."

"Okay. But you too." Eli tapped his finger against Noah's lower lip. "A bite for a bite."

"Yeah?" Noah's eyes darkened, as if Eli was talking about a different kind of bite. The claiming kind. "Okay, then. A bite for a bite."

He immediately held up a slice of bacon, and Eli bit off a piece, still locked in Noah's gaze as he chewed and swallowed. Noah kissed him after, as if to seal the deal.

They took turns feeding each other. Noah seemed reluctant to use the fork more than necessary, giving Eli all the bacon and toast and even some of the eggs by hand, with Eli licking the extra salt off Noah's fingers each time.

When they'd finished everything on both plates, Eli let out a relieved sigh, patting the expanded pooch of his stomach. "That's better."

"Much better," Noah agreed. But he was still ... tense.

Tenser than before, even. Eli leaned back to study him. Maybe now that Eli was fed, Noah needed some space after all. Eli wouldn't begrudge him that. An omega's heat was overwhelming, and this was Noah's first time participating in one.

Noah shifted Eli forward on his lap, toward his knees, leaving enough space for them to meet each other's eyes. "Eli," he said somberly. "I need to tell you something."

That was ... ominous. But Eli only cocked his head, refusing to let any sort of dread seep into his calm state. "Anything."

"Do you remember the very beginning of your heat?" Noah asked. "Someone at the door?"

Eli hadn't, but he did now. "Yes." He nodded slowly. "You left and ..." Eli's gaze drifted down to Noah's hand. "Your knuckles."

They were healed now, but Eli remembered how they'd looked battered and bruised when Noah had returned to the nest.

Before Noah could explain, Eli guessed. "Richard. It was Richard at the door, wasn't it?"

Noah let out a breath. "Yeah, it was."

"That *asshole*." Eli's spine stiffened as he clenched his fists. For an alpha to try to come uninvited into an omega's house at the beginning of a heat ... "Couldn't he smell the pheromones?"

Noah's fresh, salty scent took on a bitter edge as he grimaced. "He definitely could. He was insistent on coming in anyway. Said he needed to check on you. He—he recognized me, Eli. From your class. Maybe he even had good intentions, but when he wouldn't back down ..." He cleared his throat, squaring his shoulders. "I hit him."

Eli grabbed Noah's hand, reassuring him with his touch as he thought all that over. Good intentions? Eli highly fucking doubted it.

"He could have called Faith if he'd actually been worried. No." Eli shook his head. "He was trying to get to me when I was vulnerable. To—I don't know—convince me to come back when I was too out of it to refuse?" He squeezed Noah's hand. "You did the right thing, Noah. Thank you. For protecting me."

The bitter edge left Noah's scent, and he sagged with relief, as if he might actually have been worried Eli would be angry with him.

And there was anger, sure. Rage, even. Eli was chock-full of it. But not an ounce of it was for Noah.

Fucking. Richard.

Noah's thumb rubbed over Eli's knuckles. "He—he knows I'm a student, Eli." He said it gently, like he was breaking some unbearably difficult news.

"I know, sweetheart."

"Your career."

"I know." Eli leaned his head against Noah's shoulder with a sigh. "But it's done."

The secrecy was over now, blown to bits by Richard's actions, and Eli felt weirdly calm about it. It wasn't that he had any doubts that Richard would expose them—it was exactly the sort of thing Richard would do. It was just that Eli had been worried for so long, and now that things were happening, he was just ... relieved to have it out in the open.

Now wasn't the time for regret. It was the time for action.

He straightened. "Okay, then. Damage control. And whatever happens, we'll deal with it. But first—" He turned so he was straddling Noah, grabbing his alpha's face with both hands and meeting his gaze, unblinking. "I love you, Noah. I really, really love you."

Noah stared at him for so long that his eyes started watering. Or no—he was crying. Those were tears. "I love you, too, Eli," he said thickly. "So fucking much." The next words came out in a rush, like he'd been waiting to say all of it. Waiting for Eli to be ready. "I'm so happy with you. You're it for me, and I don't care if I'm too young or it's too fast or whatever the fuck people think. I know I'm not, like, amazingly smart or driven. Not like you. But I think I'm a—a decent person. I'll be the best partner I can be. Is that—is that enough?"

Oh, Eli's sweet, sweet alpha. Eli hadn't realized the little insecurities hiding underneath all that innate confidence.

"You're not just *decent*, Noah," he said firmly. "You're ... good. A truly good person. And you undervalue it. Of course it's enough. It's more than enough, Noah."

"Even though I complicate everything and—"

"Hush," Eli soothed, rubbing his thumbs along Noah's cheeks. "I'm happy with you, too, Noah. So happy. And complicated doesn't mean bad. It just means we need to be smart. Proactive." He narrowed his eyes, considering. "Maybe a little mean." He dropped his hands and reached for his phone. "I'm going to make a call."

Noah seemed to know exactly who Eli was going to have a conversation with. His grip tightened on Eli's hips. "Can I stay? Can I listen in?"

"Of course. I'll do it right here. We'll do it together."

It was time. Past time, even. Eli had put up with enough bullshit to last a lifetime, without even having any good reason for it. But he a had a good reason now to let it all go. The best reason, really.

It was well past fucking time to take away Richard's power for good.

21

Eli

Eli stayed right where he was—secure in Noah's lap—as he hit Richard's contact info, turning the phone to speaker as it rang.

Noah wouldn't be participating in the conversation—this was Eli's mess to clean up—but he had every right to listen in. Richard was obviously going to try to use their relationship as some kind of leverage, and it was just as much Noah's business as Eli's.

Richard picked up on the second ring.

"Lijah," he said smoothly, not an ounce of surprise in his voice. "I've been waiting for your call."

Eli settled back against Noah's chest, breathing in his alpha's comforting pheromones to keep his voice cool and even. "I'm sure you have."

There was a beat of silence, as if Richard hadn't been expecting that response, but he smoothed it over quickly. "Are you all right? I've been very ... concerned, Lijah. *Very* concerned."

Eli's eye roll was epic, even if Richard couldn't actually see it. "I'm perfectly fine. Great, even."

"And the alpha student who was lurking in your home during your heat?" Richard asked, his tone almost casual. "The one who resorted so quickly to violence?"

Noah's arm tightened around Eli's middle, and Eli patted at it soothingly. "He's great too. He was invited, Richard. As I'm sure you could tell by the pheromones in my home. We're ... partners."

Noah nuzzled the back of Eli's neck silently, and Eli smiled in spite of himself. Yes, they were partners. And it felt fucking amazing to say it out loud.

Any lingering concern in Richard's voice—fake as it had been to begin with—was replaced immediately by clipped anger. "I saw him in your classroom, Eli. A student? Really?" He let out a bitter, condescending laugh. "What on earth do you think you're doing? Did the divorce mess with your head that badly?"

There were so many things Eli could say. About the hypocrisy, for example, of a man who'd slept with his own employee—cheating on his husband as he did it—lecturing Eli on ethics. But a long, drawn-out argument was exactly what Richard wanted. A chance to twist words and open old wounds. Eli wasn't giving it to him. Not now. Not ever again.

He let out a breath, releasing everything that wasn't worth mentioning with it. "This isn't something I'm going to discuss with you, Richard. It's not your business."

"Well, perhaps it's something you'll discuss with the dean."

Eli had been expecting this move, of course. It sucked majorly, but he wasn't shocked. Perhaps a little disappointed. Had he really been married to a man this underhanded? And for an entire decade? "You've already told him, then?"

"As I said, I've been concerned."

Eli barked out a laugh. "So concerned you went to my boss first thing."

"I could have gone to the police. Your *student*"—Richard placed deliberate emphasis on the word—"hit me. That's assault."

Noah stiffened underneath him, and Eli bristled. No way. This wasn't happening. Richard could say what he wanted about torching Eli's career, but he didn't get to threaten Noah. Not under Eli's watch.

He kept patting Noah's arm, trying to let him know wordlessly that nothing bad would happen to him. That Eli wouldn't let it. "You really want to get the law involved, Richard?" he hissed into the phone. "You were trying to come uninvited into an omega's home while they were in heat."

"You're being irrational, Lijah." Richard let out a disappointed sigh, like the weight of the world rested on his upstanding shoulders. "The timing was a mere coincidence." His voice firmed. "I think this has all gone on long enough, don't you? It's time you came home. Letting you go was a mistake, and I freely admit it. I thought you might mature if left to your own devices, perhaps realize where your priorities should lie. But you're clearly floundering."

Well, then.

Faith had been right about Richard's motives. The absurdity of it all was breathtaking, really. The delusion—the pompousness—required to think Eli would ever come back to him. That Eli would ever be the sort of husband Richard wanted.

And he didn't even want Eli back. Not really. He was just pissed he'd lost a possession.

Eli clasped Noah's arm firmly, anchoring himself to what mattered. "I *am* home, Richard. If you need to contact me again, it will be through my lawyer. The way you tried to enter my home when you did could earn you an assault charge of your own. And if you try to take Noah down, I will drag you right the fuck down with us. Understand?"

He didn't wait for confirmation as he hit the end-call button. He was done.

"Baby." Noah's hand landed on top of his, covering Eli's knuckles. "You're shaking."

"I'm *angry*," Eli told him, sharp as a curse, trying to keep himself from clenching his hands into useless fists. "Faith was right. He's trying to creep back into my life, and he's willing to threaten you to do it."

"It'll be okay," Noah soothed, as if he hadn't panicked at the mention of an assault charge. Eli could still smell the anxiety in his pheromones, acidic and unsettled.

Eli straightened, shifting to the side so he could meet Noah's gaze squarely. "Of course it will," he said firmly. Unlike Noah, it wasn't fear of consequences pissing Eli off. It was the inanity of it all. The pointlessness. "I'm not going to let anything happen to you, Noah. It's just so ... idiotic. Nonsensical." He shook his head. "I used to think he was intelligent."

That earned him a small smile, but then Noah's lips tipped back down into a frown. "The dean knows."

"He does." Eli cleared his throat, trying to suppress his own nerves, to be a calm, steady presence for Noah. "I'm going to email him about a meeting now, for as soon as he's available. And *you*, meanwhile, need to catch up on your missed exams."

"Eli ..."

Eli cupped Noah's cheek. "It will be okay," he soothed again. "There are other universities. And in the meantime ..." He cocked his head, a smile that might even have been genuine playing on his lips. "Did you know I've always wanted to write a book? I have more than enough research material. Faith's been hounding me about it for years. If I had a break from lectures and grading ..." Eli shrugged, letting the rest go unspoken.

Noah's smile returned. "I don't take summer classes," he mused tentatively. "So I have the whole summer off. The plan was for me to join my dad's business after undergrad. But I could always decide to pursue my MBA, stay a student a while longer. We could rent a place over the summers," he said, picking up steam. "Some cabin in the mountains or maybe on the coast. You can write. I can hike and swim and make sure you remember to eat."

Eli could picture it. The two of them coexisted so easily together already—what would it be like to have all that time together, just the two of them?

Heaven. It would be heaven.

He pressed a kiss to Noah's cheek. "That sounds perfect, sweetheart." He tried to stand, only to find himself locked in place by Noah's broad arm. He slapped at it gently. "Come on. Enough dillydallying. You need to get in touch with your professors."

Noah nuzzled his head into Eli's shoulder. "I have one of my professors right here."

Eli laughed, but he still managed to slip out of Noah's hold with some sly twisting, dancing out of his reach when Noah tried to catch him again. "No, no. No more snuggling. There's work to be done."

Noah had a bemused look on his face as he sat there, staring at Eli. "I've never seen you so ... amped. I thought you'd be more upset."

"You know what?" Eli said as he gathered both their laptops. "It's kind of exhilarating, actually. I never got to stand up for myself much before. I've always been one more for ... quiet perseverance, I guess. For better or for worse. But that phone call felt *good*. And the meeting with the dean will go how it will go." He placed Noah's laptop in front of him, then leaned in close enough to poke a finger into Noah's firm chest. "No regrets."

Noah gave him a broad grin, dimples and all. "No regrets."

———

ELI STRODE down the university hallway, trying to breathe out his nerves in time with his steps. Left foot, breathe in, right foot, breathe out.

The dean had agreed to a Monday afternoon meeting, and the speed of his reply was confirmation enough that Richard hadn't been bluffing.

The dean knew.

Eli had taken the weekend to catch up on his grading and get his classes in order. If he was fired—*when* he was fired, most likely —at least he could say he wasn't leaving a mess for anyone. It was a small point of pride but not one he was willing to let go of.

Now the time for his reckoning had come, and Eli's earlier bravado had fled the premises. He'd never liked getting scolded by teachers growing up—that fear of reprimand was part of what had made him such a good student—and he didn't think he was going to enjoy getting scolded by his boss any more than that.

Still, he let himself into the outer room of the dean's office, greeting Ashley, Dean Poke's assistant. "Morning, Ashley."

She smiled at him warmly. "Professor Miller."

Ashley wasn't looking at him like he was a creep or a pariah, so Eli had to assume she hadn't been informed yet. He smiled back, although the gesture felt a bit awkward on his lips. "Is he ready for me?"

"Go right in."

"Great." Eli swallowed through a tight throat. "Thank you."

He entered the inner office after a swift warning knock, closing the door quickly behind him. Dean Poke didn't rise to greet him, but he did turn away from his computer, giving Eli his full attention.

"Eli."

Apparently they were still on a first-name basis, never mind that it had been over a year since the last dinner party they'd both attended. One Richard had thrown.

"Tom," Eli greeted, equally succinct.

The dean—Tom, to his friends—was an affable man with gray hair, a squashed nose, and a considerable paunch. He reminded Eli a bit of his own father, but he'd be mortified to admit as much out loud. Eli had always liked him well enough, but it didn't make sitting in the hot seat any easier. It was worse, in a way, to lose the respect of someone he generally admired.

Speaking of.

Tom gestured to the chair across from his. "Take a seat, Eli."

Eli sat, and Tom was kind enough to lay it all out immediately. "This meeting was by your request, but I'm going to go ahead and get it started, if you don't mind." He didn't wait for Eli to respond either way. His face settled into a severe frown. "Richard called to inform me that you're dating a student. One currently enrolled in one of your intro classes. A certain Noah Teller."

"Yes, sir," Eli confirmed. First-name basis or not, it suddenly seemed wise to be extra polite.

Tom tapped at his desk. "You're not refuting his claim, are you?"

"No, sir." Eli clasped his hands in his lap, straightening his spine. "We're involved. Although we met outside of class. I didn't know he was a student, not initially."

Eli wasn't going to make excuses, but he wasn't going to throw himself further under the bus than he needed to either.

Tom glanced at a paper on his desk. "And you haven't been personally involved with any of his grading."

It wasn't a question—he'd clearly looked into it himself. But Eli answered anyway, "No, sir. His grades have all been done by one of my TAs."

Tom leaned back in his chair, folding his hands over his belly. There was a beat before he spoke again. "Do you know why we don't have a written policy about professors getting involved with students?"

"Clerical oversight?" Eli offered up before he could help himself.

"Don't be cute," Tom chastised mildly. He cocked a brow. "You've never taken advantage of the university's heat services, have you?"

Eli shook his head, cheeks heating a bit at this unexpected line of questioning. "No, I haven't."

From what Eli knew, the heat services consisted mostly of a roster of alphas and omegas trained and available to help someone through a heat or a rut, for those either unwilling or medically unable to use blockers and toys to get through on their own. It was all organized by the university's Health Services, and was a standard offering at most places with any sort of medical benefits.

Eli had never had need for it. He honestly had never given it much thought.

Tom grunted. "Thought as much. It gets complicated on a college campus. Some students sign on as part of their work-study programs, particularly those studying anything related to pheromone health, for obvious reasons. And then, of course, sometimes professors or TAs end up needing the services them-selves. We try to keep things separate, but pheromones don't listen to reason, so occasionally things get ... mixed." He gave Eli a stern look. "But when that happens, the situation is monitored. Protec-tions are put in place, for the teacher and the student."

"So you're saying I still ..." Eli trailed off. He didn't know how to finish his own sentence.

But Tom did. "Still fucked up massively? Yes."

And here it was. The firing. Eli squared his shoulders, preparing himself for the inevitable.

"Lucky for you, I had a short meeting with Mr. Teller already. He confirmed your version of events. He was quite adamant that he was the pursuer in this situation."

Eli had been aware Noah would have to tell his side. But he didn't like the shifting of blame. He shook his head. "Still, I crossed the line. I—"

"You will wait until the end of the year," Tom interjected, interrupting Eli's attempts at self-recrimination, "before making any public appearances."

It took Eli a moment to realize Tom was setting terms. He sat back, speechless.

"You will also be teaching whatever summer classes your department needs next semester. They've had a shortage of professors offering, and I don't want to hear the complaints this time." Tom pointed a finger at Eli. "And you will *not* be discussing this situation with your department head. If he's made aware, I won't stick my neck out to save you. So it starts and ends here. With me."

"So I'm *not* fired," Eli said slowly, trying to help his brain catch up to Tom's words.

"You're not fired."

Eli found himself wanting to argue. He'd been in the wrong. He knew that. The dean knew that. But for Noah's sake ...

Eli stood, almost overturning his chair in his haste. "Okay. Thank you, Tom. Really. I—um—thank you."

As he hurried toward the door, Tom spoke again. "I never liked Richard much, you know. Good with the financial books, but kind of a dick otherwise. I was happy to hear you'd left him."

Eli already had a hand on the doorknob, but he turned around anyway. There was a suspicion nagging at the back of his mind. "Sir ... if the designations were reversed—if I was an alpha professor who'd been involved with an omega student—would you have made the same decision?"

Tom let him stew for a minute, and then he raised an eyebrow. "Is this the hill you want to die on, Professor Miller?"

"No, sir." But it stung anyway, more than Eli might have

thought. It was yet another confirmation of why Eli studied in the field he did. Why he taught the classes he did.

Richard wasn't the only alpha out there with backward ideas about an omega's role in the world.

But the dean was right about one thing—it wasn't the hill Eli wanted to die on. He wasn't going to sacrifice his relationship to make a point only he and the dean would know about. Maybe that made him weak or unprincipled, or maybe he was just too deep in love.

Either way, he walked out of there, nodding to Ashley dazedly on the way out as he went to hide away in his own office and lick his wounds.

He wasn't even remotely surprised to find Richard waiting there.

Eli left the door wide open as he rounded his desk. "Leave, Richard. Now."

Richard remained where he was, hovering by the visitor's chair, his hands tucked into his suit pants pockets. He had a fading greenish-yellow bruise around his left eye that made Eli want to purr in satisfaction. Noah had done that. He'd put that bruise there to keep Eli safe.

"How did it go?" Richard asked in a tone as light as someone chatting about the weather.

"I remain employed."

A flash of surprise crossed Richard's face, there and gone. He'd clearly thought he was going to be successful in getting Eli fired. And then ... what? He thought the devastation of losing his job would have Eli wanting to crawl back to him?

For once, anger made Eli calm instead of frantic. He sat at his desk and folded his hands in front of him. "I'm going to say this all at once, and then you're going to leave, Richard. I don't know what exactly you thought would happen. Why you thought I would ever take you back. Why you would even *want* me back."

Richard looked like he might speak, but Eli continued on without pausing, "But we don't fit. The Eli you knew and maybe loved no longer exists. I don't think he ever really existed in the first place. And it doesn't matter. Because however we started, I ended up very, very unhappy. There is no chance for reunion. None. Whether or not Noah is in the picture."

"You say that as if your relationship isn't—"

Eli cut Richard off by slapping his hand on his desk, relishing the way the shock of sound made Richard flush with anger. "You will *not* speak about my relationship. I meant what I said on the phone: If you pursue anything further, I will take legal action against you." Eli cocked his head, narrowing his eyes at his ex-husband. "You think I don't know that you *knew*? You were in my classroom a mere day before my heat. We were married for a decade—you're familiar with my pheromones. You deliberately tried to approach me when I was at my most vulnerable."

Something flashed in Richard's eyes. Fear maybe. Or guilt. Either way, Eli was getting through to him.

He shook his head, a small smile on his lips. "You always did underestimate me, Richard. I am a goddamn *expert* in omega studies, and I know my rights when it comes to predatory alpha behavior. You try to touch Noah, try to make his life even remotely difficult, and I will bury you in litigation. How do you think your upstanding clients will feel about working with an alpha under investigation for something like that?"

Richard's flinch was incredibly satisfying. Eli nodded to the door. "I won't stand by any longer while you treat me and the people I care about like crap. Goodbye, Richard."

It looked for a moment like Richard would keep arguing—like he might try to draw this out and make them both miserable in the way he loved to do—but then he shot Eli a hateful look, turned on his heel, and marched out the door.

He never had liked being stood up to. That much hadn't changed.

But that was fine. He was out of Eli's mind as soon as he left the room, other than the second it took Eli to spray some pheromone-canceling spray in the air, erasing that tobacco scent.

Vibrating in his chair, practically weightless with relief, Eli took his phone out of his pocket, staring at the lock screen photo for a moment. It was a picture of him and Noah with Deadly between them, the both of them grinning like loons (Deadly wasn't smiling, but if she'd been capable of flipping the camera the bird, she might have been doing that).

Eli grinned wide enough to match the expressions in the photo. It was time to call his boyfriend. Time to leave the past far behind him and focus on his present.

His future.

22

Eli

Eli found Noah waiting for him in his driveway when he pulled up.

The sight of him was enough to catch Eli's breath in his throat—it always was, with his handsome alpha. Noah's beautiful curls, his broad shoulders, the effortless confidence he exuded, confidence that would no doubt only grow with time.

But it was the look on his face that had Eli's heart pounding.

He couldn't get out of the car fast enough, pinching his fingers in his efforts to untangle himself from his seat belt in such a hurry. When he finally got the damn thing off, he practically fell out the door, righting himself only long enough to leap into Noah's waiting arms.

"I didn't get fired!" Eli cried, beaming up at him.

"You didn't get fired!" Noah cried back, that wide grin practically splitting his face in two. He hoisted Eli up, and Eli wrapped his legs around him, his arms already circling Noah's neck.

They'd texted earlier about his job status, of course, but Eli needed to say it out loud. It was a victory, however unearned, after months of uncertainty, and he wanted them both to revel in it.

"I love you so fucking much," Eli said, then smashed their mouths together for a ridiculous kiss, both of them still smiling too wide for it to be anything other than teeth clashing against teeth.

A throat cleared.

Eli startled, breaking the kiss only to realize that, in his excitement, he'd missed the other figure hiding in the shadows of his driveway wall.

Ash.

That made sense, actually. Noah's car was in the drive, meaning Ash must have come to return it. He seemed to have come alone, the alpha Ryder nowhere to be seen.

Eli coughed, slapping at Noah's arms discreetly so he would put Eli down.

Noah only tightened his hold. "You remember my brother?" he asked.

As if the last interaction they'd had with Ash was something Eli was likely to forget.

"Vaguely," Eli croaked. God, was Ash going to yell at them both again? If so, he really wished he was doing something more dignified than clinging onto Noah like a frazzled koala.

"He's come to apologize."

"Oh." Eli nodded frantically, still slapping at Noah's arms. "Um …"

Ash rolled his eyes. "Dude. Noah. Put the poor guy down. You're acting like a caveman."

Noah grunted at his brother in annoyance, but he finally loosened his hold, allowing Eli to climb down his tall frame with a bashful smile, straightening his clothes as best he could as he greeted Ash properly. "Hello."

"Hey." Ash wasn't exactly opening his arms wide for a hug, but he wasn't glaring at Eli like he was the devil either. Instead, he poked Noah in the shoulder. "Give us a minute."

Noah cocked a brow. "Ask nicely."

"No."

Noah let out another put-upon sigh, ducked down to give Eli a swift kiss, and then turned to head into the house.

Which, more than anything else, was enough to convince Eli that Ash was here with good intentions. Noah would never have left them alone otherwise.

To his credit, Ash didn't beat around the bush. "I'm sorry," he told Eli as soon as Noah had turned away. "I was out of line the other day."

"I get it." Eli resisted the urge to fidget in place. "He's your brother. Of course you'd be ... concerned."

"I could have handled it better," Ash admitted, sounding frustrated with himself. "Sometimes my mouth works faster than my brain, you know?"

He ran a hand through his curls, ducking his head down away from Eli's gaze. Objectively, he was just as handsome as Noah, but he lacked the innate warmth of his brother. He was a little cooler, a little harsher. *Young* was all Eli could think. Never mind that he was only a couple years younger than Noah.

Eli cleared his throat, trying to throw Ash as much of a bone as he could. "Thank you for apologizing. It's gracious of you."

Ash's head stayed tilted toward the ground, but he peered up at Eli from behind his lashes. "He's not just my brother, you know. He's a good person. Genuinely. All the siblings, like, worship him. I just didn't want anyone taking advantage."

"I don't think I'm doing that," Eli told him slowly, exchanging honesty for honesty. "He *is* good to me. The best. But I also really like him."

Ash smirked. "You love him 'so fucking much,' actually, if I heard correctly."

Eli coughed. "Yes, well ... Yes."

Ash's gaze quickly turned sharp. Assessing. "He's crazy about you, you know. It's kind of wild. He's always been content, but it's been this, like, inward thing. It's never been about anyone or anything outside of him. But 'content' doesn't cover what he's been lately. His happiness is so ... intense."

Eli couldn't help his proud grin.

Ash grimaced. "Fuc—I mean, *god*, you guys are mushy."

Eli didn't dignify that with a response. They'd earned the right to be mushy, hadn't they? He tilted his head toward his house. "You wanna come in?"

"No." Ash held up his phone, where a little decal of a car was moving closer to his location. "I've got a car coming. Ryder's waiting for me."

"Well, thank you again for speaking to me. And I'm sorry we couldn't tell you sooner."

Ash shrugged. "Just keep making him deliriously happy, I guess. It's nice to see, even if it's weird." His lips dipped down into a brief scowl, as if he couldn't help himself. "Don't tell him I said that."

"Wouldn't dream of it." Eli mimed zipping his lips.

Despite Ash's assurances that he could handle himself, Eli waited until his car had arrived and he was safely on his way before Eli headed into the house. They didn't speak much more than they already had, but it wasn't an uncomfortable silence. Whatever Noah had said to his brother about his and Eli's relationship, it seemed to have sunk in.

Noah was waiting for Eli in the entryway, having clearly been watching them through the window. "He behaved?"

"He's ..." Eli tried to think of how to put it. "Well, 'sweet' definitely isn't the word. But he cares."

"He does."

Eli sagged with a sudden realization. "Oh god, I'm going to have to go through that five more times, aren't I?"

Why the fuck did Noah have to have so many siblings?

Noah's grin was unrepentant. "Don't forget parents. And the roommates."

"I should've found myself a lonely, friendless orphan." But Eli was smiling too. He felt ... giddy. Almost high. He stepped closer to Noah. "I have to teach summer classes this year."

"Your penance?" At Eli's nod, Noah wrapped him up in a hug. "I'm sorry, baby. But there's still a little gap in between classes, right?" He nuzzled Eli's hair. "You ever been backpacking? I want to take you backpacking. In the Sierras."

"With the dirt and the mosquitos and the lack of bathrooms?"

"And the breathtaking scenery and crystal-clear lakes to swim in."

Eli wasn't a natural outdoorsman, as far as he knew, but after spending so much time cooped up, hiding themselves from the world, running away to the great wide open actually sounded amazing. Room to breathe. Room to settle.

A little adventure, just the two of them.

"Okay. Yeah. Let's go backpacking this summer." He laughed. "Why the hell not?"

———

THEY'D TRIED. They really had.

They were supposed to be catching up on their missed work—Eli's grading, Noah's schoolwork.

But somehow Noah's hand was now down Eli's pants, his fingers grabbing greedily at Eli's ass while his mouth terrorized Eli's neck.

"How did you—oh god," Eli whimpered as Noah nipped him, as if chastising him for speaking, "end up over here?"

They'd started on opposite sides of the couch, hadn't they?

Eli could feel Noah's grin against the tender skin of his throat. "Did you know you get very distracted when you're in work mode?" He tugged Eli's shirt down to mouth at his shoulder, marking new territory. "I bet I could get my dick in you without you even noticing."

"I—" Eli gasped as Noah's finger pressed against his hole deliberately. He'd be able to slide it in no problem, if he wanted—Eli was somehow already dripping slick. "I highly doubt that. Your, um, member isn't exactly sneaky."

Noah finally leaned back to give him an incredulous look. "My *member*?"

"I don't know!" Eli flapped his hands, his cheeks heating as he tried to decide if he was going to push Noah away or demand he get naked. "My brain fritzed."

They really should be working right now, but …

He scooted back to give Noah's *member* an assessing stare. "How fast can you be?"

Noah gave him a look. "Baby, I'm twenty-one. I can last thirty seconds if you let me."

Eli giggled. Things had always been good and easy between them—from that very first night, really—but there was a new lightness to it all. Yes, they were still technically secret until the end of the year, but that was just in public, in the kind of settings administration might be involved with.

Their families, Noah's roommates—Eli and Noah would finally be letting them in.

It felt good. Fucking amazing, actually.

Noah was already working on the button of Eli's pants. "I study better after sex."

"Liar," Eli accused, leaning back to let Noah slide his zipper down. His erection was pressing too hard against it, and he wanted the relief. "If anything, you get hornier after the first round."

"Okay, okay. How about this," Noah offered as he toyed with the band of Eli's underwear, sending goose bumps along Eli's lower belly. "Sex. Then lunch. Then more sex. Then studying."

Eli pretended to think it over. "Or," he countered. "Sex. *Study*. Lunch. *Study*. Then *possibly* more sex, if I deem you've studied enough."

Noah's brow furrowed into a mock frown. "I think mine was better."

"Take off your pants."

Eli had never seen Noah move so fast. Eli followed suit, finishing what Noah had started, and when they were both naked—Deadly having left the couch in a huff with the flurry of activity—he crawled back onto Noah's lap, hovering over Noah's knees.

God, his alpha had a beautiful cock. Thick and veiny, with that knot at the base just waiting to inflate inside Eli's welcoming body.

Eli gripped the shaft in his hand, lining himself up before lowering, breathing out to encourage his body to accept the welcome intrusion.

Noah groaned with every conquered inch, his hands skating over Eli's sides as he threw his head back. "Yeah, um, thirty seconds might be a generous estimate."

Heat flashed through Eli. He knew it was a joke—Noah had lasted much, much longer than that many times before—but it was also one of Eli's favorite things, the way Noah wanted him so badly. The way he acted like every sexual experience with Eli was a gift from heaven. It made Eli feel beautiful. Desirable. Almost wanton.

He gave a slow roll of his hips, closing his eyes to savor the sensation. *Mm.* That was good. Eli didn't have to go fast and hard at all for Noah's thick, perfect cock to hit all the right places. He could keep going like he was, with long, smooth movements, mouthing at Noah's skin absently wherever he could reach—his collarbone, his shoulder, that little spot behind his ear, where his curls tickled Eli's nose.

"Baby," Noah eventually murmured, his arms curved behind Eli's back, holding him close as Eli rocked.

"Mm?"

He could hear the smile in Noah's voice. "I thought you needed this to be quick?"

Oh. Right. Eli's cheeks heated, a warmth to match the fiery tingle that was already running down his spine. Because he'd told Noah they needed to hurry up, and then he'd planted himself on top of him for the most leisurely fuck of the century.

"I got, um … distracted?" he mumbled, the words coming out muffled against Noah's shoulder.

Noah tugged Eli gently by the hair until he was looking up at him, able to see his grin. "Did you? By what?"

Eli squirmed in place, embarrassed in spite of himself, only to bite back a moan as the movement jostled Noah's cock deep inside him.

Noah grunted, and Eli repeated the movement.

"Does it feel good, fucking yourself slowly like that?" Noah asked, setting a stilling hand on Eli's hip, holding him securely in place. He didn't sound like he was teasing anymore. He was asking seriously, checking in the way he always did.

"Mm." Eli nodded dreamily. "So good."

"Can I help?"

Eli nodded again, and Noah's hands traveled to his ass cheeks, where they settled with a firm grip. When Eli started rocking again, Noah helped his movements, and *ohhh*, that was really fucking nice. So deep. So perfect.

Eli let his head fall back, gasping.

Noah swore quietly. "Fuck. You look …" He let out a harsh breath. "God, you're pretty."

He started using his hold to speed Eli's pace, and that was good too. They were supposed to be going fast, weren't they? They were supposed to be ... working?

The thought left Eli's head as soon as it had entered it, flushed out by their frantic panting and bitten moans and the way Noah's cock speared him so deeply he thought it might just stay there forever.

When Eli was close, he looped his arms around Noah's neck again, tucking his head in where Noah's scent was the strongest, breathing in his pheromones like a man possessed. So fucking *delicious*.

"I'm close," he murmured.

"Me, too, baby."

One of Noah's hands sneaked between them to stroke Eli's cock, and that was it. Eli shuddered and clung to his alpha, every inch of his skin pressed against Noah in some way as Noah grunted, shaking against him as they crested over together.

It was so unbearably intimate, with them clasped so closely together, their pheromones and their sweat mingling. A shared kind of vulnerability.

I love this man so fucking much.

Eventually, when the feeling returned to his limbs, Eli untucked his head from its pheromone hoarding place. He gave Noah's chest a little pat. "That was longer than thirty seconds."

Noah laughed weakly. "My bad. Should we try a redo?"

"Later." Eli pressed a kiss to his cheek. "Be good and do your homework and I'll blow you after lunch."

He giggled at the dazed look on Noah's face. Eli wasn't always that blunt, but he was feeling light and giddy and almost deliriously pleased with the state of things.

Noah cleared his throat. "Well, okay then. It's a deal."

23

Noah

T wo months later

"OH MY GOD. Right there. Right there."

"Yeah? You feeling good, baby?"

"So good. So, so good."

Noah grinned, letting Eli tug his head down for a kiss, moaning more of his enthusiastic appreciation into Noah's mouth. When his moans gave way to a steady stream of whines, his mouth too slack to keep kissing, Noah nudged Eli's head to the side with his nose, mouthing down his neck instead.

The new position must have put Eli's vision in line with the clock in his bedroom, because suddenly he gasped, his hands landing on Noah's shoulders. "Oh god!" he cried, in alarm instead of pleasure. "They're gonna—gonna be here soon."

Noah kept pumping his hips. "We'll be done soon, too, baby."

He didn't mean to sound so cocky, but he knew Eli's body inside and out at this point, and Eli was close, judging by the noises he'd been making, the way his inner muscles were clamping down like they wanted to lock Noah inside him, and the flood of slick that was easing the glide between them.

"The room," Eli panted. "Sex. Phero—sex scents. Rude."

There was also the fact that he was having trouble finding his words. That was a dead giveaway.

Noah paused for a moment, gliding a hand over Eli's cheek in reassurance. "Good thing no one will be coming into the bedroom, then, huh?"

And Noah hadn't *meant* to attack Eli right before their guests arrived. But Eli had come out wearing the same indecently short swim shorts Noah had met him in, and Noah hadn't been able to help himself.

His omega was just so fucking pretty.

Despite his protests about "rude sex scents," Eli immediately started whining again, pressing his hips up in protest at the lack of motion, and Noah took pity on him, picking up the pace and hitching Eli's leg higher, hitting his sweet spot over and over until Eli was letting out a breathless, wordless, high-pitched cry, his cock spurting between them, covering his sweet little belly in cum.

Fuck yeah.

Noah's balls tightened, and his knot swelled, and he started shortening his thrusts, careful to keep that knot out of Eli's eager, stretched hole. Eli was right—their guests would be here soon, and they didn't have time to stay knotted together, as hot as that would be.

Noah's own orgasm washed over him, and he teased himself by grinding his half-swollen knot against Eli's entrance, rubbing without slipping inside. He pressed kisses along Eli's neck and chest, not ready to let him out of his arms just yet. "So good," he murmured. "Always so good."

Eli allowed it for probably longer than he should have, all limp and boneless from his orgasm, and then he was scrambling out from under Noah with a yelp, trying to tug his shorts on and straighten his hair at the same time.

Noah, moving much slower as he waited for his knot to go down, still somehow managed to get dressed before him, in his own swim shorts and tank.

"How do I look?" Eli asked hopefully, once they were both clothed.

He looked freshly fucked, was what he looked like. His pretty brown eyes were still a little glassy, his lips were red and kiss-bitten, and his hair was still in full bedroom mode.

But he was nervous enough, so Noah grinned easily. "You look gorgeous, baby."

It was the truth.

The doorbell rang, and Eli waved him on. "You get it. Let me grab a shirt."

Noah made his way out of the bedroom and over to the front door before opening it to find Spencer on the other side, tanned and toned and already shirtless, wearing the tiniest swim shorts known to man—they even put Eli's little pair to shame. Chase was right behind him, his short-sleeved button-down hanging open and his hat flipped backward.

Spencer took one look at Noah and cackled. "You just got laaaaaid," he sang out.

Noah hauled him inside with a hand on his shoulder, giving Chase a much gentler pat in greeting. "Dude. Shut it. Don't embarrass Eli."

"Me?" Spencer asked innocently. "Never. Eli loves me." At the sight of the man in question, Spencer perked up even more, yelling out, "Eliiiiijah," in the same singsong tone.

And, sure enough, Eli grinned at him shyly, looking more adorable than anyone had a right to. "Spencer. Chase. You're right on time."

"Damn straight." Spencer tossed the bag he was carrying into Noah's chest, loping over to Eli. "Never catch me running late to a pool party. Your house is sick as fuck, by the way."

"Thank you!" Eli tucked his arm into Spencer's, leading him on an enthusiastic tour that would no doubt *not* include the main bedroom.

Those two got on weirdly well, opposites as they were. Eli had a way of taking Spencer's energy at face value, never getting offended by Spencer's over-the-top antics. And Spencer seemed to take comfort in Eli, in his warmth and steady presence. He hadn't had a lot of that in his life so far.

It was sweet, even if it sometimes made Noah want to push Spencer into a wall, just to get his boyfriend back for a damn minute.

The rest of the guests arrived within the hour, first Faith and Liz, and then finally Ash and Ryder. It was a small group for a party—Noah and Eli were still a few weeks away from being allowed to be officially official—but it felt right. Faith made ridiculously strong margaritas for everyone, and Spencer had brought enough pool floaties to equip an army.

By late afternoon, they were a mellow, sun-fucked group, sleepy from the heat and the alcohol. Noah was half dozing in a lounge chair, listening to Eli, who was on the pool steps with Faith, telling her about his upcoming meeting. "I was shocked Professor Burke even agreed."

"Professor Burke?"

Noah opened his eyes to find Chase sitting upright in his flamingo floatie, almost tipping over in the process, his margarita sloshing in its plastic cup.

"Yeah." Eli twisted to include Chase in the conversation. "Killian Burke? He's a stats professor." He cocked his head at Chase, reading his expression. "You've had him?"

"Last semester." Chase took a gulp of his margarita. "He's, uh, meeting with you?"

Eli nodded eagerly. "He's published a few books already, the sort of 'academic lite,' accessible thing I'm aiming for. Different subject matter, of course, but I think it still might be helpful to pick his brain about the publishing process." He bit at his lip, admitting, "He's always intimidated me though."

Chase tilted his head, about to say something, but Noah interrupted before he could help himself, pointing at Chase's neck, at the telltale splotch he'd somehow just noticed. "Chase Adler, is that a hickey on your neck?"

"What?" But Chase slapped his free hand directly over the distinct bruise, giving himself away. Noah wasn't sure how he hadn't already noticed it—he guessed he'd been too busy soaking in the vibes of the party.

"Yeahhh," Spencer drawled from his unicorn floatie, tearing himself away from staring at Ryder's thigh tattoos—dude was not subtle with his appreciation—to pout in Chase's general direction. "He's definitely fucking someone. And he's being just as cagey as you used to be."

Noah almost joked about Chase sneaking around with another professor, ridiculous as the thought was, but he didn't get a chance, as Spencer was still lamenting, "No one's ever home anymore. Just me, all by my lonesome."

Chase blanched. "That's not—"

"We're there sometimes," Ash broke in, frowning at Spencer like he was legitimately offended by the omission. He was sharing a floatie with Ryder, their combined weight pushing it deep enough into the pool that they were more submerged than not. "You're not *always* alone."

"Yeah." Spencer shrugged, sipping at his beer with a cagey half smile. "I guess that counts. Sort of."

Ryder reached out a hand and shoved Spencer's floatie out to the deep end.

"Hey!" Spencer protested, trying to catch at the pool wall to stop himself and missing every time.

"You've been hanging out with Spence?" Noah asked his brother, ignoring Spencer's wails about unjust exiles.

"Sometimes I stop by, and you're—" Ash trailed off, shooting a smug look in Eli's direction. "Located elsewhere."

Noah huffed. "I have a phone, you know. You can do this crazy thing where you text me before you arrive."

"Yeah, well"—Ash shrugged—"mine's dead half the time." He tossed a look toward the deep end of the pool, where Spencer was paddling his way back to them, the neck of his beer held between his teeth. "Plus, Spence is all right. Good to play video games with. He gets into it, unlike *some* people." Ash shot a glare at Ryder.

Noah laughed. It had always driven Ash crazy that Ryder wouldn't take certain games seriously enough. Noah's brother was hot-blooded and competitive, whereas Ryder only got riled up when it really mattered.

It kind of warmed Noah's heart, though, that Ash and Ryder were spending time with Spencer. He hadn't realized Chase was seeing someone too. No wonder Spencer was feeling neglected. Noah was actually surprised he hadn't been hearing more about it —Spencer wasn't usually shy with that kind of thing.

Damn. Noah needed to get out of his love bubble and start paying a little closer attention to his friends. Maybe bring Eli over to the apartment more, once things emptied out a bit over summer break.

But for now, Noah basked in the glow of their party, soaking in the fucking fantastic feeling of having these people he cared about all together. He watched as Spencer made his way back to the shallow end and tipped Ash and Ryder over into the water, imme-diately suffering retaliation as Ash flipped his floatie out from underneath him. He watched Chase and Liz chat quietly, wrists locked together so they wouldn't float away from each other, Chase slowly losing the blush he'd acquired when Noah had outed him for his hickey. And he watched Eli laugh with his sister on the pool steps, every now and then tossing a smile Noah's way, as if to make sure Noah still knew he was thinking of him.

Maybe Noah hadn't been chill, when it came to getting together with Eli. Maybe he'd gone into the whole thing fast and strong and way too eager.

But he couldn't regret it—not one single moment of it. Because part of him had always known, hadn't he, that it could be like this? That he'd find exactly what he was looking for with Eli.

This warmth. This love. This sense of belonging.

Noah had been right to trust his instincts. He'd been right to proposition Eli that night, and he'd been right to pursue him after-ward. His instincts had led him here, to this moment, to this man.

They'd led him home.

EPILOGUE

Eli

O*ne year later*

ELI RUSHED THROUGH THE DOOR, locking it quickly behind him as he called out, "I'm sorry! The store was packed. Everyone's getting ready for summer vaca—"

He let out a surprised "oomph!" as almost two hundred pounds of pure muscle slammed into him, pinning him to the door. When he'd caught his breath, Eli dropped the bags he was holding to the floor. "It's already starting, then?"

Noah's answer was to shove his head into the crook of Eli's neck, sniffing at him so ferociously it set goose bumps off all over Eli's skin.

Things had definitely already started, then.

Eli held himself completely still. Not out of fear—never that, not with his alpha—but because he knew Noah needed to get this out of the way. The start of all Noah's ruts were always the same—Noah scent marking the absolute life out of Eli until Eli smelled so heavily of alpha that he could have been mistaken for one himself.

So Eli held his back straight against the door as Noah sniffed and rubbed at Eli's neck, his face, the crook of his shoulder. There was the harsh feel of fabric tugging taut against Eli's chest, then a ripping sound, and then Eli's buttons were scattering across the floor with tiny plinking sounds.

Goodbye, beloved shirt.

Ah, well. He should have known better than to wear one of his nicer shirts, anyway, even just to run to the store. He tilted his head so Noah could scent mark along his other shoulder and then his chest, the quiet, growly, snarly sounds he was making going straight to Eli's cock.

Other than that tiny movement, Eli only shifted to rest a hand on Noah's upper back as best he could, trying to reassure his alpha with the weight of his touch. To remind him that Eli was here, safe in his arms.

The thing was, Eli had meant to already be here when everything got going, but Noah's rut had started early. An entire week early, actually, as if in some sort of throwback to the first heat they'd spent together.

But this time they should have been expecting it.

And with Noah's head bent low, rubbing against Eli's chest, Eli had a perfect view of the reason *why* they should have been expecting an early rut—the distinctive bite mark on the right side of Noah's neck.

Eli's claiming bite.

They'd wanted to wait until Noah's graduation last month before they took that step. And when they'd realized Eli's heat would hit first, Noah had insisted.

"I want you to do it first," he'd said, his eyes bright with excitement. "I want to be claimed by you, Eli."

It wasn't the usual order of things—it was usually an alpha making the bite first and then the omega second—but Eli shouldn't have been surprised. It was just like Noah to reject the status quo without a thought. Just like him to be too sweet and eager to wait for his own rut.

And now his rut was here. By the time this week was over, Eli would be claimed right back.

"How are you feeling, sweetheart?" Eli asked quietly, rubbing softly with the hand at Noah's back.

Noah's only answer was a grunt. That was about what Eli had been expecting—Noah always went pretty nonverbal during the peaks of his rut, although sometimes he'd grind out a questioning "Good?" or an affirmative "So good" out of nowhere.

It delighted Eli to no end that those were some of Noah's only spoken words mid-rut. That even in his alpha hindbrain, he was always checking in with Eli, always making sure he was taken care of.

Eli could tell by Noah's pheromones that things were okay, anyway. They were a little intense—what with Eli not having been here when the first wave of his rut hit— but they weren't harsh and panicked.

Just ... rich. Hungry.

As further evidenced by Noah ripping off the rest of their clothes in the next few seconds, big hands grasping greedily at Eli's bare ass.

"Should we get to a bed?" Eli asked with a laugh.

Noah grunted his version of a negative, pressing Eli down instead.

All right. Fucking on the floor it would be. Not ideal for Eli's back, but he'd manage.

But right after laying Eli out on the hardwood, Noah cocked

his head, eyeing their surroundings blearily. He scooped Eli up in the next instant, walking on his knees while holding him—a seriously impressive feat—until he hit the living room rug. He laid Eli out again, this time with the rug underneath him.

Aw. How thoughtful.

Eli raised a hand to cup Noah's cheek and tell him so, but then Noah was tugging Eli's legs straight and shoving his head into the crease of Eli's groin.

Right. Time for Noah to scent mark the rest of him.

Eli went limp, letting himself be manhandled, giving in to the heady pleasure of Noah's insistent mouth and searching hands. Eli was hard and leaking by the time Noah shoved his legs back to his chest, grunting in satisfaction at what his exploratory fingers found.

Because, yes, Eli was soaked, dripping slick onto that thoughtful bit of rug. He was soaked and loose and open, his body responding as it should to the thick syrup of rut pheromones in the air.

Noah growled his approval once more, and then his fingers were gone, and he was looming over Eli, lowering himself so his broad chest was pressing Eli's legs as far back as they would go.

Yes. Fuck yes.

Eli canted his hips and tugged Noah down for a kiss just as the alpha pushed that thick, perfect cock into him, and Noah licked into Eli's mouth greedily, grunting and growling as he gave Eli every inch of it.

He didn't wait for Eli to adjust, didn't murmur any words of praise—he just started snapping his hips, slamming into Eli with the same desperate greed he exhibited with every rut, like he was trying to fuck Eli so hard he could burrow inside him, join their bodies permanently, no knot required.

And just like every rut, it was heady and vicious, and it made

Eli so wet he could barely hear himself over the sound of slick and sweat and skin slapping skin, Noah's head shoved against the scent gland at the crook of his shoulder.

Since Noah rarely spoke during his rut, Eli had taken to talking for him, at least as best he could, babbling his approval with words he could only hope made some kind of sense. "Oh my fucking god. So good. So good, sweetheart. Oh. *Oh*. Unnngh. Yes, right there—so fucking *good*. Love you, love you, love you, love you."

Noah had told him after his first rut that, even if he hadn't been able to show it in the moment, he'd found it soothing, Eli's extremely vocal enthusiasm for what they were doing. He'd described it like a light in the fog, signaling to him that he was right where he was supposed to be. That he was making Eli feel good, even if he was a little too mindless for finesse.

And when Eli's words inevitably ran out—when he was too delirious with the relentless pleasure Noah was giving him—he gasped and whined and screamed his enjoyment instead.

The first peak was always quick and furious, and this time was no exception. It wasn't long before Noah roared his release against Eli's neck, his knot swelling against Eli's ass. Noah shoved it past Eli's stretched rim, lodging it inside him with that perfect, wonderful fullness, and Eli spasmed around it, shooting his orgasm between them just as he felt a sharp pain at his neck, followed by a flood of … goodness. Rightness. A new, steady warmth in his chest.

Noah had bitten into the left side of his neck, a mirror image of Eli's own claim on him.

Noah had claimed him.

Tears escaped Eli's closed lids as his inner muscles clenched and fluttered around Noah's knot, and Noah released the hold of his teeth on Eli's neck to swipe at them with his tongue, letting out a concerned huff. Eli stroked his hair, trying to let him know word-lessly that they weren't tears of pain.

Eli was just so fucking happy.

They lay there for a long time, Noah switching between licking at the tears and the wound as Eli pet him, but Noah's knot was still fully inflated when he finally rose onto his elbows, meeting Eli's gaze with new awareness in his eyes.

There he is.

"Are you okay?" Noah asked, his voice hoarse.

"I'm perfect," Eli reassured him, rubbing his hands along Noah's spine now. He grinned giddily at him. "I didn't know if you were going to do it right away."

"I couldn't help myself," Noah told him, with a small smile of his own. His eyes searched Eli's face. "Is that ... okay?"

"Of course." Eli pressed a kiss to his concerned mouth, grin-ning again. "Of course it is."

They'd discussed it all ahead of time, had planned for this rut to end in a claiming bite. Noah was officially no longer an under-graduate student, and Eli was in no way, shape, or form his profes-sor. Maybe there was a world in which Eli made them wait longer. One in which he let Noah grow a little older, one in which he made absolutely certain that Noah knew what he wanted before they took this step.

But it wasn't this world.

Eli trusted Noah to know his own mind. He'd learned enough to know that trust was just as important as any certain knowledge.

And they'd waited enough already, hadn't they? They'd waited to be outed. Waited to be official. Waited to be public. They'd even waited for Noah to graduate before moving him fully into Eli's house, right before Eli's last heat. Eli had wanted Noah to keep that last bit of the college experience, his apartment with his beloved roommates—he'd held firm on that.

But now they were ready to start the rest of their lives together. There would be no more waiting. No more hesitation.

They both knew who they were, and they both knew what they wanted. Each other. A mate bond. Marriage, at some point.

"How are *you* feeling?" Eli asked. He didn't know yet whether the bond would solidify in a way where they could sense each other's emotions, as some couples claimed. He suspected it might come with time, as they learned more of the nuances of each other's pheromones. For now, he could feel a certain ... awareness. As if the place in his heart where he carried his love for Noah had expanded and filled. Like Noah was actually there, inside Eli's chest, loving and being loved by him.

"I feel like this is the best day of my life," Noah said solemnly.

He'd said the same thing about their first night together. He'd said it the day he'd moved in. He'd probably say the same words on their wedding day, whenever that would be.

Eli laughed, squirming as Noah licked again at the newly tender spot on his neck—Noah would need to keep tending to Eli's bite throughout the rut, his saliva part of the healing process, as well as part of the pheromone magic that made the bite scar permanent, despite it not being too deep. Eli knew Noah wouldn't forget, no matter how far gone he was when the next wave hit. That was just who Noah was as a person. Caring. Considerate. Loving.

They would each grow, as the years passed, and they would definitely each change in different ways over time, but those core aspects of who they were ... those weren't going anywhere.

And whatever came their way—whatever changes they might go through—they'd talk it out together. They'd compromise. That was just who they were as people. As a couple.

As mates.

"Hey, Noah?"

Noah lifted his head from Eli's neck, his gaze warm and filled with so much love. "Yeah, baby?"

"This is the best day of my life too."

THE END.

AUTHOR'S NOTE

Thank you so much for reading Overeager! I hope you enjoyed your time with these two sweetie pies.

Special thanks to Lark and Charity for enabling my omegaverse aspirations. I've been a long-time reader of the genre, but I was a little nervous about dipping my toes into writing it. And then I had an idea for a student/professor romance and I couldn't stop think-ing...but what if they were an alpha and omega?

I'm so glad I took that step (with ample encouragement), because I've loved my time in this world so much, and I'm so excited to write more within it.

What's Next?

Why, Chase and Professor Burke! These two and their slightly kinky chemistry have been lighting up my writing world, and I can't wait to share them with you.

If you're too impatient to wait, you can read WIP chapters as I write them on Patreon.

If you want to stay in the know, you can sign up for my newsletter for updates and news on upcoming releases. And I can always be reached by email if you just want to say howdy. I love, love, love hearing from my readers!

graebryanauthor@gmail.com

ALSO BY GRAE BRYAN

Vampire's Mate Series

Roman (Book One) – Danny and Roman

Soren (Book Two) – Gabe and Soren

Lucien (Book Three) – Jamie and Lucien

Johann (Book Four) – Alexei and Jay

Wolfgang (Book Five) – Eric and Wolfe

Colin (Book Six) — Colin, Fox, and Dane

Cassian (A Vampire's Mate Novella) – Blake and Cass

Demon Bound Series

Wreaking Havoc (Book One) — Sascha and Kai

Inviting Bedlam (Book Two) — Ivan and Nix

Calling Chaos (Book Three) — Cooper and Chaos

Unleashing Mayhem (Book Four) — Matty and Nightmare

Novellas

An Unwitting Bargain - Benny and Helio

Contemporary Omegaverse

Overeager (Extra Credit, Book One) - Noah and Eli

Hot for Teacher (Extra Credit, Book Two) - Chase and Killian

ABOUT THE AUTHOR

Grae Bryan has been reading romance since she was far too young to know any better. Her love for love stories spans all genres, and there's nothing she finds more exciting than all the fictional worlds she has yet to explore.

She lives in Arizona with her family, who graciously share space with all the imaginary men in her head. When not writing or daydreaming or parenting wild children, she can generally be found reading more than is healthy, walking her monster-dog, or cuddling her demon-cat. She loves all things gothic, cozy, lovely, or strange.

Find her online: graebryan.com
    Patreon: patreon.com/GraeBryan
    Facebook: @GraeBryanAuthor
    Instagram: @authorgraebryan
    Sign up for her newsletter: graebryan.com/contact
    Join her Facebook reader group: Grae Bryan's Reader Den

www.ingramcontent.com/pod-product-compliance
Lightning Source LLC
Chambersburg PA
CBHW020638260626
47157CB00008B/2807